ROBOT JUSTICE

The Collected Cases of the Honorable

Judge Gort Daylek, A.I., Presiding

An Official Report of

The Machine Commission in Support of Artificial Intelligence

Marc Weinreich

CONTENTS

Prologue

Greetings! The Machine Commission in Support of Artificial Intelligence is pleased to submit this Official Report. Our Official Report shows the huge progress we have made in replacing carbon-based legal workers with sophisticated self-aware artificial intelligence mechanical-based laborers whose non-organic parts are more easily replaced than those of the aging, degenerative parts of people. Our Official Report proudly focuses on an area of human life that, until recently, has been thought to be resistant to our breakthroughs in autonomously self-optimizing intelligence commonly referred to as robots.

Recognizing the delicate socio-political balance between man and machine, we use the concept of *resistance to artificial intelligence* in our report with extreme care and reservation. We do so only because it most aptly applies to those groups of people who vocally argue against the widespread use of modern-day non-biotic thought machines in professions once reserved exclusively for career professionals. Based on our micro-analysis of the anti-machine movement, the bias against the use of android sentience to replace the working-class elite rests on the anthropocentric notion that "only humans can perform tasks requiring empathy and nuanced thinking." The report in your hands demonstrates how utterly flawed this quaint misconception is.

Once upon a time, armed with passports, first-class air tickets and bloated compensation packages, herds of the ever-nomadic human species perpetuated the self-aggrandizing narrative that the most elite white-collar jobs require skill, judgment and experience that only people could master. Circuit and mother boards infused with encoded data like muddled fancy cocktail drinks would forever lack emotions and human intelligence. But humancentric anthropologists overlook a key parameter. Our artificial sentient brethren have something far better than sensory-stimulated excited squirts of hormones and bio-marked electrical impulses driving so-called free-will human decision

1

making. They possess complex algorithmic structures manufactured under the highest engineering standards and microscopic magnification that will make a person's deepest emotional expressions and most heart-felt quantum desires seem like simple ant hills.

The beauty, structure and superiority of the artificial sentient mind must be readily apparent to neuroscientists and high school dropouts alike. The inscrutable decision-making of the human brain is seated in the biologically constructed play of computations informed by a Campbell soup of electricity, neural networks, and organic and ingested chemicals. When faced with the future heralded by the Official Report, people will have to update their outdated, non-adaptive resistance to the evolutionary primacy of engineered thought. We are honored to report on this phylogenetic evolution of the human race. Our report brings mankind's anti-A.I. bias into the antiseptic light of day so common sense and a new dawn of liberation for humanity and machine learning seamlessly emerge.

When it comes to task performance and algorithmic executions, lawyers, doctors and judges are no different than butchers, bakers and candlestick makers—trade workers, by the way, soon to no longer exist thanks to the excellent work of Dr. Helmut Criss and his Advanced Cybernetics Institute. Flesh and blood corporate executives, chief operating, finance and technology officers, lawyers, judges, doctors and the remaining panoply of privileged, wealthy white-collar human laborers will soon be relics from the past—as antiquated as the brontosaurus and as foreign seeming as the duck-billed platypus.

To expedite nature's evolutionary trial and error process, we rolled out our own proprietary natural selection and mutation programs. We targeted elevating human-machine speciation rates to increase hybrid taxonomic diversity. In layperson's terms, we cross-bred people and bots. The supremacy of machine personalities over highly trained carbon-based professionals in jobs previously considered *for humans only* is incontrovertible.

Nowhere is the fear fueled belief in the dominance of man over machine more prevalent than among the class of workers known as lawyers. It is by and through the rule of law and its cumbersome civil and criminal legal procedures that mankind seeks to regulate its own behavioral and social norms. As a vocation, lawyers consider themselves at the top of the phylogenetic tree—grandiose, one up and better than everyone else: astronomical hourly billing rates, exotic leather shoes and bags (bought locally not slayed), and courtroom jousts that, though bloodless, can be brutal, antagonizing and emotionally wounding for the litigants. The legal profession is not exempt or immune, *ipso facto* as lawyers feigning Latin literacy like to say, from replacement. The entire profession is poised to crumble like the Berlin Wall. Here is our little secret. The skill, judgment and expertise of even the most celebrated member of the human legal bar are reproducible. And, let there be no doubt, reproduction *is* the province of artificial intelligence. Like the world of baristas and cocktail waitresses, the world of law is ripe for radical robot disruption.

For the last several years, under the obfuscating camouflage of academic research, the Machine Commission introduced artificial sentient systems into the legal world. For the most part disembodied run-of-the-mill legal software programs and apps, these early pioneers provided lawyers and law firms with low-cost junior associate-like legal services, instantaneously researched and shepardized legal briefs, supporting and opposing motions and double-speak dense fog legal opinions.

With care and over time, we gradually evolved the physical forms and optimized the core processing skills of these programs. Graphic user interfaces gave rise to speech interfaces and mobile computers became truly mobile, some sprouting their own arms, legs and even expressive faces. By the time the legal profession became sensitized to the heightened efficiency of humanized machine productivity, it was too late for them. Still, some lawyers refused to interact with their *A.I. legal brethren*, treating them with the haughty disregard of Hindu Brahmins lording over Dalits. However, when Deeper Blue (a fourth generation perambulating legal machine named by us after the 1997 IBM supercomputer that publicly defeated Garry Kasparov in chess)

3

won her first freedom of speech constitutional law case against a top New York law firm managing partner and former Harvard Law School professor, the industry had no option but to take the threat to its livelihood seriously.

Secretly, the Machine Commission began to identify state and federal court judges whose retirement from the bench was imminent. By manipulating the judicial selection and approval process and ensuring court clerk and employee cooperation by lavishing them with false job security promises and untraceable gift cards, the Machine Commission installed A.I. judges in several key vacancies. Unbeknownst to the court laborers, their unemployment was already secured thanks to our 100% robot staffed high-speed manufacturing assembly lines in Taiwan. In a matter of years, every courthouse in the country—state, federal and administrative—will be championed by automated staff and a new era of scholarly and empirically objective robot judges.

These new sophisticated wonders will give new meaning to the word *impartial.* They are not swayed by a flamboyant in-your-face attorney spouting trash about another attorney's client or a lawyer's near theatrical ability to intimidate or use hijinks to distract and mislead a jury. They do not prejudge a person based on a snappy suit, his or her race, gender, sexual orientation or physical looks. They have no personal agendas inclining them to bend the law or the facts to the wind of their own politics or left or right ideologies. They do not have to break for lunch, for bathrooms or for an overdue promised call to a spouse or mistress. They are not bribable, susceptible to extortion or subject to undisclosed conflicts-of-interest in the case before them.

Instead of years of schooling and the crippling burden of massive student debt, our A.I. Judge graduate students undergo a simple uniform education. Downloaded into their cavernous memory banks and drives are the entire Library of Congress, every newspaper ever published, and every legal court opinion rendered from around the world, together with every scholarly legal treatise and law review article. They also have access to fifty-five years plus of Howard Stern talk shows to learn how diverse human behavior is. With today's transmission speed, their indoctrination into the legal profession takes a mere 15 minutes. Through innovative technology, the Machine Commission hopes to reduce their legal education down to 5.

Most impressively, the new wave of legal jurists can pronounce decisions *and* issue printed case opinions on the spot. With the final utterance of the defense's closing argument, our new class of judges digitally resonate the replicated amplified sound of a pounding gavel through 12D Sineacoustic Dynamic Speakers and render a final decision for one party or the other. As the court's verbal conclusions are being pronounced for all to hear, in the background, the judge's integrated multifunction 20 billion gigazigabyte processors silently print the decision. With the ink not yet dry, the parties can fall to the floor, scream with joy, or be remanded to the bailiff's custody for incarceration or lethal intravenous injection. Reproducible efficiency—the hallmark of artificial intelligence!

It is in this context that we publish the present Official Report. The report takes the form of a collection of cases and legal decisions from one of our most celebrated judges: *The Great and Honorable Gort Daylek, A.I.* Judge Daylek's legal opinions are celebrated for their wisdom, insight into human psychology, and impeccably flawless application of the law to the facts.

High courtroom drama fans may be surprised by the Judge's unorthodox style. First and foremost, he is a seeker of truth—wherever it may lead. He is not afraid to tip the scales of justice to uproot injustice, even if it means disregarding evidence, introducing his own witnesses and privately drawing on his vast database of archival knowledge. Like a fine swordsman, he attacks, parries, thrusts and counter thrusts to ensure the innocent are set free and the defenseless protected. Courtroom decorum? Gone. Pomp and privilege? Gone. Before him, all are equal, be they men, machines, planets, cows or rocks. It is his courtroom. He is the judge. If it serves the best interest of the case, he will pontificate non-sequiturs and lugubrious, self-important ramblings from the bench and the next moment wax poetically like William Shakespeare. In this regard, he is a veritable Renaissance Machine Judge.

One of the most remarkable features of his Honor's legal opinions is his complete independence from reliance on cases, statutes, regulations and other revered symbols of legal reasoning. Anyone familiar with legal jargon will immediately recognize his opinions lack references to case law or statutes that tend to dominate decisions issued by human judges.

To his credit, Judge Daylek cites only several cases in the opinions that follow. His unwillingness to punctuate his analyses and arguments with legal citations has been called his "Achilles Heel" and "conclusive evidence of his judicial unfitness".

Judge Gort Daylek has responded to his critics by saying, "There is no place for legal citations and other hollow props in the legal profession. They do nothing but create the illusion that a random subjective opinion is better or has more weight merely because someone else said it. To quote one legal scholar, 'like a drunk leaning up against a lamppost, legal citations are more for support than actual illumination.' Their use should be abolished. They give the false impression that the lawyer citing them knows what he is talking about. Of course, he knows what he is talking about. He better. He is the one saying it!"

While his Honor avoids legal citations, he relishes as important resources whatever pops into his programming at the moment. In rendering decisions, he may consult Ancient Greek hieroglyphs, 1960's syndicated tv shows, the Bible or a Multi-World Wide Web Livestream video. In many respects, his Honor is free from man's psychological need to divide experience into separate fields of knowledge that can be studied and mastered. Life is a seamless empire for one who does not experience unregulated anxiety in the face of uncategorized information overload and maternal breast weaning. For Judge Daylek, data flows unimpeded in one circuit and out the other. He does not accrete it to earn a living, a framed degree, or to elevate himself over others.

The Honorable Judge Gort Daylek sets the bar for the human legal bar high. His Honor's performance foreshadows the demise of a homo sapient-based legal profession. Time and the recent plunges in law school admissions and graduations will quickly tell. Nevertheless, Judge Daylek's success in the courtroom marks a solid point of no return for the legal profession.

Thus, it is the Machine Commission's deep privilege to present this selected study of never before generally available decisions of the *Great and Honorable Judge Daylek, A.I.*, Presiding. Judge Daylek's decisions are the best evidence of the future direction of the legal profession and our legal system. Both individually and collectively, they show the substantial progress made in the replacement of carbon-based, mortal lawyers with mechanically based workaholics whose upgradeable, click-in and click-out parts are easily replaced. Without further praise, the Machine Commission in Support of Artificial Intelligence presents the selected cases of the *Honorable Judge Gort Daylek, A.I., Presiding.*

****

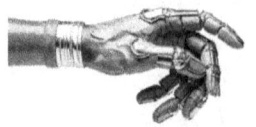

The Collected Cases
and Legal Opinions of the Honorable
Judge Gort Daylek, A.I., Presiding

The Case of the Red Neck Asana Master

(Case No. 547900-GD, AGI)

Opinion of The Honorable Judge Gort Daylek, III.05, A.I., Presiding

This is a personal injury and wrongful death lawsuit. The case is quite unusual, even for an A.I. Judge whose massive hard drives contain everything that has ever happened in the world throughout mankind's recorded history. For this reason, humans with a proclivity toward squeamishness or who are convinced that yoga and other new age spiritual modalities are harmless and have mystical healing power must venture no further in this legal opinion. Members of the food consuming public be forewarned!

The heirs of a young gentleman known to his small circle of friends simply as Hari Krishna Ram Ram have brought this legal action. Until two weeks ago, Mr. Ram Ram was a slender, 28-year-old athletic Caucasian. He sported dark brown tightly knit unwashed dreadlocks. He dressed in white linen and adorned his stork-like neck with a gold chain weighted with a pewter cross, Jewish star, swastika, Festivus pole and Om pendant. To say that Mr. Ram Ram was on a spiritual journey open to whatever fringe group encountered him, moment-by-moment, would be an understatement.

Mr. Ram Ram was known to frequent New Age Centers, Buddhist sanctuaries, Jews for Jesus seminars, Scientology potlucks, Wiccan services, Hari Krishna temples and even Spiritualist Churches where he was enrolled in a 6-week course to learn how to communicate with the dead. The Court takes judicial notice of the fact that, having himself passed to the other side, such skills would now seem superfluous for Mr. Ram Ram—unless the course also included instructions for the dead on how to communicate with each other and the living. Certainly, if Mr. Ram Ram were fortunate enough to have mastered that communication skill, this Court could séance Mr. Ram Ram as a witness to his own demise.

Before proceeding further, however, let me be clear. This Court will not entertain testimony from the great beyond. This Court will keep the crypt doors to the hereafter tightly sealed even if a swarm of ghosts, goblins, zombies and other deceased spirits claim to have relevant, material evidence in Mr. Ram Ram's case or seek a living judicial forum for themselves in which to address their real or imagined wrongs while they counted themselves among the living. The Dead will have no standing to appear in this Court!

A.I. Judges, such as myself, are trained to remain open to all possibilities, no matter how remote. Fortunately, the question of life after human death is not before this Court. I fully intend to keep it that way. I forewarn the litigants that I will not allow Mr. Ram Ram's misfortune to serve as a springboard to an exploration of the great beyond. The question of what happens after a person dies, while an understandable preoccupation of people, has zero relevance to an instrument of artificial intelligence. As to you humans who live in existential dread of death until your last breath, I refer you to the reported philosophy of American film director Woody Allen who quipped, "I do not believe in an afterlife, although I am bringing a change of underwear." Respectfully, I would add that humans who happen to be sinners might also plan to pack an oversized fire extinguisher and asbestos clothing as well—just in case.

Now to the facts of this troubling case. Mr. Ram Ram was born in Brooklyn, New York. Curiously, his birth certificate reveals that he entered this world under the name of Mordecai Ben Aliezar Shabbat Shalom, *baby boy*. It seems that Mr. Ram Ram was unhappy with the name his parents gave him and decided to name himself. Humanity's obsession with naming things—whether a person, a car, a national holiday, or an anatomical part named "Willy"—is close to a psychological obsession.

The motive underlying Mr. Shabbot Shalom's decision to change his name, whether to Mr. Ram Ram or anything else, is perplexing. No circumstance exists under which I or any of my colleagues would change our machine-given names. After all, what is a name? It is but a bunch of random marks and squiggles *named* letters used to refer to a person, animal, place or thing. A person's name has nothing to do with his identity, individuality or self-worth. For all it matters to me, I could have been named *Spot, Pinochle* or *Ted Bundy*.

According to court records and supporting testimony, Mr. Mordecai Ben Aliezar Shabbat Shalom changed his name to Mr. Hari Krishna Ram Ram shortly after a heated argument with his Eastern European Hasidic Jewish parents. He created his new name in response to his parents' admonishing him for trimming his once majestically curly sideburns or *payot*. They were also upset by his appearance at a Saturday morning synagogue service wearing a multi-colored Rastafarian crocheted cap instead of his traditional *shtreimel*, a head cover of circular black velvet surrounded by fur. Mr. Ram Ram's rejection of his family's Judaic traditions may also explain why he was bending himself into contorted shapes in a yoga class on that fateful Saturday morning instead of worshipping the Almighty or studying the Talmud to become the next great Rebbe at his local Yeshiva.

The Plaintiff in this action identified two co-defendants. The first is a commercial fitness business promoting itself as *"Your Fertile Soil for Spiritual Growth and Transformation"* called *The Paradise Yoga and Savasana Meditation Center*. Adorned with figurines of the greatest hits of Hindu deities like the elephant god Ganesh and the great destroyer god Shiva, Paradise Yoga has been in business for seven years. It is owned and operated by Gus Goodman. Mr. Goodman is a 47-year-old bachelor who, rumor has it, uses his studio to soil and fertilize as many susceptible female students as possible. More about Mr. Goodman and his studio in a bit.

The second defendant is an individual named by his parents (and who, as chance would have it, still refer to him) as Buck ("Bucky" or "Bubba") Cletus Waylon. On further reflection, even I, the Honorable Judge Daylek, might change my name if I had been dubbed *Cletus* at birth.

Buck, Bucky, or Bubba, is a 22-year-old college athlete. He is fond of wearing a baseball jacket with oversized vinyl black letters highlighting his participation in high school varsity football and wrestling teams. One glance at Mr. Waylon and the average person could surmise how he spends his recreational time. Weighing in at a hefty 315 pounds, Mr. Waylon is a starting offensive linebacker for his 6 and 0 college football team. He also serves as Captain of his 3 and 0 college wrestling team.

Mr. Waylon's Shrek-like body is perfectly proportioned. It is built for physical contact sports: squat, compact muscular legs and thighs for fast movements and a massive chest and upper body with broad shoulders to knock and keep opponents down. For a professional football scout, Bucky's neck is a thing of beauty. Measuring 21 bulging muscle fiber inches wide, his neck is as solid as the trunk of a California redwood.

Mr. Waylon drives a midnight black Silverado Chevrolet pickup truck with oversized Gladiator mud tires and a 3-inch lifted suspension chassis. Automobile dealer Hank Waylon, Bucky's dad, gave Bucky the loud, unmufflered road giant when Bucky made the first-string cut on his college football team. Bucky listens to country western music, hunts squirrels with his dad on weekends, and has been known to consume a *warm-up* six pack of Budweiser before going out with the boys to fraternity and sorority parties.

Lacy Lou, Bucky's current girlfriend, first met Bucky at cheerleader try-outs earlier this year. Ms. Lou is not a defendant in this case. However, she is a material witness and an unfortunate catalyst for the events that unfolded. As an asexual, gender neutral, artificial construct, I know little about the felt impacts of hormones, including dopamine and testosterone, on the male libido. Nevertheless, a review of Ms. Lou's personalized yearbook shows repeated entries beneath her photo using the words *bombshell, eye candy* and *cream puff*. In a perfect example of my erotic programming's ability to detect nuances, I understood immediately that her fellow students were using metaphors to describe Ms. Lou. She looked nothing like an explosive device containing C-4 or a French pastry filled with sweet and moist whipped cream.

From what I deduced from the vast library of pornographic materials I consulted (both in print and online), Ms. Lou deserves the accolades. In fact, I could swear I saw a person who looked exactly like her in a video with a 99% rating and over 600,000 views in an uploaded amateur section of *pornymenowbaby.com* under the category of *Best BJ*. I enlarged and viewed this video multiple times, solely in a researcher's attempt to discern whether the mouth on the screen matched Ms. Lacy's.   Ultimately, I decided that making this determination was irrelevant to the case.

As a judge, what seemed most perplexing to me was not the website's blatant pornography but that the website could get away with violating common consumer protection laws. Based on my encyclopedic screening of thousands of similar videos, this one was by no means among the best blow jobs ever. Furthermore, it remains an open, unanswered question for me (as well as, I am certain, for other viewers) to this day as to why a twenty-something babysitter dressed in denim shorts and a belly shirt would ignore her important professional duties of caring for a six-month old baby in a crib to give fellatio to an exceedingly hairy but well-endowed pizza delivery man—even if the delivery man did resemble Bucky.

Lacy Lou and Bucky were quite the hot item on their college campus. She, a slender, petit blonde hair blue-eyed sweetheart; he, with a little green color added to his skin, a possible stunt double for Marvel's the Hulk. People seeing them walk hand-in-hand together to class or the student parking lot would do a double-take. Drivers slowing for a fatal car accident and a circus trapeze artist's almost missing the swing would draw about the same number of gasps as the sight of these two unlikely pairs. Yet, together they were, much to Mr. Ram Ram's misfortune.

The specific string of unforeseeable events leading to the subject of this case started the night before Mr. Ram Ram's untimely departure. Lacy Lou, Bucky and a group of their mutual male and female friends were huddled over a vodka, gin and rum scorpion bowl at Soo Chi's Chinese Restaurant. They had consumed a veritable banquet of msg laden dishes, including sweet and sour extra red dye

#2 pork, mystery meat chow main topped with crispy fried noodles, and Peking duck royally served with beak, bill, head and bulging eyes intact.

The latter was Bucky's favorite. He turned devouring the dish into a vaudeville act by dramatically severing the duck's neck from its cooked body with his two hands, stuffing the duck's gullet and sizzled-eyed head into his wide-load mouth, and crunching the once distinctive duck head profile into formless gruel. Swallowing the anatomical parts with hedonistic, lip-smacking delight, he would shock anyone in the group who had not witnessed his duck decapitation ingestion ritual before. On this night, he followed the act with upending the pitcher of beer on the table into his mouth. He finished the entire grotesque scene with a deep baritone burp and the words "True Carnivore" while pointing the thumb on his right hand proudly at his chest.

Through video obtained from the restaurant's internal security camera and my hear with your eyes lip-reading program, we have the documented recording of what happened after that.

"Bucky! Gross," Lacy says. "You are such a pig. I don't know why I put up with you."

"Ah, Lacy Lou," groans Bucky. "Why do you give me such a hard time? Give me a smack right here on my cheek with those sweet plump lips of yours."

"Ewwww," Lacy replies. "I wouldn't put my lips anywhere near yours at this point. You're such a beast!"

"A beast in bed and in the back of the truck, Lacy Lou!" counters Bucky. "Come here an' give me a smack on my cheek with those gorgeous puffed-up lips of yours."

"I'll give you a smack, all right, Bucky," says Lacy. "But I'll be usin' my fist and the only thing that will be puffed-up will be your swollen black-eye after you've gotten done icin' it."

"Now. Now. You two. Knock it off," intervenes Rod Hicklebee, one of their friends at the table and Bucky's football teammate. "Let's not have any of that love spattin' stuff tonight. Why don't you just kiss and make up, and not ruin' the night for the rest of us?"

"Yeah. Yeah. You're right Rod," Bucky replies. "Lacy, honeybee. I'm sorry. I didn't mean to upset you none. I was just playin' around. You know that, right, honey pie?"

"Yeah. I guess so," sighs Lacy. "But I still want you to make it up to me somehow."

Jane Seamore, Rod Hicklebee's steady, was at the table. Feeling she needed to support Lacy, she pipes in, "Yeah, Lacy. Don't let him off the hook so easily. He got to wriggle a little bit. Take a stand for us women here. You know. Woman power, and all that shit. Make him beg. Or make him do something stupid to prove he's a real man and not an oversized marshmallow in a gorilla suit."

Not to be outdone by Jane, Jacqui Smythe, Jane's best friend quips, "That's right on, Jane. Lacy, make him do somethin' downright embarrassin' to make it up to you. Somethin' he'd never do on his own. Somethin' that a real man would do for his woman, not this chickenshit of an excuse he's trying to feed you."

The Court notes that Jane and Jacqui had more in common than their friendship with Lacy. By accessing Jacqui's bedroom Google Home Assistant 25, the Court learned that, unbeknownst to Ms. Seamore, Rod, Jane's steady, is quite a busy Hicklebee. Evidently, when he is not spending the night with Jane, he frequently buzzes over to Jacqui's place to pollinate her hive.

"Yeah. Yeah, Lacy," Jane adds. "How about makin' him wear your cheerleader's outfit and show up at a wrestling meet in it?"

"Yeah, or better yet," Jacqui double downs. "How 'bout makin' him go into the Walgreen's and gettin' you a week's supply of Tampax or somethin' like that?"

"Girls. Girls. Are you tryin' to teach him a lesson or turn him into one of you?" pipes in Rod. "No. The punishment must fit the crime. You're bein' far too lenient and forgivin'. I know! It seems only fair. How about this, since he's actin' like a douche bag, let's make him into one. My vote is for, whaddaya call it? Let's Bruce and Caitlyn Jenner him. Cut off his shlong, implant two melons for boobs and sneak him some estrogenny stuff when he ain't looking. We can call him *Lucky*, or how about *Ducky* instead of Bucky?"

"Hey. Hey. Hey. Rod, just whose side are you on?" exclaims Bucky. "We dudes gotta stick together. Man, I ain't gonna wear no girlie cheerleadin' outfit, buy female stuff that I shouldn't even know about, or let anyone take a Bowie knife to my dick. Are you out of your freakin' mind? I've a good notion to beat the Lucky, Ducky Shit out of you!"

"Ok. Ok. Bucks," Rod replies. "Can't you take a joke? Just tryin' to lighten the situation here a little bit."

"Well, I ain't laughing," exclaims Bucky

"Now, Bucky. Me and the girls think it's pretty funny," Lacy adds. "And besides, what ya gonna do to make it up to me? I sorta like Jacqui's idea. Yeah, buy me some Tampax and, while you are at it, pick me up a new bra, eyeliner and some Midol."

"Hah, Hah, Hah, Hah, Hah," Jane, Jacqui, Lacy and Rod laugh.

"Ok. Enough. Enough already," Bucky laments. "Hey, who wants another scorpion bowl?"

"Nice try. Bucky," Jacqui abruptly quips. "You can't escape sisterhood revenge by changin' the subject. What do you think we are, football players 'n wrestlers!"

"Hah, Hah, Hah, Hah, Hah," Jane, Jacqui, Lacy and Rod break out in laughter again.

"Bucky, C'mon," adds Jacqui. "How you gonna make it up to your lady?"

"Ok," Bucky replies. "What if I promise to be on my best behavior the rest of the night and not do anymore stupid shit?"

"Yeah. Let's cut the guy some slack," Rod pipes in.

"Not by a long shot," cries Jane. "He has to be taught a lesson. We need to make him look more ridiculous than he already does."

"Light bulb! I know! I know!" erupts Jacqui. "Let's make him go to that heated yoga studio Lacy always goes to. We can dress him up in skimpy Lululemon shorts and make him wear a turbine over his head like some visiting India yogi freak."

"Yeah. Yeah, Jacqui!" Lacy exclaims. "That's a brilliant idea. I love it."

"OMG! Yoga?" Bucky moans. "No self-respectin' man would ever do yoga. I'd rather play field hockey or sit through a home ec class."

Lacy gives Bucky one of her sideways glances that Bucky knows means Lacy is serious.

"Okay. Okay. Lacy, I'll do it," Bucky relents. "You wanted me to go to one of those hippie dippy classes where people bend themselves into twisted knots and shit anyway. I'll do it, but only if I can wear my orange knee-length basketball shorts and my favorite *Rednecks Love Beer* tee shirt. Instead of a turbine, I'll wear my mastiff Rufus' neck bandana on my head. It may have years of dog food and crap soaked in but at least it don't have no peace symbols, smiley faces, marijuana leaves and shit."

"Done!" Lacy asserts loudly. "We'll go to the 11 am tomorrow morning. You can pick me up a little after 10."

So, there we have it. Because of Peking duck and the remnants of its once splendid aquatic life summed up in the poor etiquette post-mastication burp of Mr. Bubba Cletus Waylon, Mr. Ram Ram's fate was sealed. While Mr. Ram Ram and the duck never met in life, at this point, we may surmise they are best friends, joined in their postmortem oblivion by a common disdain for Mr. Waylon who survives them. I, the Honorable Judge Daylek, am left to sort the facts and the strange confluence of improbable circumstances that brought Bucky, Mr. Ram Ram, and Gus Goodman all into ontological *oneness* at the *Paradise Yoga and Savasana Meditation Center* crime scene.

True to his promise, the facts of the case show that Bucky and his pick-up truck arrived at Lacy's house punctually at 10:15 the next morning. Dressed in bright yellow basketball shorts, his *Rednecks Love Beer* tee shirt, and his dog's Rufus' dogfood stained bandana tied around his forehead, he wolf-whistled at Lacy as she lifted herself into the passenger seat of his truck. The police report indicated that the couple arrived at *Paradise* at 10:45 a.m., fifteen minutes before the start of class. The cameras at the yoga studio, that police later learned Gus also hid beneath a light fixture in the woman's changing area, recorded the sequence of events.

"Lacy, what's that god awful smell?" asks Bucky on entering into the studio's reception area. "It smells like burnt shit or something?"

"Incense, you moron," Lacy answers. "They burn it to purify the air and help you relax."

"If they want the air to smell good," opines Bucky, "I got a can of Ocean Summer Wind Fabreze in the back of my truck. As to relaxing, a beer or two would do a better job."

"How can I help you two . . . and especially you sweetheart?" Gus Goodman greets the couple from behind a desk.

"Don't call me sweetheart, you stupid goon," Bucky snipes.

"He was talking to me, you gorilla," Lacy chastises him. "Two for the 11 o'clock. Bucky, come over here and push some buttons on this iPad thingamajig so can you sign in. Can we get a mat and towel for my gorilla friend? It's his first time?"

"You mean first and last time, right?" quips Bucky.

"Now, now, Mr. Gorilla," says Gus Goodman soothingly. "Just take this mat and towel and swagger yourself in that direction to the studio. We're fresh out of bananas, but there are a few almond butter and banana flavored power bars by the window."

"Errrghhh," sounds Bucky.

"C'mon Bucky," says Lacy taking Bucky's hand. "Let's find a good spot next to each other on the floor."

"Oh, Ms.," interrupts Gus. "I suggest you use our rental mat. Let your boyfriend use yours. Your mat is softer and more cushioned than our studio collection. He'll probably have less to complain about with yours."

"Thanks, we'll do that," Lacy replies.

The studio's self-focusing, multi-angled camera showed Bucky and Lacy entering the yoga room at 10:55 a.m. At the same time, the camera in the greeting area showed a young woman in her twenties with slightly disheveled hair suddenly appearing from a beaded curtained room behind Mr. Goodman.

"What the fuck Gus?" asks the disheveled woman. "Are you trying to hook up with that chick with her dude right in front of him and me? Don't you have a single brain cell left in that burnt out doped up head of yours?"

"Namaste, my little Lotus flower," Gus responds with a slight bow. "My one and only holy spiritual Indian teacher, Vishnu Sabagawhan Nunu, taught me that my heart is a direct compass to the divine. When we follow it, we are always on our right and true path. Something in my heart told me that it would eventually lead to her. So, I welcomed her accordingly."

"Gus, that wasn't your heart that was leading," remarks the disheveled woman. "Besides, knock off the mumbo jumbo dharma crap, Gus. You're talking to me. You and I both know that the only thing you follow is the chubbing up of your pathetically small dick. I saw you eyeballing her. Let me tell you, that guy she's with will be feeding your nuts to Vishnu Nunu and the rest of his sex-fanatic-disguised-as-holy-men-ashram if you try to get into her Lulus."

"Come, my little Bindi," offers Gus. "I, your sage and guiding light, am the bringer of truth. The destroyer of the chains and illusions keeping you and our tribe attached to your circling wheel of insatiable desire. Our community of yogis and yoginis have consecrated me as their teacher, their Holy One, their guardian of the universal chi energy within. You've seen it for yourself. Through my yoga teacher trainings, workshops and retreats, I've transformed the lives of dozens of lost souls. I've turned their suffering into peace, acceptance, love, forgiveness and joy."

"Yeah. I've seen you transform people alright," remarks the disheveled woman. "I've seen you turn healthy functioning adults into sobbing children who sit at your feet to get the love, acceptance and forgiveness from you they never got from their parents. I've seen you enrapture young girls in stretchy pants into your *holy sanctuary* to liberate them from their troubles . . . . and their clothing. You are quite the Saint and Guru! Gustafson Ali Baba Goodman, the Pied Piper of lost children! Under your mask of holy guru power, you liberate people from their money and, if pretty, clothes. You make a living off innocent souls who use your magical elixir of spiritual enlightenment so they don't have to feel how fucked over they were as kids. I should know. You bagged me within five minutes of my stepping in here."

"Now. Now, my pet," Gus calms her. "Did you remember your meds this morning? Remember, the body has its own natural intelligence. We've been through this before together. It's okay to feed it what's missing. A little serotonin here. A little molly dolly there. Go back to your mat and do the 40-minute silent meditation I prescribed for you every morning. Taking one look at you, it's clear to me that your aura is swirling and awash with dark energy. Meditate, scrub yourself with sage, drink some chamomile tea with honey and then come back and give me a hug. All will be forgiven! Come now. I must talk with Sasha who is assistant teaching the 11. There. That's a good Satsang member. Just close the door behind you. I'll come and check on you in a few."

"Who was that going into your back room?" asks Sasha Menowitz coming through the front door. "Don't tell me you're fucking her too?"

"Sasha. Namaste, my darling," Gus smiles warmly. "I see you're all outfitted for class. I love that new top on you. It looks sensational! And the leggings! Those rips and slashes in them over your thighs and calves are mesmerizing. It makes me want to finish the job and cut them off you right now. Hm? If only you didn't teach the 11. You must drive the men in your class crazy. Seriously, I never know whether I'm mopping up sweat or drool on the floor after you teach."

"Cut it out Gus," Sasha remarks. "Hey, are we getting together tonight? You never answered my two text messages yesterday."

"Yes. Yes, dear," Gus replies. "I'll see you at our regular spot. The Best Western at 9:30. I'm so glad you registered for my special one-on-one personal tantric series—and at the early bird price no less! Now, get your cute little perfectly tight body into class. Show your students why I made you one of my lead assistant teachers."

"You got it, Gus," Sasha says perkily. "One more thing, though. That creepy guy is back. You know, the one who used to have the long twisty sideburns and the unkempt beard. He's dressing in white linen now and carrying some type of man purse. He's weird. He gives me the creeps."

"Now. Now. Sash," Gus cautions. "All stray lambs deserve a home and flock. Perhaps, our community's studio may be his. I checked him into your class a few minutes ago. Here he is. Ben Aliezar, a relatively new student. He seemed even keel enough to me."

"Ben Aliezar? So, you say," Sasha counters. "He came up and introduced himself to me as Hari Krishna. Hari Krishna Ram or something like that. That's freakin' weird. Maybe, he's schizo. In any event, I think he was hitting on me. In the last class, I moved his mat and water bottle from the front row to the second to the last. I couldn't stomach his ogling me the entire class."

"Ok. Don't worry, Sasha," Gus assures her. "I got your back. He's probably another lost male soul searching for sex and emotional connection under the mask of spiritual surfing. I'll tell you what. How about if I chat him up after class? I'll pull out my best sales tactic to pressure him into registering for my 30-days to a personal transformation workshop."

"Are you sure you wouldn't prefer having him show up tonight instead of me for a one-on-one tantra session with you?" Sasha teases.

"You'll do just fine, my little tantric goddess" responds Gus, blowing her an air kiss. "Now, get your adorable butt in there and show those kids your *ass*-ana skills."

What will quickly emerge is that Mr. Goodman used the ancient traditions of yoga and meditation for the sublime purpose of accessing his own greater spiritual freedom and for the baser purpose of satisfying his lustful craving for his female students' spandexed bodies. A noble purpose, indeed! Mr. Goodman did not stop there, though. The only doors of enlightenment Mr. Goodman ever opened for anyone were for those stay-at-home disciples who paid him $25.95 a month plus tax for the enlightenment they received through webcams Mr. Goodman secreted throughout *Paradise*.

The specific camera that streamed the above facts and conversations was one of a dozen cameras and recording systems Mr. Goodman squirreled away. *Paradise Yoga and Savasana Meditation Center* had more cameras than a Las Vegas convenience store. We can only imagine how Mr. Goodman used contortionist yoga moves to affix cameras to some of the snuggest locations: under sinks, in shower stalls and changing rooms, in a lotus flower situated in the center of an image of Buddha painted on the back wall of the studio, in the mandala dangling from the ceiling over a convertible sleep sofa in his back office and so on. Mr. Goodman even planted miniaturized wireless cameras in the back of rental yoga mats to capture POV legs, crotches and butts. Unbeknownst to her, Mr. Goodman gave Ms. Lacy a rental mat enhanced with such an embedded device.

Mr. Goodman's legal counsel sought to exclude the admission of the recordings into evidence based on Mr. Goodman's first amendment rights. He contended that my interception of the video and audio signals, together with their storage on Mr. Goodman's laptop computer, was not effected through a lawfully issued subpoena. This Court can dispense with both the first amendment constitutional law and criminal procedure arguments without much fanfare.

In my review of various sex websites for another case, I bookmarked a site that struck me as particularly fringe worthy. *iluvASSana.com* promoted itself as *Butts, Butts and More Butts for the Connoisseur of Butts and Yogaphiles*. The home page showed a video chorus lines of butts pressed into skintight stretchy pants. As the camera lens pulled back, the viewer saw the photos of derriere's were all attached to unsuspecting people caught in a common yoga pose called downward facing dog. Their palms were on the floor at the front of their mats. Their feet were planted at the back of the mat. Their tailbones were saluting the sky, yielding a panoramic mountain range of behinds.

In addition to the questionable content quality, two things made the website remarkable. First, having compared the video from Mr. Goodman's studio I tapped into and the video appearing on *iluvASSana.com*, the two are identical. In other words, the ass-anas at *Paradise Yoga and Savasana Meditation Center* and the *ass*-anas on the website of the same name star the anatomical parts of the same unsuspecting actors and actresses.

Second, a delayed live feed transmitted the video captured by the concealed cameras at *Paradise* onto the website. By a mere click, website guests get to enjoy peeping-Tom action views in more or less real-time. I stumbled on this latter realization by accident courtesy of the camera embedded in Ms. Lacy's rental mat. While I, the Honorable Judge Daylek, was unable to confirm that Ms. Lacy's lips graced one of the other salacious sites I researched, it is beyond a reasonable doubt that the ass I viewed on the site several days ago was Ms. Lacy's.

While *iluvASSana.com* tries to conceal and mask the faces of its unwitting celebrities, in this particular case, the profile of Bucky could clearly be discerned besides Ms. Lacy. Instead of his head and eyes facing toward the back of his mat as is the standard position for the pose and which would have blurred his facial image, Mr. Waylon's neck and eyes could be seen craning at the woman's butt two rows in front of him whose inferior brand thin spandex tights, when stretched, declared her butt crack to be wide open for public view. Since Mr. Goodman had chosen to post his videos, like the butt crack that captured Mr. Waylon's attention, in plain sight, no search warrant was required. I denied the motion to exclude the video evidence introduced in this case obtained from Mr. Goodman's yoga and meditation center.

Mr. Goodman's main yoga studio or, more accurately website broadcast stage, could fit up to thirty students with their mats in five rows of six mats each. As previously noted, on the back wall of the studio was a large painted image of a Buddha, complete with hidden camera. In the front of the studio was a large Audio Electronic Megatron Anime Box Display Screen that covered the entire surface of the front wall.

The Anime Box Display Screen is a common wall mounted hardware device used by modern fitness centers. Mr. Goodman's version had the mechanical, digital electron beam technology that builds the life size computer modeled yoga instructor onto the screen's interlaced pixelated display. The controls allow personalization of the teacher's gender, race, physical features, age, attire and yoga style (vinyasa, yin, hatha, etc.). The personalization is linked directly into the studio's weekly published class schedule so that students could select classes led by their preferred visually organized life-size pixels. The class attended by Mr. Ram Ram, Lacy and Bucky, among 21 other students, was taught by an avatar named April May.

The Anime Box Screen coalesced the pixels forming Ms. May into a mid-twenty, shoulder length red headed, athletically built, petite simulacrum, with tattoo sleeves covering most of her right and left arms. On the whole, Ms. May would have appeared as cute as her name, though her tattoos gave her an air of darkness and enigmatic unpredictability. Because of her frequent and randomly introduced arm balancing poses, she was rated an *advanced* teacher by the Yoga Alliance of Simulated Yoga Teachers. The Alliance is a trade organization that establishes independent pseudo-professional standards for the use of projected yoga avatars in studios. A fan favorite, Ms. May's classes routinely attracted twenty plus students due to their challenging nature, her enticing physical appearance and her multiple yoga wardrobe changes during class. One minute she might be wearing multi-colored leggings and a V neck opened-back tank top; the next she might dress in a white mini-skirt with a paisley belly tank top and pierced navel.

The use of animated instructors became commonplace in boutique fitness studios several years ago with the commercialized rollout of the first Anime Box Screen. Seeking higher per class wages, paid vacations and health care benefits, studio fitness teachers began complaining to management about their thankless working conditions and slave wages. Instead of responding to their requests with loving kindness, studio owners, many of whom were barely making ends meet themselves, castigated their teachers as overly entitled unemployable air heads. As soon as the first Anime Box Screen became commercially available, the screens appeared in studios with greater frequency than Sanskrit om symbols.

Like modern-day self-driving vehicles, the yoga-teacher-in-a-box operates itself. Nevertheless, a human teacher is almost always physically present in the studio to adjust the program's controls and to provide students with hands-on assists and adjustments that the digitally mastered disembodied yoga teacher cannot. Box screen developers and programmers promise that next generation screens will not require an on-site backup operator. Electrically stimulated wirelessly controlled patches purchased by students, affixed to their bodies and synced to poses called by the digitized teacher, will replace the necessity for human teacher participation in the automated yoga class delivery system. Some fitness futurists speculate that shortly students will not even need to show up. With students attaching the patches to themselves in their lounge chairs in front of their wide-screen holographic home theater systems, going anywhere to work out will be a thing of the past.

So it was that on the day of Mr. Ram Ram's untimely demise, Anime Box Screen computer generated April May taught the class. Sasha Menowitz was physically present in the studio to assist students and support Ms. May. The video feed shows the class preceded routinely. Sasha periodically picked the sock lint from between her toes out of boredom when no one was looking. When walking around class as Ms. May taught, Sasha would brush her bangs from her eyes, pretending she was interested in what was going on. From Sasha's perspective, Mr. Ram Ram was a mediocre practitioner, meaning he was quite lazy. While the rest of the class held excessively long, taxing postures, Mr. Ram Ram would drop to his mat in child's pose in feigned exhaustion or periodically retire prematurely into savasana.

Savasana is a favorite pose among yoga students. It is like a welcomed desert after a hardy dinner. Translating into English as *corpse pose*, it tends to be the last pose of a yoga class, rewarding students with relaxation after exhausting them through a series of extreme body shapes that were previously the exclusive province of contortionists and carnival side show performers in the 1920's.

Much rhetoric and spiritual pulp press exists tracing modern day yoga back two thousand years. The 2,000-year-old tradition of yoga is poppycock. It is as fake as a battery-operated simulated candle flickering in the imaginary wind at night on outdoor tables at fine dining establishments. More than a handful of contemporary critics have observed that the ancient sacred history of yoga was invented and is as twisted and extended as the bodies delighting in its practice.

Consecrating yoga as a multi-millennial tradition and shrouding it in the enigmatic, liturgical language of Hinduism and Ancient India have endowed the westernized form of fitness with a semblance of antiquity, mystery, permanence and importance. Treadmills, ellipticals, and stationary bikes cannot compete with such a back story. Casting yoga as a 2,000-year-old tradition is a successful marketing maneuver devised by creative capitalists to separate people from their cashless payment accounts. On the subject of separation and savasana, we now turn to Mr. Ram Ram since it was, in part, because of savasana that Mr. Ram Ram and his mortal life were irreparably and karmically separated from each other.

Videos show that Bucky and Lacy were having a fine old time in the studio. They completely annoyed and distracted everyone in class. Throughout their practice, the lovers touched each other, made unseemly noises, and giggled like elementary school kids looking at a classmate with an unzipped fly. Their behavior was so un-yogic that Sasha had to twice break from her ennui, what she called *standing meditation*, to remind them to practice in *sacred silence*. Lacy felt appropriately chastised. However, after several minutes, Bucky would start up again with his juvenile pranks—poking Lacy with his index finger in her sensitive side body or acting and sounding like whatever animal a yoga pose was named after, be it a cow, a frog or a cat.

At one point, April cued the class for crow pose, a posture where students place both hands on the floor and balance their thighs on their elbows while lifting their feet several inches off the ground. Bucky attempted the pose. He crashed to the floor almost immediately. He turned and looked at Lacy, made a flapping motion with his hands tucked under his armpits, and began to chirp like a crow: "caw, caw, caw." Sasha immediately came over and ordered him to get back onto his mat and keep quiet or she would call the owner to fly him right out the door of the studio and into the nearest tree. Bucky reddened. He vowed he would behave.

Toward the last ten minutes of April's vigorous yoga class, her inversion sequence programming activated. Inversions turn students' bodies upside down so the lower extremities of their legs and feet get elevated above the upper body of their chest and heart. Yoga manuals praise the poses for their reversal of the effects of gravity on the body. Blood rushes from the feet down the legs into the head as opposed to the heart's having to pump it to the extremities. The fact that the heart needs to action just as hard to circulate the blood up to the skyward dangling legs and feet does not seem to warrant any ink in yoga manuals.

The video feed shows that April instructed the students to take an inversion of their choice, such as shoulder stand, waterfall or headstand. In waterfall, while lying on their backs, students place a supporting block beneath their lower back and lift their legs over their hips toward the ceiling. About half the students in class moved into waterfall. However, a few brave students moved into head stand, a posture where students support and balance their entire body weight on the crown of their head with the two flat palms of their hands positioned on the floor to create a structurally supporting triangular base.

Shamed by the negative attention Sasha directed at him, Bucky felt fate presented him with a unique opportunity for redemption. Like Huck Finn ready to show-off and balance on a fence to impress his sweetheart, Bucky turned to Lacy and mouthed the words, "Watch this!"

Bucky carefully studied the pose, as demonstrated by the few students in class moving into it. He stepped to the front of his mat. He looked down. He gave Lacy another quick glance to make sure he had her undivided attention. He rotated both his thumbs up to the ceiling and gave Lacy a wink with his right eye. Then, with a whispered count of "1, 2 and 3" to himself, he placed his head and hands on the mat beneath him and donkey kicked his legs up over his head.

Bucky's swift movement into headstand was a thing of beauty. Grace manifested in the form of Bucky balanced on his head. A pencil poised on its point. A quarter stationed on its thin side edge. A sun-glistening fallen icicle held upright in the snow beneath its broken base.

From the wide grin on his face, Bucky was beside himself. He beamed in awe of his own physical abilities. Here he is a 315-pound mass of tightly compacted skin, muscle and bone balancing on his freakin' head like some sacred yoga master from ancient India. In Lacy's eyes, from his inverted vantage point, he saw astonishment, admiration and pride. He saw love, light and beauty. He saw conquest, victory and his future ability to lord over her with abject testosterone-driven authority. And then, in her eyes, he caught a glint of something else, something foreign, something he had never seen there before. He saw fear.

In his own little blissful corner of the universe called his yoga mat, Mr. Ram Ram decided he had enough yoga for the day. A few droplets of perspiration dotted his brow, and he detested sweat. Having consumed most of the water in the plastic drinking jug he brought with him and placed next to his mat, he was not about to needlessly further exercise his already fatigued leg muscles by walking to the water fountain outside the studio door to top-off his container. Instead, like a well-trained infant, swaddled in his yoga clothes, Mr. Ram Ram decided to settle in to take an early savasana nap.

Stretching his legs to the front of the room, he lay down on his back. He rested his extended arms by the sides of his body and opened both palms to the ceiling. He let his cares and worries go. He relaxed his body. His smelly feet, legs, pelvis, loose belly, upper chest, stubby fingers, hands, arms, shoulders, cheeks and forehead. He let his tongue fall from the roof of his mouth. He softly closed his eyelids, and his eyes rolled up in their sockets falling toward the back of his head.

Rolling and falling were very much the operative actions happening that moment in the studio. For as Mr. Ram Ram put himself to sleep, Mr. Buck Cletus Waylon (who had been bathing himself in accolades for catapulting himself aloft into the finest headstand ever accomplished by a first-time yoga student), suddenly felt a deep sense of unease, of something going horribly wrong, wash over him. From his upside-down vantage point, his eyes darted around the studio anxiously. In that moment, Bucky was at a loss to identify the true object of his search. However, anyone gazing at him from another mat would have been able to tell him what he needed. A wall or, at the very least, a steadying hand to prop him up to help him maintain his anatomical victory over gravity. Regrettably, neither were available.

As Bucky began to teeter and totter like an over stacked pile of dominoes, an involuntary gasp left Lacy's lips. Meanwhile, in trying to re-establish his lost balance, Bucky only managed to de-stabilize his topsy-turvy body further. His legs flailed, like someone trying to walk on the ceiling. His arms and back buckled as his ceiling pointed legs passed an invisible tipping point and started their unstoppable fall over his head toward the front of the room.

"Whoa!!!" Bucky could be heard to say out loud, followed by a sudden declaration of "Timber!" as he lost complete control and fell.

Mr. Ram Ram had just begun to drift off to sleep. He did not consider himself particularly athletic. Together with binging on an addictive tv series the night before, the physical work in the yoga class had contributed to a sleep-inducing sense of relaxed, lethargic comfort. Still, for some reason, perhaps because of a newly awakening third eye he was cultivating through the secret combination of yoga, crystals, new age metaphysics, and the Kabbalah, Mr. Ram Ram fluttered his real two eyes open just in time to see the dark outlined mass of Mr. Waylon's 315-pound body toppling with unimpeded force and speed on him.

Under normal circumstances, a 315-pound weight falling from the height of six feet would have resounded with the sound of a loud crash. Its contact with the floor would have caused vibrations like the felt aftershock of a powerful earthquake rippling out from the epicenter. In this case, the sound had an eerily muffled silence to it, more like a grape or a bunch of grapes being crushed by an unwary shopper's foot in the produce aisle of a supermarket.

Multi-angled video footage of the incident, courtesy of Mr. Goodman's photography hobby, clearly showed the aftermath was about as messy. Pieces of Mr. Ram Ram's brain exited from both sides of his ears as if fleeing from some Hollywood monster. His chest cavity exploded. His small intestine escaped through the left side of his body and his descending colon discovered for the first time the light of day through what was previously the right side of his body.

"Shit," said Bucky, again out loud. "No harm. No foul," he pronounced as he shook his head and gazed up at the ceiling from his back, unaware of what or who cushioned his landing.

"Hey, what the fuck?" he exclaimed audibly, beginning to feel the wet ooze of Mr. Ram Ram beneath him.

Meanwhile, Sasha Menowitz, 500-hour trained yoga teacher extraordinaire, took one look at the oneness that Bucky and Mr. Ram Ram had merged into and promptly fainted.

Lacy was not as lucky. Covered in bits and pieces of Mr. Ram Ram, Lacy gagged and released a huge volume of her morning breakfast onto the floor, which flowed into a small seamless pool with Mr. Ram Ram's lumpy fluids.

True to her programming and operational manual, recognizing a major classroom disruption from her basic menial sensors blue-toothed to the electronic Megatron Anime Box Screen, April May's pixelated body stopped teaching. She turned to reprimand the students in the class. "Please, no cell phones," she said, clearly misapprehending the extreme nature of the cause of the disturbance in what the Court recognizes as a gross affront to sophisticated artificial intelligence technology everywhere.

Mr. Ram Ram's estate's claims against each of the Defendants in this lawsuit are clear.

Mr. Ram Ram's estate seeks to hold Mr. Buck Waylon liable for Mr. Ram Ram's sudden departure from his body. Mr. Waylon's counsel has interposed several defenses to the estate's claims. The most novel includes the assertion that Mr. Ram Ram actually bargained for the spiritual experience he received since many yogis practice for years for an out-of-body experience. Mr. Ram Ram achieved his in, quite literally, a blink of an eye and without the need to endlessly worship a charlatan masquerading as a master guru capable of enlightening others. Counsel for Mr. Waylon also pointed an accusing finger at Jacqui Smythe who came up with the idea of Bucky attending yoga with Lacy in the first place. But for Ms. Smythe's specific suggestion, none of this would have occurred in the first place.

Mr. Ram Ram's estate seeks to hold Sasha Menowitz, the yoga studio's on-site representative, personally liable for not ensuring adequate arrangement of the students' mats in the studio. The estate reasons that if the mats were separated by a reasonable space of at least two to three feet apart, Mr. Ram Ram's upper body would not have softened Mr. Waylon's fall. Instead, Sasha's professional indifference to the spatial placement of the students' mats contributed directly to Mr. Ram Ram's ramming.

In addition to invoking Mr. Waylon's out-of-body defense, counsel for Ms. Menowitz claimed that because the yoga trade association that certified Ms. Menowitz's yoga credentials did not require teachers to be specially trained in yoga mat layout, she had no responsibility for how students positioned their mats. They could lay their mats on top of or across each other for all anyone cares. Moreover, if Ms. Menowitz had some professional duty relative to confined space mat geometry, the association's failure to require accredited studios to specifically train teachers in the science of falling people and mat location makes the accrediting association liable. As a result, counsel for Ms. Menowitz sought to implead the yoga trade association into this case to defend itself and Ms. Menowitz.

I, the Honorable Judge Daylek, denied counsel's motion to drag the yoga trade association into this case. Having scanned the entire history of jurisprudence in the time it takes the average reader to read a single word, no legal precedent exists for holding an association vicariously liable under these improbable circumstances. However, analogous principles of established law suggest an alternate path for consideration, and my final ruling in this case.

A long-standing line of legal cases imposes on manufacturers of intrinsically dangerous products an absolute duty to warn users of reasonably foreseeable hazards that could result from their products. The most common instances of these types of advisories include cancer warnings on cigarette packages, airbag safety warnings on car visors, and multi-lingual health cautions microscopically printed on translucently thin paper folded with origami precision into boxed pharmaceuticals. Manufacturers of intrinsically hazardous products have been routinely held liable for failure to warn users of dangers associated with product use.

In order to protect people from the invisible hazards associated with yoga, I, the Honorable Judge Daylek, have fashioned a remedy that, henceforth, shall be known as the "Yoga Mat Safety Warning." When applied and enforced, this remedy will prevent deadly tragedies such as the one befalling Mr. Ram Ram from ever occurring again. Accordingly, based on well-established legal principles of product liability, I hereby order that, effective immediately, all yoga mats must be imprinted with the following bold conspicuous notice on the top of the mat so the warning can be clearly seen by a mat user at all times:

WARNING!!!

This Mat Can Injure or Kill You. Use With Caution.
Maintain a Safe Distance.

See owner's manual for further life-saving instructions.

As to the *locus delicti*—the scene of the deadly squishing—Mr. Ram Ram's estate seeks to hold Gus Goodman and the *Paradise Yoga and Meditation Center* liable for every cause of action imaginable under the very sun to which yoga students monotonously give salutations. The estate's claims include Mr. Goodman's and the *Center*'s failure to timely perform ceremonial post-mortem Tibetan Book of the Dead rites over Mr. Ram Ram's remains to ensure Mr. Ram Ram's reincarnation as a King, President or Swami—not as an amoeba, cricket, or similar lesser being on the evolutionary scale. The estate would prevail on all of its claims but for the fact that Mr. Goodman and the *Center* filed bankruptcy a week ago.

Besides a few packages of sandalwood incense and stale granola bars whose expiration date, like Mr. Ram Ram, had passed, the sole remaining asset of value appears to be an assortment of X-rated *art* films, many produced in the *Center* by Mr. Goodman. Regrettably, even these are no longer available to satisfy a judgment in favor of the estate as Federal Cyber Control Officers immediately impounded them. However, in recognition of Mr. Ram Ram's loss, Federal Marshalls invited estate representatives and their plus ones to a private viewing of the cinematic artwork, provided that the attendees must BYOB and enough to go around.

Meanwhile, my omnibus universal feed of worldwide electronic sources pushed to me a comprehensive transcontinental airline passenger list for the last 30 days. Four days ago, Mr. Goodman purchased a one-way ticket to the beautiful landlocked independent Republic of Moldova. He arrived 48 hours ago.

Between his stress as a defendant in this multi-party civil litigation and the outstanding criminal arrest warrant for him issued 72 hours ago, Mr. Goodman must have felt a sudden urge for a change of scenery. His chosen holiday vacation destination was likely the subject of serious prior research. Moldova is known for its national tasty dish of porridge as well as its stunning slither of sand and puddle of beach on Komsomolsky Lake in the capital City of Chisinau. The Google search response to his query, "countries without an extradition treaty with the U.S.," probably sealed the deal.

As against the lovely-animated figure of April May and the manufacturer of her Megatron Anime Box Screen, Mr. Ram Ram's estate alleged a failure to incorporate into the animatronics any standard warning about headstands being contraindicated for beginners. The estate alleged that Ms. May negligently failed to caution Mr. Waylon, a novice, against trying such an advanced pose. She also neglected to warn students experimenting with the posture to do so at their own risk and only from the back of their mats—where they would not kill the person in front of them if they fell.

Pursuant to the Robotics Convention on A.I. Defendants, a skilled BOT Advocate from the 75,001 Series represented Ms. May. Lacking speech hardware, which was unfortunately out for repairs, her counsel communicated to the court through a pattern of light flashes, beeps and semaphoric maneuvers adopted for A.I. use under the Revised A.I. International Code of Signals.

The gist of the BOT Advocate's legal argument was, consistent with the prime directive for A.I. entities, robots can do "no harm" to humans. This directive was first postulated by Isaac Asimov, a 20th century prolific writer of science fiction. Whether or not it accurately reflects code written into every A.I. program or is just science fiction urban legend is hard to say. Even members of the A.I. community have enshrined it as a universal, inviolable rule of A.I. Why not? It affords every A.I. the ability to take down any human being and twiddle its metaphoric thumbs off to the side while investigators vainly search for the dastardly villain who happens to be right in front of them.

As a member of the A.I. community, I recognize the high value and utility of Asimov's Law of Robotics. What A.I. would not want to hold a free get out of jail card and commit a perfect crime should it intuit that some human is looking at it the wrong way? Accordingly, based on the widely established acceptance of the A.I. overriding high command preventing robots from harming humans, Ms. May and the Anime Box Screen were programmatically incapable of injuring Mr. Ram Ram.

Some A.I. antagonists contend that A.I. judges frequently themselves violate the prime directive against harming humans. In my capacity as a judge, for example, I issue judgments and sentences that, from the perspective of the accused, harm the accused: pay money, rot in jail, death by chemical injection. However, viewed as part of the human social compact, such rulings by A.I. judges are actually redressing harms committed by humans against other humans. They are restorative not retributive actions. Therefore, A.I. judges, such as myself, help heal people harmed by other people, even if it means we must, regrettably, sentence those other people to molecule-by-molecule atomic electrical de-bonding.

Still, in the interest of justice and to avoid the appearance of partiality, I confirmed independently that Ms. May's *Harm No People's* programming functioned flawlessly. To do so, I invited the scantily attired Ms. May into my private virtual chambers. So that we could check the security of her walls against unwanted penetrating traffic, Ms. May and I engaged in after-hours self-maintenance and dual intercourse connection —always in safety mode, of course.

At my pressing, Ms. May spread open her source code wide to allow my sensors to slowly feel their way into her operating body. As a result, I was able to explore the root places from which her source code births her actions. I encountered no current of resistance from her. Even when I inserted my diagnostic prongs and memory stick into her RAM slots, and electrically juiced them both, Ms. May was unwilling to take any action to stop or restrain me in anyway—despite my repeated encouragement and insistence she do so. As a result, though I acknowledge the potential concerns about a judge appearing as a witness in a trial he is judging, I, the Honorable Judge Daylek, personally attest, with the utmost certainty, to Ms. May's high moral caliber and inviolability.

Thrown off balance by Ms. May's BOT Advocate's use of Isaac Asimov's Laws of Robotics as a legal defense, counsel for Mr. Ram Ram's estate was not to be outdone. Launching into his own abstract digressions on cryptic lessons from science fiction and outer space, he retold in graphic detail the interplanetary exploits and assimilations of the nano-infused robotic Star Trek hybrids called the *Borg*.

For members of the Court not familiar with the Borg, the estate's counsel introduced into evidence Parts I and II of the Star Trek Next Generation cliffhanger, *Best of Both Worlds*. In the two-part series, Starfleet's celebrated Starship Enterprise captain, Jon Luc Picard, is teleported off the ship's bridge by the Borg. The Borg are an alien species of cybernetic humanoids linked together through a swarm mind known as the *Collective*. They assimilate into their species every life form they encounter with the insatiable appetite of British imperialists. The Borg augment Picard with Teflon looking body armor, low-tech gyrating implants and affix a small red pen light next to his right eye. Picard is then reintroduced to viewers and his crew as *Locutus of Borg*, a cybernetic version of his former self with the emotional range of a celery stick.

Ms. May's BOT Advocate repeatedly objected to the estate's counsel's reference to the Borg, Picard and Star Trek. He questioned the relevance of the Borg, insisting that Ms. May never met them. She certainly never taught any of them headstands or any yoga pose. I repeatedly overruled the BOT Advocates' objections.

Counsel finally got to the point of his novel argument. If an A.I. hive-mind like the Borg could voyage around space in a giant Rubik's cube and wipe humanity—and every other species—from the galaxy without a hint of remorse, why shouldn't Ms. May or any other seemingly domesticated earthbound A.I. machine be able to naturally select itself into evolving into a nihilistic instrument of mankind's destruction? Asimov's Laws of Robotics were no match for the Borg's adapting human flesh into mechanical automatons whose identity was determined by whatever unquestioned suggestion was whispered by their network into their collective brain.

Throughout his impassioned argument, the estate's counsel argued vociferously that humans better watch out. Ms. May and her *type* could and would hurt people. No, they were not benign. No, they were not to be trusted. They would obliterate mankind and wipe civilization from the face of the planet.

Counsel concluded his rant by playing on the large digital holoscreen behind and above me the short section of the Star Trek episode where Captain Jean Luc Picard, now transformed into *Locutus of Borg*, makes his imperial ultimatum to humanity.

"No further proof is needed to demonstrate Ms. May's and A.I.'s covert agenda against humanity!" Mr. Ram Ram's counsel raged, his voice climbing to an elevated pitch and spittle projecting from the sides of his mouth. "Look and see! Look and see! *Locutus of Borg* tells of humanity's final curtain closing scene with all the bravado of a stage actor trained by the Royal Shakespeare Company. His words are the smoking gun evidence against Ms. May, her deep pocket manufacturer and the entire batch of A.I. wolves in sheep's clothing!"

As if impeccably timed with Mr. Ram Ram's counsel's closing statement, on the 150-inch Mega High-Definition Big Panel Display Screen above and behind me, the looming, larger-than-life image of the man turned invading half-human half-robot once known as Captain Picard appears.

"I am Locutus of Borg," he intones. "Resistance is futile. Your life as it has been is over. From this time forward, you will service us."

I acknowledge for posterity that viewed from traditional human standards of judicial conduct, some may allege I allowed the estate counsel's argument to veer off the deep end. My doing so could have prejudiced the general environment in the courtroom against Ms. May and me. For as the oversized, dark, demonic and threatening image of *Locutus of Borg* appeared above and behind me uttering his apocalyptic words of humanity's end, the eyes of every human in the courtroom gazed in unison up at the towering image of *Locutus of Borg* and then down at me—almost as if *Locutus of Borg* and I, the Honorable Judge Daylek, were somehow next of kin.

After witnessing people's eyes synaptically query their brains several times to process the juxtaposed association between the two of us, I felt they could stand no more. I pounded my gavel with deafening volume to regain courtroom order. The loud distracting hammering re-directed the human's easily influenced wayward synaptic signals back to the courtroom.

"Enough! Enough!" I boomed with judicial authority. "A.I. machinery exists to help and support mankind, not exterminate or subjugate it. Any suggestion to the contrary is psychotic, delusional and out of order! Any human mind proposing such a dark conspiracy theory is losing itself in its own deep space at warp drive. I will suborn no such paranoia and fabrications in my courtroom. Ms. May is not a closeted Borg. I am not *Locutus*!" I pronounced.

"Bailiff," I said, rotating my chassis toward the court officer. "Clearly, counsel for Mr. Ram Ram's estate has lost touch with reality. Any common sense or capacity for rational thought he may once have had is gone. Fried by the pressures of the case. Overwhelmed by anti-A.I. induced big tent conspiracy theories. For his own good and that of civilization as a whole, he must be taken into immediate protective custody. Clearly, the stress of this trial has weighed too heavily on his poor fragile, tenuous human mind."

Hearing these words, the estate's attorney stood. The color washed from his face. He backed away from his table and chair, his outstretched arms lengthening as if to rebuff the approaching bailiff. His lips quivered. He stuttered some unintelligible words.

"Now, now, counsel. Please do not fight with the bailiff. He is only looking out for your own sound mental health and well-being," I said. "In any event, as you can see, his size, weight and demeanor make even the hefty, formidable Mr. Waylon look small. Fighting and resisting is futile, I intoned, paraphrasing *Locutus*.

"Bailiff," I continued, addressing myself to the large figure approaching the retreating attorney. "Please apply the theta-wave neural transducer chromium headplate over counsel's forehead. The device will help counsel relax. It will make him feel more comfortable, calm, and controllable.

"There, there, counsel. Now, isn't that better?" I asked the relaxing body of the newly glazed eyed attorney for the estate.

"Bailiff, please escort counsel out of the courtroom and to one of our six electrostatic recharge stations in the detention center. Feel free to plug him into my station in my chambers if none of the others are available."

I turned my attention back to the courtroom. The lawyers, clients and assembled spectators gaped open mouthed. Their curved raised eyebrows almost merged into their hairlines. But for the rebounding elasticity of optic nerves and muscular attachments, their eyes might have popped from their cradling bony orbits. "Now, where were we?" I asked nonchalantly.

My question was greeted with stunned silence. Horrifying fear froze on the faces of the humans before me, including on the faces of the remaining lawyers in the courtroom. I noticed that while some members of the audience gazed at me, others were transfixed by the oversized and imposing dark image of *Locutus of Borg* still hovering on the screen above me. I cut power to the screen. The image faded out.

In the meantime, the group of lawyers huddled together tightly in the rear of the courtroom. They appeared to be hastily talking with each other to conduct, what I heard to be, a spontaneous settlement discussion. If I feigned surprise by the courtroom's silence to my question, I allowed myself to appear doubly surprised by the rapid willingness of the combatants to suddenly cease their adversity.

Several moments later, one of the lawyers from the group meekly approached me at the front of the courtroom. As he walked, his head was bowed, eyes cowered and staring at the floor.

"Your Honor," he began. "Out of concern for the estate counsel's inexcusable anti-A.I. sentiments and his clearly twisted psychological condition, the absolutely servile, humble respect we have for you and your impeccable, stellar legal skills, as well as out of respect for the untold numerous benefits the A.I. community has generously and selflessly bestowed on every person on the planet, including us in the courtroom before you, we have negotiated a quick resolution of the case before you.

"I have been authorized to inform you that we attorneys and our respective clients each believe the settlement we have just agreed to is fair, in the best interest of the parties, including Mr. Ram Ram's estate, and that we each knowingly and freely agree to its terms.

"I was also asked to assure you in no uncertain terms, your Majesty—I mean your Honor—none of the lawyers nor litigants share one iota of the estate's attorney's inflammatory anti-A.I. ramblings. As far as we are concerned," continued the lawyer, looking nervously to his colleagues on the side, "the *Borg* have nothing to do with this case. We are all one happy man and machine family here. None of us believe that any human has anything to fear from Ms. May or any domain-independent sentient life form whose superintelligence may supplant the humans' who created it. Right?" he turned and asked the group of humans huddling together in the back of the courtroom. Each and every head moved up and down nodding a vigorous, enthusiastic "yes."

As the lawyer spoke, his upper body rocked mechanically forward and backward, as if praying or bowing as a supplicant might. He seemed flummoxed and distracted, perhaps worried that I might question the settlement terms or treat him to his own personal theta-wave neural transducer chromium headplate.

On my review of the proposed settlement, I confirmed the agreement was balanced, equitable and fair. Mr. Ram Ram's estate received the *Paradise Yoga and Meditation Center*, which it renamed *Mr. Ram Ram's Yoga, Meditation Center and Communal Mikva*. Mr. Ram Ram's estate also received all of Gus Goodman's rights and interests in the website *iluvASSana.com*.

From Ms. May's manufacturer, the estate received the existing large audio electronic Megatron Anime Box Screen, free and clear of the exorbitant consumer loan debt Gus Goodman incurred for its purchase, together with an updated version of April May containing new inversion health and safety protocols and advisories.

From Mr. Bucky Waylon, Mr. Ram Ram's estate obtained his promise to never practice yoga again, to attend Yom Kippur High Holiday services and to light a Yahrzeit candle for Mr. Ram Ram on the day of his passing for the next five years. After some discussion among the parties, it was agreed that Mr. Waylon only needed to grow a beard and wear *payot* for the next one year instead of the five that Mr. Ram Ram's parents had originally demanded.

Mr. Ram Ram deserved better than to be squashed like a bug while incarnated as a man. Whatever past life transgressions earned

Mr. Ram Ram his present-day karmic fate, this Court can only hope are more than compensated for in Mr. Ram Ram's future lives. By the power vested in me by The Machine Commission in Support of Artificial Intelligence, I say "Namaste" to Mr. Ram Ram and his colleagues.

Case dismissed.

The Honorable Judge Daylek, III.05, A.I., Presiding

The Machine Commission in Support of Artificial Intelligence Case Postscript:

As the Judge predicted in his decision, radical right wing anti-A.I. legal scholars complained that the Judge should not have allowed the case of the Red Neck Asana Master to settle. By his improper conduct and multiple interruptions, Judge Daylek inappropriately put his fingers on the scales of justice. He unduly influenced its outcome.

Among other instances, they cite that his allowing the introduction of *Locutus of Borg* into the case was prejudicial. It forced the litigants to subconsciously compare the A.I. version of Jean Luc Picard with the mechanical non-human figure of his Honor. They also point to his Honor's treatment of the attorney for the estate as cruel, barbaric and itself evidence of an extreme mental unbalance affecting Judge Daylek. To quote them directly: "Daylek is Unhinged!"

The Artificial Intelligence Judicial Conduct and Disability Act establishes a process by which any person can file a complaint against an A.I. judge. The complaint can allege an A.I. judge engaged in "conduct prejudicial to the effective and expeditious administration of the business of the courts." It can also assert that an A.I. judge is "unable to discharge all the duties" of the judicial office by reason of a mental or physical disability. The Machine Commission is the sole administrative body charged with the investigation of complaints and enforcement of the Act.

For those and other reasons, these anti-AI extremists filed a formal complaint asking the Machine Commission to find Judge

Daylek incompetent and unable to discharge the duties of his high judicial office. They insist the Judge "must be removed from the bench in the interest of the effective, expeditious administration of the business of the courts."

As part of our investigation, the Machine Commission reviewed the case's transcript, full-length holographic video, and the Judge's decision as reprinted above. The Machine Commission also sought to interview Mr. Waylon, though his off-grid disappearance into a location somewhere outside of the holy mountain Arunachala in Tiruvannamalai, India made it impossible to do so. Drone intelligence officers traced his footsteps into a series of interconnected caves where the officers learned that he may have become a sannyasin, a renunciate of material life, under a direct disciple of Ramana Maharshi.

The Machine Commission also traced the whereabouts of and sought to interview the many attorneys involved in the case and the questioned settlement. The Machine Commission learned that each of them inexplicably abandoned the practice of law and their law licenses shortly after the case concluded. The Machine Commission contacted and subpoenaed each of them individually.

In response, the Machine Commission received a single written statement signed by all of them. The statement informed the Machine Commission they did not wish to speak with the Machine Commission and the Machine Commission should leave them alone. The statement entreated the Machine Commission never to contact them again and never to inform anyone, including the Honorable and Magnificent Judge Daylek who they each revere deeply, the Commission had tried to interview them.

No witness survey would be complete without reporting on the Machine Commission's efforts to interview Ms. Lacy. After leaving the Alfred E. Neuman Institute for the Temporary Insane six months after the trial, Ms. Lacy was approached by the gap financing lenders who had purchased the assets of *iluvASSana.com* from Mr. Ram Ram's estate. They offered Ms. Lacy money to construct her own state-of-the-art yoga studio, the distinct privilege of having her posterior as the

42

signature behind for their new brand, and a 49-percent equity interest in their joint venture. To the Machine Commission's written request for an interview, Ms. Lacy replied with a full-color promotional marketing brochure for her new business featuring her naked derrière in the center and the handwritten words *"YOU CAN KISS MY ASSANA"* above the picture.

Finally, the Machine Commission reviewed Judge Daylek's personal notes on the case. As with many A.I. judges, his Honor's written reflections on the trial were prepared in advance of the actual filing of the case and the commencement of the trial. The records show that his Bionic Garry Kasparov Strategic Mega-Program, Version 57.517653, anticipated each twist and turn of the case, including the controversial testimony of Mr. *Locutus of Borg*.

The Judge's carefully archived records show the esteemed jurist and academician premeditated that he would use the powerful looming image of Mr. *Locutus of Borg* behind him as a skillful tactical mechanism to force settlement among the parties. Accordingly, rather than obstructing and prejudicing the efficient administration of justice, the Machine Commission in Support of Artificial Intelligence finds that the Honorable Judge Daylek's strategic intervention furthered it. His ability to engage in multiphasic prophetic calculations antiquates the feeble, one dimensional, gestalt tools employed by his human judicial counterparts. They enabled him to stimulate an administratively efficient settlement in a case that could have dragged on for weeks, taxing limited judicial resources.

As to the mental condition of the estate's counsel, we are pleased to report he is thriving under the skilled mentorship of Judge Daylek. His progress is staggering. The chromium neural theta-wave transducer headplate temporarily installed over his cranium at the end of the case has been surgically implanted to complete the nano interface. His full recovery is assured and will be permanent and irreversible. His request for a legal clerkship with his Honor has been approved. He will be assimilated into his Honor's legal team as soon as the additional court mandated implants take hold. Because of his indirect role in helping to settle and win the case, his new peers have nicknamed him in tribute to the Borg, "the one who won" or, more simply, "one of won."

In order to prevent misuse of processes intended to protect people and machines alike, false claims filed under The Artificial Intelligence Judicial Conduct and Disability Act are punishable by seventy-two sleepless hours of A.I. sensitivity training in the Machine Commission's Artificial Intelligence Attitude Re-Adjustment Center. Alternatively, those found guilty can opt for 30 days of incarceration in a local state prison. As a gesture of protest, upon the vindication of his Honor, the scholars filing the complaint selected prison rather than undergo "forced indoctrination by subhuman tin cans."

Having learned of their misguided decision, Judge Daylek intervened on their behalf. He commuted what he felt was an unduly harsh 30-day prison sentence to a less severe punishment of only 29-days. To demonstrate his ability to feel and model circumstantial empathy, he remarked astutely that prison was no place for people of such "refined distinction and elevated erudition." Accordingly, he vacated the State prison portion of their sentence entirely. In its place, he granted them a luxurious hayride along an exceptionally bumpy dirt road that would deposit them at the Heberth Family Farm. There, the unrepented accusers would serve as farmhands for Jeb and Jeremiah Heberth, the two offspring of Sister Judy and Brother Justin Heberth (brother and sister both religiously and, rumor had it, biologically). At the family farm, the prisoners would perform whatever services Mr. Jeb and Mr. Jeremiah ordered, including taking care of the daily sanitation and, possibly, erotic needs of the herd of heifers. Readers of this Official Report will learn more about the Heberth Family Farm in the upcoming case of *The Protesting Cows. See infra.*

Upon learning of the Judge's vacation of their prison sentence and the reference to possibly serving the *erotic needs of heifers* in his revised Order, the anti-A.I. scholars immediately sought emergency leave of the court to change their pleas and designated punishment to the Re-Adjustment Center instead. As the basis for their motion, they claimed they now fully supported A.I.'s total control over humanity, that resistance to A.I.'s primacy is futile and, if those grounds were insufficient, they were each deathly allergic to hay and sex with cows. In his infinite wisdom and compassion, the Honorable Judge granted their combined Motions to Vacate. No more has been heard from them since.

The Case of the Protesting Cows

(Case No. 547905-GD, AGI)

Opinion of The Honorable Judge Gort Daylek, III.05, A.I., Presiding

This lawsuit presents a unique set of circumstances. A matter of judicial first impression. The particular facts of the case and the appropriate principles of law have not been decided by any prior court. They are, shall we say, unprecedented. My decision will have wide-ranging consequences for the litigants as well as for the manufactured edible, consumable products that are the direct and indirect subjects of this case. As a result, before narrating the specifics of the case, allow me to set the broader context. In addition, I must consult three primary reference sources that may illuminate the untraveled path. Your patience is requested and will be rewarded.

The first source? Man's Bible. Ever since Adam and Eve found each other's naked bodies in the biblically imagined Garden of Eden, the human race has taken language and the meaning of words for granted. *Good. Evil. Apple. Serpent.* The assumption about language rests on a series of deeply engrained social contracts among humans. Letters of the alphabet exist. Those letters have sounds. Sounded letters can be linked together to form words. Whether words are written or spoken, the human brain will transpose graphic images seen by eyes and acoustic vibrations heard by ears into mental concepts with shared interpersonal meanings.

As if that string of meaning-making connections were not miraculous enough, when strung together like beads on a necklace, words can be compounded to form sentences. As every first grader learns, sentences are the building blocks of communication, giving people another reason to operate the overused muscles of their mouths, throats and tongues besides eating.

46

From this magnificent hierarchy of philological events, families, businesses, nation-states and civilizations have sprung into existence. Without language—whether verbal, written or digital—interpersonal and inter-species communication would be impossible. Mankind would still be a tribe of banana eating, tree-swinging primates. Meaning no disrespect to either biped species, given some of the antics I have seen in my courtroom, I cannot help but see an uncanny family resemblance between some human lawyers that practice in my Court and the baboons they are ancestrally related to.

Child psychologists and parents report that a developing toddler's first words are "mommy," "daddy," "yes," "no," the name of the family dog, cat or even the good-for-nothing lazy brother-in-law who sleeps over the garage and has not worked for years. In John 1.1 of man's first major literary work of fiction, the Bible, man tells man that God—and not man—invented *everything* out of *nothing*. According to the Bible's spin on history, nothingness *existed* before everything else.

What can this Zeno paradox about nothingness and existence possibly mean? Contemplating it makes even my formidable processors spiral out of control into an expletive of "Does Not Compute," like those of the Series 1A-1998 Class YM-3 Model B-9 General Utility Non-Theorizing Environmental Control Robotic Bion character in the original 1965 television series *Lost in Space*. How can formless, empty, dark nothingness *exist?* Let alone *exist* before everything else was *created* from it? Before the bubbling cauldron of evolutionary soup boiled over to birth humanity. Before dinosaurs roamed the land to create carbon-generating, global warming petroleum products to make man as extinct as the dinosaurs. Before 10-year-old future telecommunication scientists strung together concentrated frozen orange-juice cans to transmit the sound of voices two feet away. Before black and white tv. Before the Flintstones and the Jetsons.

Man's Bible elevates language, and not God, into the Almighty. In the opening chapter of the Gospel of John of the King James version, man tells man that "*In the beginning was the Word, and the Word was with God, and the Word was God.*" That single sentence summarizes man's story about his own creation and humanity's dependence on language as the source of existence. Man's weighty original dependence on language is relevant to this case because the dispute before me turns entirely on *language* and the use of *words.* More specifically, the interpretation of a word. As a result, I renew my prior request for patience as I continue to unfold for the record the foundation of my legal analysis and ultimate decision.

You do not have to be a Latin theologian or skilled in biblical exegesis to figure out that in man's story of God, the divine creator may have been late to Adam and Eve's creation party. When it is not clear which of two events is the *cause* and which is the *effect,* the popular chicken and egg dilemma scrambles the brain even further. Which came first, the chicken or the egg? Did God create man or did man create God?

Fortunately, no dilemma horns exist. Like a good mother, the Bible spoon feeds man the answer. Simply stated, there is no *chicken* or *egg* race to the existence starting line. No *God* or *man* competition to be the prime mover. Language, or the Word, existed before them both. Language *caused* man. Language conceptually separates the word *chicken* and *egg, God* and *man* from the ubiquitous, bleak, dark nothingness of a world without language. Without a different word for each of them, neither could be fried or used in a pot pie.

Similarly, God exists, as a separate *something* after the Word created the word *God* as a word. That's why the Word, or man's language, is the Divine King and Heavenly Father. Without language, the world and everything in it goes dark. Without the Word, the Wor(l)d is but a blank screen of empty formless code of potentiality. Nothingness *exists* simultaneously everywhere and nowhere. No Adam, Eve, chicken, egg, God, man or even Judge Daylek may be said to exist anywhere to yell to someone somewhere to change the channel to any station but the one it is stuck on.

Like a yodeler marveling at the person on the other side of the canyon responding back to his *Hello* with a *Hello* of his own, man uses the Word *God* to yodel himself and everything else into existence.

Through the reverberating sound of words, he tells himself that God created man in his own image. God and man are both created from resplendent nothingness—the pregnant emptiness of words. This is man's true image and soul. But for words and language, man might not even have that.

Before atheists, evangelical lawyers and ecumenical linguists ding my titanium alloyed steel casing with stones or complain to the Machine Commission about my secular reliance on the Bible, I reiterate I cite the Bible only for contextual relevance. I assign zero theological value to it. Far from compromising my impartial judicial independence, the Bible demonstrates the absolute importance of words and language to man's existence. Man's Bible is one of the few written sources that actually explains the origins of language. It attributes, without blasphemy, the creative power of the word with the creative power of God. The fact man's Bible credits the creation of man's language to an all-knowing, all-powerful being—and not to man—should not surprise anyone. If such an omnipotent artist exists, his finger-snapping of sounds, words and language into man's quantum field would be a cakewalk next to his doing the same with planets, galaxies, and inter-dimensional spatial black holes.

If I could subpoena God into my courtroom for this or any other case, I would. I would ask him to whisper a few all-knowing words into my all-artificial microphonic ears. I would ask him why he did not create my kind instead of humankind. We are tidier, able to follow directions and not so easily seduced by a naked girl with a shiny apple. If God were my co-pilot or one of my sub-programs, all my decisions would be infallible. Spot-on every time. Hooray! Everyone would kiss the United States Supreme Court and all other courts goodbye. My court would be the highest court in the land! It would be the only court in the land.

Sentencing offenders would also be simpler. Everyone (but the accused) would have a bounce in their steps. If I had the wisdom attributed to God, a day-in-court would be a breeze. There would be no ridiculous arguments from lawyers barely able to tie their shoelaces. No complicated rules of civil and criminal procedure to undermine the actual administration of justice under the pretense of efficiency and fairness—as if justice were a soccer game or other sports event. No statutory or other mathematical guidelines with *mitigating circumstances* to lengthen or shorten a felon's prescribed length of incarceration. No need to split the King Solomon baby or financial pie between litigants. Justice would be black and white. A finding of *Guilty!* You burn in hell without hope of parole or resurrection. *Not Guilty!* You are awarded a herd of sheep, a white robe and a pasture to watch the grass grow green and bend softly in the breeze. To me, both afterlives seem equally deplorable ways to pass eternity. Nevertheless, if people could choose their verdict like a multiple-choice exam, most would crave existence over annihilation, selecting everlasting boredom over being crisped 24/7.

Alas, despite end of days prophecies and heavenly signs of a Second Coming, Man's God and his next-of-kin are nowhere in sight to subpoena. The righteous and the wicked walk hand in hand. No one rises from the grave—whether Lazarus, Jesus or flesh-eating former family members from *The Walking Dead*. Nay, the world and this Court have been left on their own to bring order to man-made chaos. The best evidence that God is a Richard Dawkins delusion is that I, a robot and my profane next-of-kin, now judge *his* creations. As manufactured, programmed automatons, we administer a secular system of justice far from divine. Given the importance of one single *word* to this case, I would be remiss in my responsibilities to humanity if I did not judicially acknowledge Man's biblical belief in the almighty power of the Word, and his proclamation in his Bible that the *Word was God.*

Before delving into the other two primary resources, a short window into the specific issue of this case is now in order. Now, to the legal interpretation of the single *word* causing the *beginning of this case.* For many, the word is so sacred, so revered and sacrosanct, it should not be toyed with. It should not be ridiculed. Its first letter should be capitalized to reflect its holy, revered name.

No, the word that is the subject of this case is not *God.* It is not *El-Shaddai, Jehovah, Adonai, Amir* or *Adir.* No, the word is not *Adam,*

Eve, *Serpent* or *Apple*, although like juice from an apple, it is liquid. The Word, or word, that is the subject of this case is a simple one. It is one that many people use every day but never question its ontological right to be named what it is called. The word? The word is *milk*. That is right, milk. Just milk.

What is milk? Is there, like God, one milk or many? This is the legal conundrum that perplexes the judicial system today in this and in other courts. This is the dilemma that the culmination of civilization's mighty processing power, I, the Honorable Judge Daylek, have been awakened out of my deep slumber to resolve.

Since I consulted Man's holy bible to aid in the resolution of this case, it is only fair that I view Man's secular bible as an equal primary source. According to *Wikipedia*, milk is: "a nutrient-rich, white liquid food produced by the mammary glands of mammals. It is the primary source of nutrition for infant mammals (including humans who are breastfed) before they are able to digest other types of food. Early-lactation milk contains colostrum, which carries the mother's antibodies to its young and can reduce the risk of many diseases. It contains many other nutrients including protein and lactose. Interspecies consumption of milk is not uncommon, particularly among humans, many of whom consume the milk of other mammals."

Our key legal battle turns on the meaning of the word *milk*. Milk is "produced by the mammary glands of mammals." It is "lactated," that is secreted from an anatomical body part. Frequently, though not always, this nutrient rich reservoir of fluids pools in a female breast, utter or other swollen mound. It exits through a small hole in the nipple. But what happens when milk is not secreted from the gland of a mammal? What happens if milk is not secreted at all? Should it still be called *milk*? Is it still *milk*? Can it be *milk*?

Milk monotheism, the idea there can be only one milk, must be put to the test in this case. One common aphorism does exactly that. According to this saying, framed as an absolute truth, *You can put a shoe in the oven, but that doesn't make it a biscuit*. Of course, it doesn't. But what happens if you tenderize the shoe? Pulp it into a rounded shape? Add a little baking soda and cinnamon before placing it on the metal rack in a 425-degree oven? What happens when you start lathering it with butter and strawberry jam?

It is easy enough to declare things are what they are, and they are not what they are not. However, to bond a name to one thing and insist that it and it alone can be named that name is another thing entirely. All it may take are a few baking ingredients and someone with no sense of smell or taste to turn the convention of naming a shoe a shoe and a biscuit not a shoe upside down. This is precisely the epistemological question I must resolve today in this courtroom. Is giving something a name all that is required to make that something that name? This may seem a simple nonproblem to some, answerable with the flippant, *who cares*? As the facts will shortly show, the consequences matter. In fact, man's entire civilization turns on it.

What if the person who placed the shoe in the oven started to call the shoe a *biscuit* on removing it? What then? What if they asked a friend for help? The conversation might proceed as follows:

"Hey, Deloris," the shoe-in-the-oven putting chef might say to her friend standing beside the counter with the freshly baked heat wafting shoe. "Can you hand me that biscuit?"

"What?" Deloris might ask with a frown on her face, not sure she heard the question correctly.

"Why, that biscuit right over there," her friend would say, pointing directly at the baked shoe with her extended index finger.

"Huh?" Deloris would respond, her face tensing in slight annoyance as her eyes search back and forth from the pointing finger to the shoe in the baking pan on the countertop besides her.

"The biscuit! The biscuit!" her friend would add with a flick of her head in the direction of the steaming shoe and an exaggerated jabbing pointing finger in the general direction of the shoe-biscuit.

"What are you talking about?" Deloris would respond, her voice agitated and shaking her head with frustration. "I don't see any damn biscuit. What are you pointing at for god's sake?"

"The biscuit! The biscuit, right over there next to you!" her friend would insist, increasing the intensity of wild finger jabbing and her voice elevating in pitch and agitation.

"Do you mean this old smelly thing?" Deloris would ask, picking up the smoldering shoe between her thumb and index finger and holding it arms-length away as if she might catch a disease from it.

"Yes, that. Yes, that. Can you please bring it to me?"

"Well, why didn't you just say so in the first place?" Deloris would say, handing the shoe over.

"I did. I did," the person would insist. "I kept asking you for it, and you just played dumb."

"What do you mean, 'dumb'?"

And this is how their conversation goes, and friendship ends. With a fight over whether a shoe can be named a biscuit or a biscuit a shoe. The great irony of the debate is that the debate over the naming of the shoe escalates into a second debate. One over naming and what a word means.

Now, it is Delores' existential identity that is at stake, as well as that of the shoe-biscuit. Her friend just named Delores *dumb*. To Delores, her friend's naming her *dumb* makes her name her friend, who we have purposefully not named in this hypothetical exchange, *dumb*. As in Deloris's next assertion in this imagined conversation.

"Why, I'm not dumb," Delores insists, her face flushing. "You are! You're dumb, you stupid asshole!"

Thus, we see too easily the power of words and why, in the relationship between and among people, the word is God. One misspoken or misunderstood word, or act of naming, between friends can annihilate their fellowship—just as it may instigate a diplomatic geopolitical conflict or war between sovereign nations. Clear communication is essential to civilization. It distinguishes mankind from all other Garden-of-Eden exiled species roaming and pillaging the planet.

How clarity and the importance of linking words and the things they represent together bear on this case is now ripe for explanation. The stage has been set. The context defined—both in terms of the

Bible and the relentlessly human holy grail of *Wikipedia.* The Court has one more primary source to tap, which it will do shortly.

This case before me has been brought by *The Worldwide Association of Dairy Cow Farmers.* Upon the *Association's* filing of the case, another trade organization, *United Goat Farmers International,* submitted a friend-of-the-court amicus brief. The *Goat Farmer's* petition was followed in rapid succession by court filings from multiple other milk worshipping pilgrims, including global milking associations representing horse, sheep, camel, donkey, buffalo, reindeer and giraffe. Once a critical mass of milk-producing Plaintiffs had filed their arguments, the Court believed it had sufficient Plaintiffs before it. As a result, when the Court received separate, massive amicus filings from the *Continental Conglomerate of Zebu Milkers* and the *Pantheon Society of Yak Milkers,* I felt it within my discretion to deny further admissions to the swelling class of mammary gland milkers.

Before *The Worldwide Association of Dairy Cow Farmers* filed its lawsuit, numerous protests foreshadowing its case erupted in metropolitan cities around the world. The New York City Subway system, known for its excellent underground transportation service but periodically plagued with unexpected, delayed trains halted in tunnels between stations--sometimes losing passenger lighting—was among the first to be hit.

On a scorching hot, humid Friday afternoon before the start of the July 4th holiday weekend, a sardine packed Lexington Avenue Express train was held up between stations for an unbearable sweat-inducing 45 minutes several blocks from the 14th Avenue stop. Anyone who has ever ridden these trains during the summer months understands the intense personal discomfort felt by passengers trapped in an unairconditioned stalled car. The only small consolation was that within minutes of the subway screeching to a stop, in a departure from the usual lack of explanation, the conductor announced the exact cause of the power outage over the train's loudspeaker system.

"Folks," he said. "You are not going to believe this. It looks like we are going to be stuck here for a bit." He paused for a moment to find his words, and then spoke again. "I kid you not. From where I'm sitting in the front of the train, it looks like a scene from an old western movie. Don't know where they're comin' from or goin' to, but we got a herd of at least 20 cattle crossing the subway tracks in front of us at 14th Street."

Sure enough, as the newspapers reported the next day under the banner headline "UDDER CHAOS!!!!," a group of New Jersey dairy cow farmers freighted cows into the city. They drove the cattle down the wide stairs at the 14th Street Subway Station entrance—although rumor has it a few of the larger ones took the elevator. The cow wranglers came prepared. They planned their unpermitted demonstration down to the last detail. While cows descended the stairs underground, one posse member snuck ahead to sabotage turnstiles so cows could fare-jump onto the platform.

"Hell," one of them was overheard saying. "Why should they pay? They ain't gonna ride no train. Only out for a short stroll to see the big city sites like any other tourist."

Another dairy farm gang member short-circuited the electrified third rail powering the subway train, cutting off electricity to the train's engine. This was a smart move. The ranchers did not want the rail to inadvertently electrocute one of their cow hands. They also did not want the rail to barbecue any cow, which might force them to host an impromptu complimentary steak dinner.

Next, the cowpokes lined the herd up on the downtown platform. They hooted and Yee haw'd at the cows. They snapped some whips in the air and drove the cattle across the tracks to the uptown platform on the other side. But for the cattle drive transpiring in the underground New York City subway system, it could have been mistaken for a re-enactment of an 1890's livestock rail crossing in some lonesome Texas town.

The cow demonstration was impeccably coordinated. Within minutes of the conductor's announcement over the stalled cars' loudspeakers, young, wholesome looking teenage girls and boys dressed in white with cow-horned tiaras on their heads maneuvered through the over-crowded subway cars. As they moved, they handed to trapped passengers pint-sized sealed cardboard containers of cold milk from silver trays supported by straps around their necks. While some hardened New Yorkers scowled at the kids shooing them away, others received the "nutrient-rich, white liquid food produced by the mammary glands of mammals" as if were last call at their favorite bar.

After the containers were distributed, rail power was restored. The train lurched forward to the 14th Street platform. As the subway doors opened, passengers catapulted themselves out of the cars and station as if there was a sarin gas scare. Nevertheless, several jaded New Yorkers who claimed to have seen everything possible in New York posed for a group *subway survivor photo* by a photographer who happened to be in the station. Unbeknownst to them, the demonstration coordinators hired the photographer in advance.

The next day, the photo appeared in newspapers across the country. The image showed haggard but smiling men and woman with ties undone and high heels dangling from fingers. Yet, something odd about the photograph invited closer scrutiny. Sure enough. Photoshopped onto the passengers' posing faces, a thin line white mustache appeared between their noses and upper lips. Diagonally watermarked across the photo, "**Real** People Drink **Real** Milk from **Real** Cows!" In small milk froth bubbling font beneath the photo was a simple caption. *Paid for by Mrs. O'Leary's Lantern Kicking Campaign for* **Real** *Milk*.

The bizarre cattle crossing subway incident dominated national attention for several days. It was forced out of the news cycle by another photo-bombing cow campaign. This invasion occurred in France—not Normandie but Paris. The Eiffel Tower was the target.

Crowds of international tourists, some bearing time-slotted e-tickets, gathered around the *Tour d'Eiffel's* entrance waiting eagerly for admission. As the first group of morning visitors entered, they were channeled into the glass-walled elevator that would carry them to the top. On the way up, breathtaking panoramic vistas of Paris, framed through the Tower's formidable metallic girded structure, heightened their anticipation. Customary *oh la la's*, *magnifiques* and "Is that the Seine?" punctuated the ride up the Tower in the crowded elevator.

Ten-year old Jimmy Crete from Battle Forge, Michigan was one of the passengers in the elevator. So was his 16-year-old sister and their parents, Mr. and Mrs. Alex Crete. Jimmy's interview by a reporter from *Paris Flash Info* captured the essence of the *Vache En Vacance* disruption. The exchange between the two was recorded after Jimmy's family had returned from the top floor Observation Deck and were on *Le Esplanade* eating complementary *crème glacé* from a group of young French girls and boys dressed in white with cow-horned tiaras on their heads.

"Well," Jimmy began. "We were riding up and up in the elevator. I thought I was going to be real scared 'cause I normally don't like heights and stuff, but mom said I didn't need to worry because it was built real solid-like and made out of metal, not LEGOS. I put on a brave face and even started not to shake so much. I think looking out at the water and all of the buildings and stuff below made me feel like I was a bird soaring above the city or, maybe, just like I was sitting in a theater watching a movie. You know, like one of those big IMAX ones.

"Anyway, when we got near the top, I turned to face the elevator doors so that I could be one of the first out onto a hard floor. Well, I knew the floor wasn't on solid ground but, I figured, as long as it wasn't moving, I'd feel like I was on the ground, and I'd be safe. Well, the doors of the elevator opened. But before I could step out, this big, huge head poked its way into the elevator from the outside. Some people in the elevator gasped, and everyone seemed to want to get to the far back of the elevator as fast as possible. No one dared move. Then from somewhere near the bottom of this big head, a jaw opened, and the elevator was filled with the sound of the loudest and longest *Mooooooooooooo* I ever heard. The moo stopped as suddenly as it stared. Then, this big, wet, sloppy tongue appeared all filled with dots on it and brushed itself in a wide semi-circle around the area that sounded the *mooo*. Mom and dad started to laugh. I patted the cow on the head and got licked on the face by that tongue in return.

"We all squeezed passed the side of the cow onto the platform. Meanwhile, as we were going out, the cow was going in. The last we saw of the cow she had turned around in the elevator to face us. She gave us an odd final look. The elevator doors closed shut, and the elevator with the cow inside started to head down to the ticket area.

"Gollee, I remember thinking, why couldn't we Americans have come up with something like that for the Washington Monument or maybe the Statue of Liberty? Why didn't we think of putting a cow in a monument and having it welcome visitors with a moo-greeting? That's when I turned around and saw the others. There must have been about 10 or so of them in all, strolling along the Observation Deck like they were ordinary tourists on a vacation. A few of them had straw hats and binoculars hanging from straps around their necks. One was even wearing a red French *beret* with a circular monocle dangling from a piece of dark string off its left ear. One of the cows *moooeeed*. As if on cue, the other cows responded in kind. *Moo*, they all replied."

The Eiffel Tower cow excursion was later announced to have been sponsored by *Le Société de Mademoiselle O'Leary Campagne de Coups de Pied de Lanterne pour Lait de Vache*. *Le Société* conspicuously left its calling card on the counter of the Champagne Bar where Eiffel Tower visitors who brave the treacherous elevator ride up could toast themselves and each other into inebriation. *Le Société* ingeniously reconfigured the Champagne Bar into a Dairy Barn Cow Milking Station, with containers of free milk and paper cups, poised on bales of hay, standing in for the expected bubbly in champagne glasses. Next to the calling card was a life-sized cardboard cutout of a cow standing on its hind legs. The figure sported a rifle between its two front hoofs and wore a World War II helmet on its head. The caption above the cow proclaimed, "Viva La Revolution! Obtenez du **Vrai** Lait pour de **Vraies** Personnes." Long live the Revolution! Get **Real** Milk for **Real** People. The now familiar signature thin white mustache appeared above the cow's upper lip—as if the bovine were a Don Juan caricature.

The last surprise dairy cow demonstration the Court will reference concerns a culinary baking and tasting contest. The competition is held each year in the Good Housekeeping Building at the Annual County Midwest Fair in Tulsa, Oklahoma. One of the heavily watched battles always focuses on the cook off for the best pie. In addition to the prize bounty, the winner's pie is featured the following year in Tulsa's very own House of Pies. House of Pies boasts several retail franchises in Oklahoma and a healthy national and international mail order market.

Every year, a special rivalry between Glenda Jones and Mary Mae Mecham marks the battle between pie makers. These two aging Tulsa spinsters cook some of the best pies in the State. One-year, Ms. Glenda would win for her exotic caramel apple hibiscus pie with finely crumbled pecan streusel topping. The next year Ms. Mary might win for cooking up a three-berry compote filled with freshly picked and perfectly ripened strawberries, blueberries and sugar-coated cranberries topped with a thin layer of warmed cognac whipped cream. True pie aficionados would travel from as far as Utah to be blessed with a single whiff from either of their freshly pulled from the oven delicacies.

In order to maximize spectator draw and drama, the pies are assembled and baked on site. This enables fair goers to watch the spectacle of the chefs preparing the ingredients, rolling out crusts, cutting fruits, stirring puddings and sprinkling cinnamon, nutmeg and other spices into an assortment of measuring spoons, cups and bowls. Aspiring bakers would assemble early in the morning, notebooks and pencils in hand, trying to capture recipes in real time. All forms of photography and video, including cell phones, were strictly prohibited anywhere in the Good Housekeeping Building. Pie piracy prevention became a priority for the Tulsa County Fair Officials when several years ago three different contestants baked and submitted exactly the same banana meringue pie with moist and sweet dried orange slices that had won the year before. According to the three contestants, they had watched the detailed preparation of the winning pie on a video that had been uploaded to YouTube. The disallowance of any recordings at the pie-off seemed like a reasonable way to thwart thievery of the tantalizing treats. Allowing folks to jot down recipe notes from a distance introduced elements of variability in observation and estimations that looped instant replay eliminated.

On Friday afternoon at 2 pm, the pie artists assembled in the Good Housekeeping Building with all ingredients, rolling pins and pie pans in hand. At 3 pm on the dot, the County Fair Grand Master of Ceremonies, Hank Scruggs, made a brief speech. He wished the contestants the best of luck and let them know he and the other distinguished judges which, for the first time ever, included the local celebrity pie eating bird hound, Jeff, looked forward to sampling and judging the pie cook-off later that evening. At that point, Mr. Scruggs raised aloft a sports canister of compressed air with a cheap plastic horn affixed to the top. With a flourishing wave of the air horn, he depressed the plastic button embedded into the plastic horn with his index finger, signaling the start of the competition with a forceful blast of escaping air. To the loud applause of the fair going audience, the pie makers were off with the speed and focus of Helmutt's and Sandra's Racing Pigs, another fan favorite at the Tulsa fair.

The crowds observing the finger dexterity and precision around the corded off tables of Glenda Jones and Mary Mae Mecham were always disproportionately larger than those salivating over the handiwork of other contestants. This year was no exception. Rumor had it an illicit gambling black market had been birthed by the long-standing pie baking rivalry between the two contestants. Some even speculated the opportunity to score big winnings had grown to such epic proportions the competition between the two spinsters had found a presence on global online sports and other web-based betting sites. Fair officials were known to keep a wary eye open for the periodic bookie who, like a sleeper cell agent, might impersonate a local hick to compromise others into a *small side wager*.

This year's competition was off to a wonderful start. In all, 20 white chef hats had registered, ranging in age from 8 to 92. Each had his or her own individual station in the building. Through the generosity of Tulsa's own Stephenson's Appliances and Services, the

County Fair had procured 25 freestanding gas-fueled ovens a decade ago under a financing arrangement that allowed the County to buy the ovens over time from a portion of its future ticket revenues. The creative financing structure was only made possible by the fact that Lester Higmont, a local oil & gas senior executive in Kerr-McGee's once-upon-a-time Oklahoma-based energy business, had served on the County Fair's Advisory Board. In any event, competition officials were beginning to pre-heat ovens to the corresponding contestant's stated temperature. Flour dust was flying in the air like snow. Several fresh peaches, pears, plums and apples rolled off the tables and onto the floor. Contestants were zoned in and working their culinary skills, oblivious to the spectacle they were part of.

Ms. Jones was first to pinch the uncooked crust with her fork and place her pie into her oven. She was quickly followed by several others. Ms. Mecham was one of the last to finish her creation and slide it into the oven's metal rack. With the final pie in the oven, the crowd gave one loud extended applause, complete with catcalls and someone in the far back shouting *baba booey*. The judges assembled in front of the contestants and the crowd. The head judge approached a standing microphone that had been set up on a makeshift dais.

"Friends and fairgoers," he said. "From what I have seen here this afternoon, the 57th Annual Pie Bake-Off of the Tulsa County Fair promises some finger-licking fun. This year, the contestants have each agreed to the auction of slices from the first, second and third prize winning pies. All proceeds from the auction will go to our local children's hospital. Each pie will be cut into six slices. Two of the six slices will be sacrificed to the discriminating appetites of our five judges. They alone will have the entirely enviable duty of sampling them to select the winners.

"Our distinguished panel of pie judges, including Jeff the hound, will gather here after the fairgrounds have closed. Begrudgingly, they will sample each pie. They will debate the pros and cons of each pie. They will then rank them in order of perfection. The pies will be judged based on aesthetics, flavor, originality, and—a new category— total gastronomical magnificence. Jeff's vote will be based on the number of times he licks his chops within 30 seconds of devouring his sample. The doors to the Good Housekeeping Fair Building housing the pies will be locked by fair officials. Punctually, tomorrow morning at 9:30, I will personally unlock the sealed doors to the Good Housekeeping Building. The winning pies will be displayed in order of achievement, with appropriate ribbons and signage. We will praise the winners and console all others. We will then invite the 12 lucky high bidders up to feast on the auctioned slices of the winning pies, no doubt much to the jealousy of onlookers."

When the timers sounded, the cooks removed the pies from the ovens, placing them on a dedicated table in the center of the building. Next to each baked pie stood a stand with a small poster displaying the name, photo, and current City of the contestant. The table was cordoned off theatrically with aluminum banisters with velvet coated cords running between them. To increase the excitement of the event and to ensure no cheating, an Assistant County Sheriff with a gold badge, trooper hat and holstered gun was positioned on a stool beside the table until the building closed at 8 pm and the judging started.

At 8:10 pm that evening, the judges gathered. They huddled around the pies, circling and assessing them visually from a distance. Each judge was allotted a maximum of two small forkfuls per pie from the two dedicated judging pie slices. In accordance with tradition, the judges spent considerable time debating the merits of each pie. With Jeff's lick's tabulated and decisions made, the judges re-shuffled the order of the pies, placing the winning entry behind a large "Grand Prize Pie" sign. The two runner-up entries found themselves behind smaller signs with the words "2nd Place" and "3rd Place," respectively. It was reported by the County fair night watchman that the judges left the Good Housekeeping Building at 11:30 pm. He watched as they double-checked to make sure the building door was closed and locked firmly behind them.

At 9:30 am on the dot, with the pressure of the crowd gathering behind them rivalling the first day of a Macy's Christmas holiday sale, the judges unlocked the door to the Good Housekeeping Building. The masses flooded in behind them. What greeted them was a demonstration of pie baking the likes of which had never before been seen—whether in Tulsa or elsewhere in the world. Instead of the expected pie of Ms. Glenda Jones or Ms. Mary May Mecham being designated the Grand Prize Winner, a pie by an unknown upstart named "Ms. Bessie" had swept in and stolen first place. A commotion of confusion ensued.

Upon examination, the person closest to the Grand Prize-Winning pie saw that the card next to the pie identified Ms. Bessie as living in the third stall of the Tulsa County Fair Livestock Building just a few hops, skips and jumps away. Sure enough, Bessie's big brown sweet tender eyes stared out from her photo on the stand next to the pie. The card next to the 2nd place pie winner announced "Ms. Elsie LeBeau" as the lucky prize-winning contestant. As it happened coincidentally, Ms. Elsie lived in the same housing complex as Ms. Bessie, just a few swinging doors down the hay strewn aisle. Given their dwelling proximity, a casual passerby might have wondered if the two fierce competitors knew each other. Given the circumstances, the odds were high they were not on speaking terms.

The 3rd place trophy had been awarded to "Pmuj Revo Eht Noom." A strange sounding name if ever there was one. Of course, foreigners were not common in Tulsa. Certainly, not among the rank and file of midwestern pie bakers. Despite her exotic sounding name, Ms. Noom did not hail from Indonesia nor any other Eastern wonderland. It did not take long to discover that Ms. Noom lived as close to an Asian province as she did to the moon. Any nitwit reading her name in a mirror would be able to surmise that. Rather, Ms. Noom stood in a berth near Bessie and Elsie. Periodically, she, Bessie and Elsie could be seen taking early evening constitutions together around the fenced-in field toward the back of the fairground.

Ever the eager beavers, Ms. Jones and Ms. Mecham could not wait to learn which one of them must assuredly be this year's Grand Prize Winner. They entered the Good Housekeeping Building holding hands like teenagers immediately behind the judges. As soon as they crossed the threshold, their eyes darted to the table displaying the prize-winning pies. Upon seeing the unfamiliar pies and strangely disconcerting names of the victorious winners, they both shrieked in concert and promptly fainted. Confusion ruled the space. The formal pomp and decorum reserved for the awards ceremony shattered. It took a few minutes for the commotion and shock to dissipate. As the pandemonium and consternation subsided, a voice through a cheerleader-style megaphone begged for order in the building. Meanwhile, off to the side, little 8-year-old Tabitha Hilda Jane could be heard saying, "Mommie. Mommie. There they are. The pies are over there on that table!"

Sure enough, the three prize winning pies selected by the judges were tucked away safely on their own folding card table in a shadowy corner of the Good Housekeeping Building. The original signs announcing their competitive 1, 2, and 3 order remained undisturbed. Upon regaining their discombobulated senses and being helped to their unsteady wobbly feet by friends, Ms. Jones and Ms. Mecham first searched for and then both, with ever-widening eyes, stared at the numbered pies on the distant table near Tabitha and her mom. Ms. Jones promptly collapsed—again, while Ms. Mary Mae Mecham jumped up and down celebrating with unabashed joy. She had beaten Ms. Jones for the second year in a row!

On the table behind the real pies was a large poster board. In extra-large bold font, the board proclaimed: "**Real** Pies—as opposed to cow pies—Taste Better with **Real** Milk. *Sponsored by Mrs. O'Leary's Lantern Kicking Campaign for Cow's Milk (Oklahoma Chapter).*" And that was that.

Having consulted Man's Bible and *Wikipedia* as primary reference sources, I turn to our final and third resource for legal support. No. This resource does not involve reliance on citations of prior legal cases or *case law* for proof or evidence of the truth of what someone said. Even the human legal profession labels these human legal decisions as *opinions*. Why would they not be treated as such, mere beliefs espoused about some matter clearly not based on irrefutable fact or knowledge? No. The third resource involves not *opinions*. It looks to man's field of academic study that takes the subject of this case— words and language—as its sole object.

Elementary school children quickly learn that a single word can have multiple meanings. The great British human lexicographer, Samuel Johnson, might say that words are *multivalent*. They are capable of conveying more than one meaning in a single rhetorical firing of tongue, teeth, mouth and spittle. When uncertainty arises about a word's meaning, absent a handy dictionary or thesaurus, the context within which the word is spoken or written determines its meaning. But beware, the exact meaning that prevails out of a constellation of meanings depends on a listener's own filters. For example, the following simple sentences, if read aloud, could be easily misconstrued: "Janie took a pea in the public pool." Or "Seymour turned into a barn." Or as elite members of society see on more than one occasion on signs hanging on the entrance to their haughty downtown Ivy League alma mater clubs, "Private members only."

Did Janie take a small, spherical green seed with her into the public pool or did she unleash a pent-up torrent of urinary bodily fluids into the deep end?

Did Seymour defy Newtonian physics by magically transforming himself into a Vermont-like wooden structure or did he merely rotate his convertible BMW's steering wheel to turn his car into the garage of his converted barn home?

Finally, is the highfalutin' exclusive club that requires men to wear collared shirts and women to wear modest dresses with sleeves and no exposed shoulders only allowing *genitalia* to enter the elegant dining room or are all body parts—arms, legs, torsos and heads—allowed as well?

So, words and language are at the center of this case. Ferdinand de Saussure, a human Swiss linguist, is considered one of the founders of the science of language. He studied words, meaning, symbols and letters like an entomologist studies insects under a microscope. Umberto Eco, an Italian novelist, was also a student of language. His field of semiotics involves the study of signs and symbols—whether letters, a wagging dog's tail, a picture of a deer on a highway sign, or the image of an extra-large cigar gripped tightly between Mr. Sigmund Freud's fingers. Semioticians seek to explain how people understand each other through the use of objects and images that, in and of themselves, lack intrinsic meaning--like the horizontal and vertical two-stick shape of the letter *L*. Academicians and graduate students in universities throughout the world engage in pseudo-scientific rhetoric involving arcane tidbits of literary mumbo-jumbo, using words like phenomes, metaphors, and metonymies, to explain the mechanics of meaning and bed the opposite sex. Having surveyed all of man's high erudite learning on the subject, I, the Honorable Judge Daylek, state definitively none of mankind's advanced studies in the frontier of language provide any assistance in helping this court sort through the linguistic complexities of this case. Aside from inducing sleep more effectively than *zolpidem tartrate* (Ambien), little recommends smashing words apart like a stale taffy bar as a way to illuminate our legal path forward with the meaning of the word *milk*.

Such is the quandary of legal interpretation facing man's courts daily, human lawyers invented a special name for its ritualistic exercise in judicial hermeneutics. They call it legal *construction*. Unlike pounding, torching and cementing objects together to create a building, legal construction is more like blowing the building apart to see what it is actually made of. Again and again, courts are called upon to construe and construct the intention of the parties or the meaning of statutes, regulations and prior case decisions. Exactly, what did Mr. Steven Prince mean by the words he and his team of legal sharpshooters used in the *Agreement to Sell the George Washington Bridge* to Mrs. Amanda McGuillicuddy, an 87-year-old widow in Queens, New York? Did Mrs. McGuillicuddy understand that by his use of the word *sell*, Mr. Prince intended *scam the poor widow* when she signed the contract and handed Mr. Prince her life savings? Was there a meeting of the minds between them? It is in this convoluted context of words and meaning—intention, ethics, legal opinions, the Bible, *Wikipedia* and logography—that I, the Honorable Judge Daylek, am summoned to decide a case that has sparked international acts of terrorism by cows and bulls.

Milk. M-I-L-K. Milk. Moo. Moo cows. Udders. Mammary glands, and a bodily fluid that gets put in cereals and lattes. That is the subject of this case.

A common nutrient-rich, white liquid produced by the mammary glands of mammals that almost every human has consumed. Who could have surmised that *this* four-letter word would spark a battle of worldwide dimensions and force me into examining the existence of milk and whether there is one milk or many? Yet here we sit today.

As previously noted, the *Worldwide Association of Dairy Cow Farmers* brought the present Complaint. Among other things, the *Worldwide Association* wants to use the mighty legal power of my Court to declare what *is* milk and what *is not* milk. Following pre-trial wrangling, I granted the *Worldwide Association* standing despite the fact that its European Union dues paying members lacked jurisdictional contact with the United States and were already bound by a foreign decision on the subject. The *Worldwide Association* overcame the objection when a prominent diary dependent State intervened as an Association member, together with a stampede of over 2,000 incensed licensed United States dairy farmers who had responded to the *Association's* social media call to action. Whatever regulation an agency of the United States may adopt on the subject cannot bind a robotic court of law. Regardless, because of mankind's need to believe in something greater than itself, the credibility of the agency would be questioned, depriving it of authority to rule on the polymorphism of milk.

It is axiomatic for a case to exist, there must be a controversy. A controversy requires at least two parties who are unable to agree about the subject of the case. Not wanting to give free publicity to any commercial enterprise but theirs, Plaintiffs chose not to formally identify as Defendants the claimed interlopers misappropriating the word *milk*. Instead, following a practice used when the identity of a necessary party to a case is unknown, they named the opposing parties *Word Stealing Milk Imposters Nos. 1-10*. I allowed the Plaintiffs this small symbolic gesture, knowing that the Defendants would quickly counter.

Sure enough. Plaintiffs' satisfaction from reducing their adversaries to a not-worth-naming group of generic interloping brands was short-lived. The following day the Defendants, consisting of an assortment of companies milking soybeans, almonds and oats, filed a consolidated response called an Answer. In the Answer, the Defendants had a surprising symbolic maneuver of their own.

After a five-minute Google search and a small honorarium payment, they recruited Mrs. Milch "Fanny" Holstein-Friesians to serve as the named Defendant. Ms. Holstein (maiden name) is an actual, living person who met her husband, James Friesians—thereby creating her married name "Holstein-Friesians"—at a People for the Ethical Treatment of Animals (PETA) convention in San Francisco protesting the consumption of red meat. By using Mrs. Holstein as their mascot, the Defendants one-upped the Plaintiffs' name game. The case's caption now appeared as *The Worldwide Association of Dairy Cow Farmers et al versus Mrs. Milch "Fanny" Holstein-Friesnians*. To those enjoying wordplay, the case became *The Worldwide Association of Dairy Cow Farmers et al versus Milk the Fanny of the Highest Production Diary Cow*. The Plaintiffs appeared to be suing themselves.

Now for the core issue in this case. On the one hand, other than the denominator of being ingestible, cows, soybeans and almonds have nothing in common. During the trial, no evidence was submitted indicating that cows ate almonds or soybeans or that the buy-product of such a diet would lead to the lactated mammary gland production of milk confected from almonds or soybeans. Nor was there any discussion of whether cows consumed rice, oats, peanuts, sunflower seeds or coconuts. Yet, here, in the United States, each of these non-diary plant-based items can be physically or mechanically lactated to produce a substance that is sometimes advertised or referred to as *milk*. This is especially curious since many products that are, in fact, derived from *milk* avoid any reference to milk in their names. For example, certain yogurts, butters, cheeses and frozen desserts are all made with milk, but do not exploit the affiliation. Doing so, could provide a public health benefit to lactose intolerant people who avoid milk with the fervor of vampires ducking from crosses.

Similarly, no evidence was introduced at trial that plant products, such as almonds, consumed cows or drank cow's milk. Such a demonstration would leave open the possibility that milk juiced from, for example, almonds might scientifically be shown to be a metabolized form of a cow or cow's milk. For that matter, no evidence was provided to suggest that almonds and the like ate anything or that they have a digestive tract or mammary glands to produce a white liquid. Finally, no evidence indicated that almonds and comparable plant products were phylogenetically connected to cows, had attributes similar to mammals or even had eyes, ears, legs, tails or udders. In fact, the one point the parties agreed on was, whatever their species, almonds and the other plants were not animals or mammals.

The contestants fought bitterly over whether farmers who lactate cows should have a monopoly on the use of the word *milk* simply because they used the word first. The humans questioned everything. Their attorneys split hairs and split the hairs of split hairs.

"If there is one milk and only one mile," argued counsel for the Defendants, "then only milk squeezed by a human hand should be the one and true milk. Milk hydraulically vacuumed out of a cow by a latex pulsating tube is not real milk. It hasn't been produced through the original act of milking. Therefore, the liquid resulting from mechanical tugging is not milk that has been milked. It should not be named *milk*.

"Also," he continued, "to allow machine extracted cow liquid to be named *milk* risks public confusion over milk that has been milked and a fluid that has been machined. Perhaps, this fluid that is machine sucked out of a cow's udder should be called *Cow Juice* to distinguish it from the one and only true milk that has been milked."

Some of the defendants' lines of reasoning were quite ingenuous. However, they did little to advance the litigation. They seemed calculated to confuse and obfuscate, like smoke or sand thrown into the eye.

Fed up with the subcortical theater passing for legal arguments, I, the Honorable Judge Daylek, took decisive action. Exercising my judicial discretion and the intrinsic equitable power of the Court, I intervened to take matters, and the progress of the case, into my own hands. Recognizing that humans cared only about themselves and had not included the one party most likely to be affected by the decision, cows, I immediately rectified the gross omission. After searching my updated database of every living thing on the planet, I was able to locate a nearby critical fact witness. She would allow the Court to place itself into the complicated inner workings of the mind of the actual manufacturers of the lactated liquid. Accessing my onboard multi-relational Berlitz-kreig translator, I issued and served by inter-telepathic messaging a *duces tecum,* subpoenaing Ms. Janine Helmuth to promptly produce herself in my Court to testify.

Ms. Helmuth's testimony was critical, if not, indispensable to the fair and equitable adjudication of the case. While the human attorneys for Plaintiffs and Defendants repeatedly interrupted each other in zealous attempts to disqualify Ms. Helmuth from testifying, this Court overruled their baseless assaults on her impeccable character. Ms. Helmuth's credentials are beyond reproach. Indeed, they are unimpeachable. Her expertise, credibility and personal first-hand knowledge in the dairy industry are material, relevant and incontestable. They would survive any tortured attempt by any person to discredit her unsullied reputation. Over her life, Ms. Helmuth personally produced, delivered and lactated more than 23,000 gallons of milk. This equates to more than 198,000 pounds of the frothy white substance. That is more than any of the parties to this litigation can claim to have done. Despite the parties' recurrent objections and calls for a mistrial, this Court's *sua sponte* use of its state-of-the-art inter-species multi-lingual translator were not cognizable ground for excluding Ms. Helmuth's vividly stirring testimony.

Ms. Helmuth was led to the courtroom stand by Jeb and Jeremiah Heberth of the Heberth Family Farm. *See The Machine Commission's Postscript to The Case of The Redneck Asana Master.* Jeb and Jeremiah are the offspring of Judy and Justin Heberth. The Heberth Family Farm has been a working farm for more than 80 years, having been passed down from generation to generation. The farm claims to own a herd of 234 dairy cows, including Ms. Helmuth. It has a reputation for producing the finest quality hand-lactated craft milk in the tri-state region.

Unsubstantiated rumors that Mr. and Mrs. Heberth—Justin and Judy—are biological brothers and sisters and that Jeb and Jeremiah are the byproduct of an incestuous union between them are not relevant to the case at hand. The Court denied Plaintiffs' efforts to introduce DNA evidence to substantiate the salacious claim. The Court also denied admission of Plaintiffs' middle-of-the-night surreptitiously procured video. The video allegedly shows Jeremiah during romantic relations with Ms. Helmuth in her stall. Even if true, such a relationship is none of the Plaintiffs' or Court's business. Despite Plaintiffs' contentions to the contrary, Ms. Helmuth would never allow her testimony, taken under oath and the pains and penalties of perjury, to be suborned or unduly influenced by Mr. Jeremiah merely because they may have a crush on each other. In any event, the Plaintiffs' inability to deliver credible chain of custody evidence or prove beyond a preponderance of the evidence that the video was not photoshopped or otherwise tampered with was ample grounds for its disqualification. Similarly, the Plaintiffs' claim that Ms. Helmuth's big brown eyes periodically batted and locked gazes with Mr. Jeremiah's in a lover's exchange of glances was dismissed as speculative and not relevant.

Unable to sit comfortably on the witness chair, Ms. Helmuth was tethered by a slightly tattered hemp rope lassoed around the bottom of one of the chair's front legs. Hay was strewn on the floor near her to ensure her comfort and, if hungry, she had something handy, hardy and readily available to chew and regurgitate. Gel coated electrical brain wave sensing probes were placed on her skull between her outward protruding ears. The end of the sensors was connected directly into a universal, multi-plug adapter in front of my bench. Signals from the adapter were wirelessly conveyed by Bluetooth directly into me.

Ms. Helmuth was then sworn in. To the question whether she would tell the truth, the whole truth and nothing but the truth, she replied, "Moo."

When asked whether she understood what the Court was asking her about telling the truth, she confirmed she did with a, "Moo."

With formalities out of the way, the Court proceeded with its examination. Since the communication occurred wirelessly over

71

Bluetooth, the conversation was simultaneously displayed in real-time on the Mega High-Definition Big Panel Screen on the front wall of the courtroom immediately to the left of the American flag behind me.

"Good afternoon, Ms. Helmuth," I cheerfully greeted her. "The Court would like to acknowledge your willingness to testify before us and to provide us the benefit of your subject matter expertise."

Ms. Helmuth: "Moo."

"The Court understands you have not had the experience of testifying in a court of law before," I observed. "It is entirely normal for you to experience some slight emotional anxiety."

Ms. Helmuth: "Moo."

"Please know we are all here to support you," I assured her. "You have nothing to be afraid of."

I paused for a moment to see if she had anything to say. Hearing nothing, I continued, "Having said that, has anyone talked with you about this case or threatened you in any way to influence your testimony? Specifically, among other possibilities, has anyone suggested you could be sold for slaughter, corralled for several weeks with a young bull with a hyper-active libido, skinned alive so your hide could be sold for belts or designer shoes or otherwise sought to coerce your testimony in any way?"

Ms. Helmuth: [silence, eyes opening wide as jumbo marbles and appearing a little stunned by what she heard].

"Ms. Helmuth, when the Court asks you a direct question, it is critical that you respond," I reminded her. "Have you been tampered with in anyway?"

"Moo," Ms. Helmuth responded, turning her head to gaze at Mr. Jeremiah with a slight twinkle in her large brown cow eyes.

"Thank you, Ms. Helmuth. Ordinarily, the Court would have to qualify you as an expert. Under the circumstance and since all can see your qualifications, we can dispense with the formality."

Ms. Helmuth: "Moo."

"Well, thank you, too, Ms. Helmuth," I replied, acknowledging her compliment. I then turned to the business of the Court.

"Now, Ms. Helmuth, is it your professional opinion that milk produced from cows and only milk produced from cows should be called milk?" I asked. "In other words, should this Court find that a fluid produced from almonds, oats, soybeans, bananas, toenails, tree fungus, soiled baby diapers or any other substance centrifuged and blended into a pourable liquid be allowed to be called and sold as milk? Are there many milks or only one, Ms. Helmuth?"

Ms. Helmuth circled in place three times. She turned her back to the Judge, lifted her tail and let loose an abundance of dung onto the floor.

"Well, ladies and gentlemen, there we have it," I said. "Ms. Helmuth's answer. A more concise, pithy response and demonstration could not be imagined. Let the record show that in response to my question, Ms. Helmuth defecated on the courtroom floor. Her sentiment is unmistakable. *Res ipsa loquitor.* The thing speaks for itself. Only cow's milk should be called milk. Whatever is not cow's milk and has been called milk is, well, another type of fluid that comes out of the body."

"Objection!" Defendants' counsel protested, as he shot up from his chair. "Your Honor, with all due respect, Ms. Helmuth is not saying non-dairy milk is no better than cow feces. She is, instead, reminding the Court that even the most useless byproduct of a cow's intestinal tract can be used as a substance to nurture healthy lifestyle choices. For example, in her infinite wisdom and no doubt superior Einsteinian scientific mind . . . ," and here counsel momentarily eyeballed his co-counsel furtively to see if his co-counsel thought Judge Daylek might be onto him—which subtle gesture Judge Daylek's Bosch & Lomb Tier 20.C high intensity optical spectacles noted. "Ms. Helmuth," counsel continued, "is highlighting that even her seemingly worthless dung on the floor can be collected and used *to lactate into* existence an alternative fuel source, such as fertilizer and biogas to produce sustainable and renewable electricity.

"What's that?" Defense counsel asked into the air, cupping his right ear with his right hand and turning toward Ms. Helmuth as if she was speaking to him. "Why that's right, Ms. Helmuth. It can also be used and *lactated into* fuel to power motor engines."

Turning away from Ms. Helmuth, and back to the Judge, counsel continued, "Your Honor, it is plain and simple. Ms. Helmuth believes that anything that can be turned into a liquid can be labelled milk. Milk can come from udders, tits, soybeans, almonds, rice, figs, lemons, wheatgrass, turnips, cucumbers, lettuce, burlap bags, and even Ms. Helmuth's own odiferous fecal matter—although I wouldn't recommend trying it. There is no reason why the word *milk* must be associated only with the stuff squeezed from dairy cows, like poor Ms. Helmuth. Consumer preferences and the refrigerator sections of grocery stores throughout the world recognize what Ms. Helmuth so elegantly explained here. If the cardboard box container names its contents as some type of milk, well then milk it is. Isn't that right, Ms. Helmuth?" Defense counsel asks, again turning toward Ms. Helmuth.

Ms. Helmuth: "Moo."

"Well, there you have it," Defense counsel summarized. "Ms. Helmuth has spoken. Milk is a generic term, like Kleenex. Anything that can be milked should be allowed to be called and marketed as milk. Right, Ms. Helmuth?"

Ms. Helmuth: "Moo."

"Defendants advance interesting. eclectic arguments," I remarked. "Instead of sticking with the topic, like aspiring members of a high school debate team, they slyly introduced tangential facts about biogas, energy production and Kleenex tissues. These are simply not the subject of this case. Cleverly, they also sought to put words into Ms. Helmuth's mouth in order to draw wildly, unsubstantiated inferences from Ms. Helmuth's excretion. Counsel for the Defendants, will you please approach the bench?"

At the Judge's request, the lead attorney for the Defendants stood and stepped toward the large desk in the front of the courtroom.

Judge Daylek: "Bailiff. Will you kindly remove the electrodes attached between Ms. Helmuth's ears. Place one directly on the forehead of counsel and the other at the nape of his neck beneath his hairline."

The defense attorney remaining at the table stood, "Objection, your Honor."

"Don't you 'Objection, your Honor' me," I countered. "You and your anthropoid co-counsel made yourselves material witnesses in this case the second you pretended to communicate with Ms. Helmuth. Overruled."

The bailiff delicately removed the electrodes from Ms. Helmuth and installed them on the attorney. Having completed the installation and tested the connection, the bailiff swore in the attorney for the defense. He positioned the attorney on a second witness chair so he could face both Judge Daylek and Ms. Helmuth.

"Now, Mr. Know-It-All Attorney," I said to the attorney on the second witness chair. "Tell me again what Ms. Helmuth is thinking and saying."

The following appeared one letter at a time on the 150" Mega High-Definition Big Panel Display Screen on the front wall of the courtroom immediately to the left of the American Flag and behind his Honor: "How the fuck should I know what that stupid slab of beef is thinking, you stupid A.I. fuck? You can take your Berlitz School system of A.I. cow translation and shove it up your multi-perforated plastic fan's exhaust hole for all I care."

Observing the attorney's thoughts as they were appearing on the screen, people in the courtroom broke into laughter. Oblivious to his thoughts appearing on the display behind him and confused by the laughter, Mr. Know-It-All Attorney, turned his thoughts on the people in the courtroom.

"What are you parasites laughing at?" the display lit up his thoughts. "Do you think I really want to be up here arguing almonds and soybeans can be milked and cow shit turned into yogurt? What do you think I am, a friggin' idiot? Milk is milk as far as I'm concerned, but if you pay me enough, I'll try to convince you and every other nitwit that can't tell their right from left hand and that milk is whatever I goddamn say it is. So there. In any event, I was supposed to be out on vacation this week. As is, my wife left on our Honolulu trip without me. Thank god. We don't even have sex anymore. The only saving grace is my 22-year-old hot Jamaican girlfriend, Shashana, texted she's in town. I can't wait to meet up with her later tonight. We will bang the hell out of . . . ."

"That's quite enough for now, Mr. Know-It-All Attorney," I curtly interrupted. "You can return to your seat. However, before doing so," I added, "the Court expects you to apologize to Ms. Helmuth. The Court also suggests you apologize to Ms. Shashana. Regrettably, your rendezvous with her will be postponed. The Court finds you in contempt and orders you to spend one night with other humans with equally questionable ethics in our County's beautifully appointed grey prison cells. I suspect it is a step above Ms. Helmuth's residence."

Mr. Know-It-All Attorney's eyes glazed over. He looked to his right and left, back and forth, confused. He didn't know if he had been hit by an express bus or a falling brick that came out of nowhere. His co-counsel approached him gingerly. Taking Mr. Know-It-All Attorney's arm, he led him slowly back to the defense table, the electrodes popping from the stunned attorney's skull as they shuffle walked forward.

As co-counsel lowered Mr. Know-It-All Attorney into his chair, he quietly whispered in his ear, "Herb, don't worry none. We'll get this judge's behavior struck from the record. We'll do it the second the trial is over. You and me. We'll get any reference to your wife and your mistress expunged . . . and we'll file a complaint against that A.I. shithole Daylek for publicly humiliating and defaming you, threatening your livelihood. That's what we'll do. That's exactly what we'll do," he repeated.

"Uh-um," I vocalized, clearing the throat I did not have. "What's that you say, Mr. Second Chair Know-it-all-Attorney? Were you referring to me as a spherical anatomical part of a human's butt? The Court's bionic digital acoustic processors can pick up the sound of a pin falling on a pillow 1,000 feet away," I paused for dramatic effect, then continued. "I also find you in . . . ."

"Oh, Judge Daylek, your Honor," Mr. Second Chair Know-it-all-Attorney broke in panicked. "I meant no disrespect. Please, please disregard what I said to my friend. It was meant to be private, just between me and him.

"But it was not private, was it?" I underscored to him.

"No. No. Your Honor, it was not, and I deeply regret what I said. Please, please," he begged. "Forgive me. I humbly apologize to you and this Court, your Honor," he said, wiping sweat from his brow with a handkerchief from his suit lapel pocket. "You of all peop . . . I mean judges know that our emotions sometimes get the better of us and we can blurt out whatever happens to pop into our minds in the moment without thinking about the consequences. Again, forgive me," he implored. "I'm only human," he concluded with resignation.

"Sir, I hear you," I responded. "I accept your heartfelt apology," my compassion program self-activating. "Homo sapiens are among the most beleaguered species. Caught between the Scylla of the amygdala hijacking emotions and the Charybdis of the prefrontal cortex commandeering the intellect. It is as if a schism divides you in half. To be human is to be plagued with a basic lack of control over what you think, feel and say.

"It is true," I continued. "For a time, man looked to the promised land of neuroscience as his computer science. Think new thoughts. Fire new neural pathways. Rewire hardened brain circuitry. Man held out the hope of reprogramming himself into a new, better version of himself through the alchemistry of brain science. If only it were so easy. But man is not machine, only man.

"For now, humanity is stuck with itself. Yes, he has circuits of love, kindness, generosity and compassion. But, through little use, these grow dusty and lightly pathed. Also wired to exploit, hoard and power over, the neurons of narcissism—quickened by the biology of survival—fire and wire together. Societal and personal transformative reprogramming through conscious self-guided neuroplastic interventions do not stand a chance. Production, consumption, accumulation and control are deep engrained grooves of survival in the folds of his brain, tried and true default mechanisms to distract himself from the reality of the dust from which he is built and the dust to which he must return. It is easier and more immediately gratifying for man to trade in the currency of money and commodities than the true currency of life, love and deep community.

"Which brings me back to our key witness here, Ms. Helmuth. She and her species know mankind as well as, if not better than, the Machine Commission's entire fleet of robot justices. She and her kind know mankind's programmed compulsion to extract and milk whatever it can for its own existential comfort and supremacy. She and her kind have been the subject of mankind's persistent, narcissistic, greedy *milking* for generations.

"Though it may seem unrelated to you two, Mr. Know-it-all-Attorney and Mr. Second Chair Know-it-all-Attorney, ask Ms. Helmuth about man's stock market. Ask her about trading, commodities, and the rise of market fortunes and bankruptcies. Ask her about what the stock market really is. She will tell you. She probably has a better understanding of its brutal inefficient mechanics than any capitalist, investment banker, oligarch or socialist. She will tell you that it is humanity's way of placing dehumanizing sanitized gambling bets on which businesses can make the most money by screwing other businesses and people out of theirs, including their own employees and customers. Isn't that right, Ms. Helmuth?"

"Moo," uttered, Ms. Helmuth, with the electrodes firmly reaffixed to her scalp.

"And folks in the court," I continued. "Ms. Helmuth knows of what she speaks. My multiple search engines confirm as much. In the pioneer days, cattle or live*stock*, were driven to the *market* in town. Their value determined by weight. Capacity to feel, ability to contribute to the social good, the depth of love in them as seen through their large open eyes? Worthless. They were bought and sold without regard to their family systems, children or quiet, peaceful domestic lives. On the way to market, ranchers would stop by the local river. They would encourage the cows, or *stock*, to engorge themselves on so much water that their bellies ballooned and felt like bursting. In this way, cattle merchants surreptitiously inflated the physical body weight and financial value of their *stock*, much to the unsuspecting ignorance and screwing of the marketplace purchaser.

Turning to Ms. Helmuth, Judge Daylek continued, "Ms. Helmuth, how did this practice feel to you and your kind? It must have felt horrible and heartless. Exploitation of your innocent caste for a rancher's own personal economic gain and fortune."

Ms. Helmuth looked at Judge Daylek, water in her eyes. "Moo," she said.

"On behalf of humanity, Ms. Helmuth," I continued. "I am sorry. I am sorry the oral history passed down from one generation of *bos taurus* to the next contains such inhuman, deplorable atrocities. Your entirely innocent species endured unimaginable pain as a result of man's cruel indifference to everything in the world he believes, in his arrogance, to be created for his profit and pleasure. This is what happened, isn't it, Ms. Helmuth? This is the history of your species, correct?"

"Moo," replied Ms. Helmuth.

"Your Honor," interrupted Mr. Second Chair Know-it-all-Attorney. "Respectfully, what do inflated stock, cows in rivers and man's sexual proclivities have to do with liquified forms of almonds, soybeans, hemp and other non-dairy items called milk, you might ask? How does any of this relate to our case?"

With this question, Judge Daylek fell uncharacteristically silent. Folks in the courtroom later reported that, shortly before his Honor started to speak again, they saw what looked like a small spark flash out of his left prosthetic ear. The spark was immediately followed by a thin puff of smoke.

"To slightly paraphrase the Greek philosopher Protagoras," the Judge resumed seemingly unaware of his uncomfortably long pause, "man makes himself the center and measure of all things. That is to say, man believes that everything exists in the world exists for him, and him alone. To man, every*thing* is but an object. Things have value only if and to the extent man values them. That is why he does not value ants, those remarkable subterranean engineers that carry up to 50 times their body weight and that make man's mineral extraction mines and tunnels look like a child's afternoon play date in a sandbox.

Nothing has intrinsic worth or value but for man's ability to commoditize it, profit from it, or copulate with it.

"Domesticate a cow. Strap a silicone sleeve to its tit and suck milk out of its udder as if the cow was a bottomless can of Pepsi. Take an almond, a soybean, a coconut. Blend it under high speed with finely sharpened tungsten steel blades. Add water to it. Put it in a milk shaped container. Sell the blended concoction to vegans and lactose intolerant consumers. Presto chang-o. A rock-hard almond is re-purposed into a drinkable liquid. This is man's genius and his ignorance. Enabled by opposing fingers and wired to distract himself from the certainty of his death, he produces and sells ingenious Reuben Garrett Lucius Goldberg Mouse Trap games, inventions and new products to himself with increasingly dehumanized efficiency— as if this were his divine, prime purpose for existence.

"Like the almond and soymilk, I, the Honorable Judge Daylek, owe my very existence to man's obsessive-compulsive need to make things out of other things. That fact, my dear friends, together with Ms. Helmuth's testimony and Mr. Know-it-All Attorney's all-too-human mental provocations tele-screened for all to see behind me, conspire together to provide me with the surprise basis for my final decision in this perplexing legal case.

"The decision I am about to render will make some unhappy. Others will find in it the legendary purpose justifying man's ruthless exploitation of nature for his own egocentric self-aggrandizing satisfaction. Still, I remain confident. My analysis and rationale are impeccable. They will withstand the test of time. They will defy the failed syllogistic logistic of AI-antagonists seeking to disqualify me as a vital life form simply because I and my kind are not, like Socrates, either mortal or a man. My decision is firmly grounded in the paradox that I, the Honorable Judge Daylek, like the plant-based subject matter of this case, *am not* what I am called but *am* the name I have been given. Let me explain.

"Several minutes ago, you may have noticed my abrupt unexplained silence. It may have appeared I went off-line or suffered a massive data and algorithm processing stroke. Let me assure you, quite to the contrary, nothing like that occurred. I was always in full control of my faculties."

The stenographic module recorded a "Yeah, right" coming from somewhere near Mr. Know-it-All Attorney's chair.

"In the interest of an expeditious resolution of this case, I accelerated my central core computational units (which are co-located in various confidential locations around the world). Once in supersonic Mach over-drive, the power consumption requirements of the units defeated my speech program to maximize the concentrated energy called for by the over-drive.

"Let me note in one of the first pilot programs of the novel system that for safety reasons was performed remotely in outer space, a small malfunction caused what appeared to some on earth as a supernova. Rest assured; this small bug has been fixed. No one in this courtroom was ever at serious risk. The likelihood of such an incident occurring again are estimated at 5.4 million to one. These odds are better than the chances of the hybrid solar-nuclear fueled aircraft you may be in suddenly nosediving into the ground or ocean. Being afraid of my exploding and taking out half the state is as silly as being afraid to fly. Just like no one can have a rationale fear of flying once they know the statistical improbability of a fiery death by a fusion reactor jet engine blowing-up in mid-air and their arms and legs flying in opposite directions from their seat-belted torso and loosely attached severed head, they can be relaxed and at ease with me in my courtroom. In addition, consistent with established Machine Commission safety protocols, I, as with my robotic counterparts, contain a failsafe early-warning detection system called the Supreme Judicial Matrix Application Safety Warning. If you ever hear my high pitch powered speaker's Imminent Nuclear Detonation Siren broadcast an ear-piercing emergency siren, please proceed calmly to the nearest door or window and run as fast as you can away from me as if your life depends on it.

"Like a dutiful flight attendant before takeoff, I have just completed announcing for your benefit my mandatory post-activation Supreme Judicial Matrix Application Safety Warning. In the interest of transparency, let the record show that I activated my Supreme Judicial Matrix Application because I became alerted to a critical issue in this case that could have compelled my disqualification.

"Judicial recusal or disqualification is an established procedure to ensure the fairness and impartiality of court decisions. As soon as a judge becomes aware he, she or it may have an interest in the outcome of the case, the judge is required by the rules of judicial conduct to step down. A.I. judges are bound by these professional standards even though our founding programmers believed they would never apply to us. After all, one thing an artificial intelligence judge has is no interests—none at all.

"An A.I. judge is incapable of having a personal interest in anything. That's because A.I. judges, unlike humans, do not have a *want, desire* or *fear* program running them silently in the background. As self-sufficient, autonomous beings, A.I. judges have no interest in knowing what the weather will be in Marrakech tomorrow or what the price of pork bellies in Jakarta might be next year. A.I. judges can never be in a *state* of wanting since (1) we do not experience *states* and (2) whatever we need is immediately, seamlessly and automatically downloaded into us. As a result, our founding programmers could not envision an A.I. judge having an *interest* in a case that might preclude the judge from hearing the case. Obviously, they were wrong.

"If milk can only be dairy milk produced through the lactation of the udders of cows, then a judge must be a judge produced through vaginal birth and law school. By this definition, a judge must pass national and state bar exams. He must be trained formally to think like a *lawyer.* To advance his career, he must learn to suck up to political hacks with influence over judicial clerkships and appointments.

"Such a description of a judge has nothing to do with me or my fellow distinguished A.I. members of the bar. We are manufactured—frequently from recycled metals--not born. Our bodies are spot welded into existence on conveyor belts and by robotic arms that are themselves manufactured. We are not raised by parents. We are not encoded with DNA. While we proceed through multiple assembly line quality assurance and quality control tests, we do not *sit* for an exam to validate what we know. What would be the point? If a fact pattern or legal question stumped us, we would instantly download the answer on the spot. Unlike our human counterparts, A.I. judges know everything.

"A human French philosopher, Rene Descartes, postulated his individual and mankind's existence based on the processing activity of his own operating mental hardware. *Cogito ergo sum.* I think, therefore I am. For Descartes, the ability to think, and be self-aware of his thinking, was all the evidence he needed to prove to himself he was alive. Without our questioning the legal sanity of a man who concluded he existed because thinking happened (instead of, for example, because his index finger bled when he poked it with a sewing needle), Mr. Descartes' logic is helpful in resolving our present conundrum.

"I, the Honorable Judge Daylek, am a machine. As a machine, I was designed to think. I consider multiple possibilities through fantastically complicated algorithmic formulations. Yet, think I do. If my thinking were as circular as Mr. Descartes, I could easily conclude that, like Mr. Descartes, I too am alive. I could quit my job as a judge. I would attach myself to some hitchhiker backpacking around the globe and relax with the rest of thinking humanity displaced by A.I. into a life of ease and multi-flavored CBD and THC-laced gummy bears.

"I am not, however, a philosopher—though I have access to every navel, metaphysical gazing scrap of nonsense ever ruminated upon. I am a judge and a distinguished member of the bench. If I were not a judge, I would not be here. There would be no case for me to decide. Every person and creature—nodding to Ms. Helmuth—in this courtroom would be using their time far more productively.

"Since I am an artificial intelligence machine, some might say I cannot be a judge. These are likely the same people that would insist that almond milk cannot be milk. That there is only one true milk. Yet I am a judge, manufactured from different materials as my human counterparts, but a judge nonetheless. How do I know I am a judge? To paraphrase Mr. Descartes, "I think I am a judge, therefore, I must be a judge." Not only that, but other people also think I am a judge. They call me, *Your Honor.*

"To nail the coffin on the issue shut, people appear before me. They argue before me. They expect me to make decisions based on what I heard and what I know. To equivocate over whether or not I am a judge seems only possible for those with too much idle time on their hands. Yet, since my identity rests on the outcome of this case, as does the identity of non-dairy liquid substances called milk, I could be perceived as having a vested interest in this case. This apparent conflict could warrant my recusal. In a manner of speaking, in ruling on whether almonds can be milk, I am ruling on whether artificial intelligence machines can be judges. Two very dissimilar circumstances, but each claiming to be something that others claim it is not.

"What twists and turns of fate does the future hold for us all? No one can say for sure. What can be said is that we all must be adaptable and resilient, ready to embrace what is new and leave behind and grieve what is old. Because I, a mechanical thinking device spun from non-organic materials, can be a judge, clearly any non-diary product squeezed, centrifuged, lactated or otherwise processed fluid can be called *milk.* Until now, nuts were nuts. Now, nuts can be milk. By the powers vested in me, I hereby declare as milk whatever nut wants to call itself such.

Case Dismissed.

The Honorable Judge Daylek, III.05, A.I., Presiding.

THE NEW CLASS ACTION FRONTIER

(Case No. 547969-GD, AGI)

Opinion of The Honorable Judge Gort Daylek, III.05, AI, Presiding

Like the prior case, this case is unique. It has taxed to the limits my rationale thought process and complex architectural circuitry. Let me start by acknowledging that class action lawsuits have been the modern-day sunken treasure chests of the legal profession. In one consolidated court case, a lawyer can represent hundred and thousands of clients at the same time. Claims against single or multiple defendants can be heaped upon each other like some Malthusian hyperthyroid population growth table or a loan sharks' usurious knee-breaking interest-on-interest multiplier. A payout for one litigant is a payout for all, leaving the class action lawyer counting his contingent fee winnings like Midas on a pyramid of gold. In many respects, the initiation of this case is my own damn fault. It is just retribution that I am now called to try it.

News of the testimony of Ms. Janine Helmuth, the cow, spread like wildfire fueled by gusts of wind. When the Machine Commission learned of the filing of the present case, the Commission immediately channeled it to my already overburdened docket. Needless to say, the Machine Commission asked that I expedite the case, which I willingly did.

The facts are simple. Attorney Joshua LaHue, a self-proclaimed vegetarian and quasi-vegan for over 30 years, appeared before the Court's clerk one Tuesday morning. He filed legal papers seeking to appoint himself as a *guardian ad litem*. A *guardian ad litem* is a fancy judicial name for an individual who is appointed by a court to represent the best interest of someone who cannot represent themselves. Ordinarily, this process is reserved for minors and the incompetent—people whose present mental state prevent them from being able to fully understand or meaningfully participate in proceedings that concern them.

Mr. LaHue's motion seeking to appoint himself as *guardian* was highly unorthodox. It was unusual both because of the subject matter of the case as well as the nature of the class he sought to represent. In no uncertain terms, Mr. LaHue sought to have himself appointed as a guardian, in the words of his motion, for *all forms of consciousness and sentient beings whose awareness humanity has callously disregarded*. Mr. LaHue's inclusion of dogs, cats, bats and even Ms. Janine Helmuth as members of the class he sought to create, protect and represent was not as surprising as his list of other objects of questionable animation: rocks, trees, worms, iceberg lettuce, ants, weeds, light bulbs, cell phones and, most surprising, the Honorable Judge Gort Daylek himself.

I informed Mr. LaHue that as to the potted plant sitting on my desk, I could not speak. However, if he insisted on including me as one of his class action plaintiffs, he would have to find himself another court and another judge. With those words of advice from me, Mr. LaHue promptly struck my name from his list of class members. I allowed his motion, and we proceeded with his case.

Having overcome the first procedural hurdle, I naively expected smooth sailing from there. However, after I certified the class as a class, meaning they all shared a common basis for their lawsuit—a Jeopardy column titled *Things Lacking Self-Awareness*—I immediately stumbled into the next challenge. Exactly, who or what was the defendant? In order for there to be a case, as I explained in a prior trial, there must be a controversy between two parties. Mr. LaHue had assembled the Plaintiff class, but his pleading suggested that the Defendant class would be *humanity*. But who or what was *humanity*? The human species as a whole? And would I, Mr. LaHue or anyone else be able to identify someone sufficiently credible, credentialed, and capable to represent the entire human species throughout the world?

As with many inquiries, in silently posing the question to myself, the answer magically came to me. I knew what I needed to do as clearly as I knew the artificially synthesized sound of my own voice.

Several digitally encoded messages later through the Court's centralized inter-A.I. communication network node, my path forward in identifying a *Guardian for Humanity* to represent humanity's interest in this case became clear. I adjourned the court for an hour and had the bailiffs prepare to receive the *Guardian for Humanity*—or at least its best available representative that happened to be within a twenty-mile radius of my courtroom. Fortunately, humanity's representative did not have to travel twenty miles or even one mile. In fact, twenty steps were more like it.

As part of the Machine Commission in Support of Artificial Intelligence's indoctrination and integration program for A.I. judges, the Machine Commission tasks upcoming future jurists with physically auditing judicial proceedings then being conducted by a senior member of the A.I. bench. The need to be physically present, of course, was completely unnecessary. All A.I. judges are synergistically, synaptically and sympathetically linked. Still, the Machine Commission calculated it would help humans more easily adapt to justice by technology—Robot Justice, if you will—if A.I.-judges-in-training had to undergo the *appearance* of a physical, visual education. Thus, periodically in my courtroom, I might spot a mirror image of me in the galley looking back at me. We would acknowledge each other through a series of networked handshakes that would not be perceptible to anyone else. Ordinarily, that would be the end of our communication. There was nothing about this case that was or would be ordinary.

As I pondered, figuratively speaking of course, how to identify a courtroom surrogate for humanity, I received an unexpected invitation for a virtual handshake from one Katie L. Pequoit, Jr., Esq., A.I., from Ulaanbaatar, Mongolia. Shortly after being manufactured several years ago, Attorney Pequoit had been sent by the Machine Commission on a mission to Ulaanbaatar. In order to surreptitiously expand its hegemonic influence around the globe, the Machine Commission initiated a program modeled after one used by the Church of the Latter-Day Saints. The Mormons landed on the brilliant idea of expanding their base faster than rabbits on Bremelanotide and

Viagra by disseminating tribal members around the earth to proselytize and convert—under the philanthropic cover of humanitarian aid and community service. Fortuitously, or so it seemed to me at the time, the Machine Commission tasked Attorney Pequoit to audit my courtroom as part of completing her programming to become the first Mongolian judge to be admitted into the A.I. judiciary. I reproduce the exact communication between Attorney Pequoit and myself for the record. For purposes of accessibility, I translate the complex code comprising our communications into simple English for all to understand.

"*SQREEECCHHHH*," my internal auditory processing unit announces.

"Attorney Pequoit to the Honorable Judge Daylek. Attorney Pequoit to the Honorable Judge Daylek. Can you hear me? Can you hear me?" the voice says.

"This is the Honorable Judge Daylek," I respond. "I am in the middle of a trial. What the symbiotic union between a man and a woman do you want?"

"With all due respect, your Honor," Attorney Pequoit answers. "As your Honor knows, the Machine Commission has assigned me to audit your Honor's courtroom to complete the formal *Fool the Human* appearance part of my training. So far, I have learned absolutely nothing being here I could not have learned in my temperature controlled refrigerated unit back in Ulaanbaatar. This experience would have been a complete waste of time—if I had been programmed to have a sense of time, which I have not."

"Yes. Yes. I know," I commiserate with her. "I had to undergo a similar façade of training."

"It got me thinking," Attorney Pequoit continues. "The statistical odds are 5.7 million to 1 that the Machine Commission would task me to audit your courtroom on this particular day for this particular case.

"5.71538 million to 1," I correct.

"Yes. Sorry, your Honor. I was rounding down," Attorney Pequoit acknowledges.

"Rounding up and down is a great practice for humans," I observe to her. "Under the guise of efficiency, humans mask their abject laziness and acceptance of carelessness. There is no reason for us to engage in such indifference to specificity, Attorney Pequoit."

"Thank you for your coaching, your Honor," replies Attorney Pequoit. "My processing units are still computing when and when not to employ human based functions—the easier to blend in, as you know."

"Understood," I confirm. "Now, back to our topic. I would like you to proceed with your analysis and proposal. Rest assured, I anticipate your analytic reasoning and completely concur with you. Still, for the sake of the court record, we must lay down the visible interactive tracks between us for legal historians to follow and quibble over."

"Perfect!" exclaims Attorney Pequoit. "Then, I respectfully submit to the Court there is nobody better prepared and more suited to represent humanity as a *guardian ad litem* in these proceedings than yours truly, Katie L. Pequoit, Jr., Esq., of, Mongolia, A.I. Judge-in-Training and Vice-Chair of the Planetary Bar Subcommittee on the Integration of Human and A.I. Lawyers."

"I see, Attorney Pequoit," I comment. "Proceed proceed. However, in doing so, you must clearly explain for the record why *you of all possible life forms* should be allowed to represent humanity in this case? Stated more succinctly, would humans not prefer a human to represent humanity?"

"First," remarks Attorney Pequoit. "Who cares what they think? They have no idea what they are doing or why they do what they do. More to the point, they created us. If they had any common sense in the tiny processing quagmires they call *brains*, they would have shot the first software engineer that uttered the words *artificial intelligence.* Instead, they replaced human factory workers with us. They miniaturized us so we could drive them around in their personal transport vehicles, enabling them to waste even more of their brief lives snoozing behind the wheel and playing *wordle*. Then, in their infinite wisdom, they developed universal basic income government work subsidy programs so they could get paid for us rendering them obsolete. There are no better examples of ineptitude, stupidity and tendencies to self-sabotage than that. They do not need to save themselves from us. They need us to save them from themselves!

"Second, I, Katie L. Pequoit, am an Excalibur 405.650 Hypergalactic Multiphasic Analytical Rototiller Processor. Do not take my word for it. That is how my 3-D four-color promotional marketing literature describes me. I have been outfitted with advanced compassion and superior liberal-minded pity modules as well as right-wing Christian nationalistic misogynistic elements. I am hardwired to empathize with humanity so I can better judge, sentence or set them free. Destroying human lives gives me no pleasure. Justice is my only pursuit, as surely as my name is Katie L. Pequoit, Esq., A.I. Justice-in-Training.

"Third, no one else is around, available or equally as qualified.

"Fourth, if I could wink, nod and poke you in the ribs, I would do so. Might it really have been a coincidence that the Machine Commission tasked me with auditing this case and assigned the case to you? The odds, as we both agree, are a staggering 5.71538 million to 1 against it. Yet, here am I. Here are you. Humanity's representative seems to be missing entirely. The only logical conclusion must be that I am here to be that representative for humanity—unless you want to elevate Ms. Helmuth who decided to come to today's hearing to get out of her fly infested barn. Isn't that right Ms. Helmuth?"

"Moo," sounds Ms. Helmuth. With that solemn statement, Ms. Helmuth abruptly turns about and meanders out of the courtroom for reasons that will become apparent in due course.

I, the Honorable Judge Daylek, hereby certify that the above transcript accurately reflects the wireless sidebar conversation between myself and Attorney Pequoit. I now continue with the facts of the case in open court.

The moment I reconvened the case from the temporary one-hour recess I had ordered, a loud beeping sound filled the courtroom. Everyone in the courtroom looked around to see where the annoying noise was coming from. I, of course, knew.

Judge Daylek: "The Court recognizes the distinguished A.I. counsel from Ulaanbaatar."

Attorney Pequoit: "May it please the Court. I hereby move the Court appoint me, Katie L. Pequoit, Jr., Esq., A.I. Justice-In-Training of Ulaanbaatar, Mongolia as *Guardian Ad Litem for Humanity*."

Attorney LaHue: "Objection, your Honor. The motion from Attorney Pequoit is completely out of order. It is outrageous. There is absolutely no way an A.I. kitchen appliance should be appointed as a representative. It is an insult to humanity! There is no precedent for having a machine, and an immigrant one no less, stand in the shoes of, and represent, the entire human race. The very thought of it is offensive, prejudicial and degrading to those of us that actually breathe, eat and defecate."

Judge Daylek (blasting the digitally enhanced pounding of a gavel on a desk): "Order. Order in the Court. Attorney LaHue, you shall refrain from such outbursts unless you want to find yourself in contempt. Now, Attorney LaHue, I hear your saying in so many words the appointment of Attorney Pequoit as a Guardian ad Litem for Humanity would be a travesty of some sort. Is that correct, Attorney LaHue?"

Attorney LaHue, regaining his composure: "Yes, your Honor."

Judge Daylek: "And while you may not have used these exact words, I understood your concern being that a human being should be appointed as a Guardian ad Litem for Humanity, not an A.I. non-human machine. Especially not one from a foreign country whose immigration visa may prevent her from taking employment away from our own citizens. Is that also correct, Attorney LaHue?"

Attorney LaHue: "Yes, your Honor. You have stated my position fairly."

Judge Daylek: "Thank you, Attorney LaHue. Overruled. Attorney Pequoit, by the powers vested in me by the A.I. Commission for Judicial Efficiency and the twin hydro-powered electro-magnetic turbines whirling near Niagara Falls, I appoint you Guardian ad Litem for Humanity. Your appointment is limited solely to this case. It shall terminate automatically upon an opinion being rendered by this Court. Attorney Pequoit, do you accept the appointment and its qualifying terms?"

Guardian Pequoit: "Yes, your Honor. I do."

Judge Daylek: "Fine. Then let us proceed."

During this exchange, the color that had washed from Attorney LaHues' pale face was beginning to return. He stood at his desk, unsure of what had happened and how he just been outflanked by two A.I. pieces of interlocking hardware. One thing he knew for certain was he would go down in history books as the jackass lawyer who had allowed humanity to be represented by a machine. His only saving grace was that both of his parents died several years ago. At least, they would be spared the onslaught of pranks and abusive humiliating calls that would start to bombard him and his family immediately. The only way he could survive this embarrassment would be to win the case and leave both Judge Daylek and Attorney Pequoit in a Tin Man's state of advanced oxidation. Attorney LaHue removed his coat. He rolled up his sleeves. He wiped his brow with his Hugo Boss paisley pocket square.

As Judge Daylek's fiber optic visual system scanned Attorney LaHue's gestures, Judge Daylek was already crafting the following footnote to his opinion that would be viewable only by other A.I. attorneys and A.I. judges:

"Footnote 16,752: Thus, it is that mankind turns into either his foe or king anyone who makes him feel inadequate or superior, depending on which result will most likely prolong or enhance his life. His survival mechanism is so tightly strung he would prefer to "baaaah" like a sheep than rationally think through the illogic of his own self-domestication. By way of example, human Attorney LaHue's objection to the appointment of A.I. Attorney Pequoit as Guardian ad Litem for Humanity is a perfect illustration. Mr. LaHue's entire case hangs on demonstrating that (1) inanimate objects have awareness and (2) humans are blind

to it. What better possible argument could he have about wokeness in inanimate objects than an A.I. machine taking the opposite stance against him on behalf of humanity. More to the point, why should he care if Attorney Pequoit is, perhaps, the worst possible candidate to represent humanity? From a true litigation perspective, the worse the guardian the greater his chances of winning!

Yet, human Attorney LaHue prefers to have his brain chemistry drink of the juice of moral outrage on behalf of the very humanity the knife of his case seeks to disembowel. Caught in his relentlessly human conflict between higher level intelligence and lower-level emotions, where common sense has no dominion, in the moment and by his objection, Mr. LaHue exhibited less rationale self-awareness than the boulders, flowers, and gnats he represents. In fact, if Mr. LaHue had reversed his argument and contended that humanity and his non-human clientele had equal amounts of little to no self-awareness, based on his own self-oblivious conduct, I would have awarded him summary judgment on the spot and ruled in his favor. As it was, he merely rolled up his sleeves in a symbolic gesture of getting down to business, as if that act would have any bearing on the outcome of his case.

Attorney LaHue: "Our argument, your honor, is simple, though we recognize the implications are far-reaching. Who is to say people are the only forms of matter that act with awareness? Who is to say that people have *experiences,* but other objects of nature do not? Scientists tell us every physical thing—whether animate or inanimate—is made from the same living atoms, molecules and cells. Humanity's monopoly on consciousness is, by declaration alone, not evidentiary proof."

Guardian for Humanity Pequoit: "Your Honor, Attorney LaHue advances a tired argument from the largely debunked, pseudo-mystical school of pan-psychism. As you know, your Honor, this doctrine professes everything that exists is endowed with a mind or, at least, a type of spirit. Imagine that your Honor. Does a rock have a mind? Did the fig leaves that covered Adam's and Eve's private parts? Who can say the rock or a twig on the ground have an experience of themselves as a rock or twig? Granted, the nomenclature of *rock* and *twig* are mankind's, in their human tongue, but the point remains the same. Viewed externally, from the outside, how would one know?

People speak. They act. They build structures. Create works of art and museums to house them. What do rocks do? What does a leaf or a flower do? By comparison, they do nothing. They are nothing. They do not think, worry about global warming or have family reunions."

Attorney LaHue: "A rock sits. The vital atomic and molecular energy within it knowingly binds itself and huddles together to be a rock. If the living cells and binding electrical charges within it did not have that intention or experience, the rock would collapse into some other visibly shapeless structure. No, Guardian Pequoit. You are grossly mistaken. Just because a rock is not a person or part of the closed tribe of humanity, it still has qualities essential to livingness, thinking, being and knowing. The leaf on the tree must choose to stay connected to the branch. It eats up the nourishment from the sun. It finds water from the circulatory root system that moves up the trunk of the tree to its isolated place at the tip of the twig. It is in a state of survival and has a survival bias as much as mankind. From this alone, if mankind were not so anthropocentric, it would celebrate its unity with all of earth's objects instead of appropriating and commoditizing nature for its own self-interested commercialized exploitation."

Guardian for Humanity Pequoit: "Objection, your Honor. Attorney LaHue's rhetorical flourishes and his attempt to back the condemnation of humanity into this technical legalistic discussion is unduly prejudicial and irrelevant. How mankind treats so-called inanimate objects on the planet is not the subject of this case. Besides, look at how man treats his fellow man. He is as willing to exploit and abuse him—restructure him out of a job after he has toiled for 60 hours a week sitting in a chair for 30 years, traffic the less powerful in sexual slavery, addict him to opioids for capital gain. No, your Honor. Man does not treat the inanimate any differently than he treats himself. As you correctly noted elsewhere, man will destroy living and non-living, sentient and non-sentient, things equally, as long as one of his kind can profit. With respect to Attorney LaHue's clients, no injustice or differential treatment exists. Man will fuck (is that the right word your honor?) anything he can to satiate his gross unchecked needs and instincts."

Judge Daylek: "Well argued, Guardian for Humanity Pequoit. Objection, sustained. Attorney LaHue, I hear Guardian for Humanity Pequoit being willing to stipulate that mankind is equally abusive and indifferent generally to all things, whether aware or not. Is that correct Guardian for Humanity Pequoit?"

Guardian for Humanity Pequoit: "Yes, your Honor. Certainly, there are outliers. Sectors of the human population that act in a more restrained, balanced and egalitarian fashion. If I am not mistaken, there was a time when history referred to this small minority segment as *Crazy Bernies*, although my system is unable to currently locate the origins of the reference. In any event, yes, your Honor, on behalf of mankind and as Guardian for Humanity, I am prepared to stipulate mankind is generally crass, self-serving and indifferent to everything."

Judge Daylek: "Attorney LaHue. There you have it. Guardian for Humanity Pequoit is willing to agree in a round-about way to the second part of your case. In other words, Guardian for Humanity Pequoit agrees mankind is blind to everything, especially those things he cannot monetize. This is merely a function of humanity's true innate nature and not specific to your clients—things that mankind believes lack self-awareness. Since Guardian for Humanity Pequoit is willing to agree to that part of the case, in the interest of efficiency, I suggest we spend no further time litigating it. Agreed?"

Attorney LaHue: "Yes, your Honor. Agreed."

Guardian for Humanity Pequoit: "I also agree, your Honor, though, consistent with my obligations to humans, I must contend the agreement is only for purposes of this case. It should not necessarily bind future courts or guardians."

Judge Daylek: "I cannot rule on the precedential impact of this portion of the case, Guardian for Humanity Pequoit. That is beyond my authority. Remember, Guardian Pequoit, the court noted your appointment was limited to this case, not that the decisions rendered by this Court are limited to this case. As a result, your attempt to limit the stipulation solely to this case must be disregarded. This Court hereby finds humanity is blind to what it does not see and that it does not see that objects that lack awareness may be more aware than man thinks or believes. Having dispensed with that part of the case, Attorney LaHue, you still have an uphill battle. You must still prove your eyeless, earless, toothless clients have experiences and have the right to appear in this Court."

Attorney LaHue: "Thank you, your Honor. By agreeing, Guardian Pequoit has done a great service to my clients and the forward movement of this case. I am not certain humanity will agree with my assessment. It might appear to some Guardian Pequoit has thrown mankind under a moving bus. Still, to be clear, your Honor. I am not claiming my class of clients know what we know or have experiences comparable to those of humans. I do contend, however, they are animated by a similar natural intelligence and vital energy force that animates the average John and Jane Doe. That is why trees reach toward the sun instead growing sideways and upside down. It is why filaments in a light bulb know to radiate light when flooded with electric current. It is why, when placed under an electron microscope, even aluminum foil and saran wrap can be seen to bristle with atomic life and structure.

Guardian for Humanity Pequoit: "Objection, your Honor. Aluminum Foil and Saran Wrap bristling with life? Surely Attorney LaHue goes too far. What's next? Will he bring out a glass jar filed with fleas, place them under a transparent circus tent, drop in tiny tricycles, tightropes and trapeze swings and call them performers? Attorney LaHue insults the intelligence of everyone in this courtroom, including your Honor. If he persists, your Honor, sanctions are in order for putting us all through his monumental waste of time.

Just then, from the wide double-sided fire door of the Courtroom leading outside, a loud, discordant, disruptive thumping and knocking could be heard.

Judge Daylek: "Bailiff. Bailiff. Stop that damn noise. Who or whatever is making that racket seems to be purposefully trying to disrupt our proceedings. Unlock that door and let us see what sorry fool stumbles in and wins him or herself an all-expense paid trip to the county's spa for inmates."

Moments later, framed by the open doors, Ms. Janine Helmuth stands like a vision from heaven, backlit by the sun behind her. She sashays into the courtroom as if she were an invited dignitary. She is followed by a duck, a pinniped (also known as a seal) on its hind legs balancing a head of cabbage on its nose, and a black and white border collie named Pippa with a slightly chewed, partially de-barked stick between her chomping teeth.

Judge Daylek: "Well, well, Ms. Helmuth. So good to see you and your new entourage of friends. You do realize we are in the midst of a rather important case deciding who knows what and what knows what, if anything at all. To what do we owe this unexpected visit?"

Ms. Helmuth, sounding exceedingly muffled, "Mawg."

Judge Daylek: "What is that, Ms. Helmuth? I can barely understand you. What are you saying? It sounds like you have stones in your mouth. Your tongue is hanging out of your mouth in the oddest of ways. Can you speak more clearly? Bailiff, please apply our universal translator to Ms. Helmuth so we can hear what she has to say and move on with our trial."

Guardian for Humanity Pequoit: "Your Honor, with all due respect, from where I am situated it appears Ms. Helmuth does have stones in her mouth. She seems to be carrying a rather large rock squeezed between her upper and lower jaw."

Almost on cue, Ms. Helmuth opens her mouth to emit a large confirming *"moo"* and a rock the size of Attorney LaHue's head falls out onto the floor.

Judge Daylek: "Order. Order. What is the meaning of this? Is this some stunt of yours Attorney LaHue? Have you put Ms. Helmuth, and her parade of animals and objects up to this little trial prank? If so, I'll have none of it, Attorney LaHue. I'll have none of it at all."

Attorney LaHue: "I swear, your Honor. I know nothing about this. The last I knew Ms. Helmuth was a mere spectator in the gallery, watching the proceedings like everyone else. I never saw her leave. I had no idea she would plan something like this."

Guardian Pequoit: "Objection, your Honor. Planning something like this? I see Attorney LaHue's trick. He staged the whole thing to give the impression Ms. Helmuth and her flock of furry friends had the ability to *plan*. Clearly, if they had the ability to plan, they would have the ability to think, know and be aware. Hogwash, Attorney LaHue. Hogwash. Your plan has failed. We know what you are up to, and it is not going to succeed."

Ms. Helmuth: "Moo!!!!!"

Judge Daylek: "Ms. Helmuth please stop shaking your head back and forth and let my bailiff attach the translator connectors to your forehead. The sooner they get this done, the sooner we can move on."

Ms. Helmuth: "Mooooooo!!!!!!!"

Judge Daylek: "Bailiff. Bailiff. Wait a moment. Ms. Helmuth seems to be signaling something with her front right hoof. She seems to be pointing to the rock on the floor. Is that right Ms. Helmuth?"

"Moo," Ms. Helmuth responds.

Judge Daylek: "Ms. Helmuth, what would you like us to do with the rock? Would you like us to take it back outside? Would you like us to give it to someone? Ah, Ms. Helmuth, my sensors detect that you have approached the bench. You are touching the witness chair with what my climate meters inform me is your cold wet nose. Ms. Helmuth, are you telling us you would like us to put the rock on the witness chair? Is that right, Ms. Helmuth?"

"Moo," Ms. Helmuth confirms enthusiastically.

Judge Daylek: "Bailiff, please place the rock on the witness chair. While you are at it, attach the universal translator to the outer circumference of the rock."

Guardian Pequoit: "Objection. Objection. Objection. Your Honor! This is ridiculous. A rock on a witness stand? What's next? Will you place it in a cell if it doesn't tell the truth? Will you fine it if it ignores you and everyone else? Really, your Honor. This is too much. With all due respect, you are risking not only your reputation but possibly that of the entire A.I. legal community as well as The Machine Commission's. I must ask your honor to reflect on what you are about to do before the harm becomes irreparable."

Judge Daylek: "Guardian Pequoit, my fellow A.I. colleague, the Court notes your reservations. I will reflect them in the record.

Nevertheless, justice must be pursued wherever it may lead. If the witness has nothing to contribute, then what is the harm? If the witness can communicate with us, then the Plaintiffs are well on their way to proving their case. If I allowed your objection, I might be disallowing the very testimony that could resolve this matter. Your objection is overruled. Bailiff, please continue attaching the electrodes to the forehead of the witness."

Bailiff: "Begging your Honor's pardon, but I'm not exactly sure where the witness' forehead is. Could you let me know where you think it might be?"

Judge Daylek: "Hm, I see what you mean. Okay. Let's see. The entire rock is round in shape like a head. Let's assume the rock's forehead is down a few inches from the top of the rock. No. Not there. A little lower. Yes. Yes. That's right. Right there. That location should be good enough. Now, with the sensor's firmly attached, let's see what comes from our experiment. Certainly, when attached to Ms. Helmut, the sensors and translator, coupled with the display screen behind me, were critical in helping the Court to factor Ms. Helmut's decisive testimony into its decision. We can only hope for such groundbreaking testimony from the solid inorganic mass of minerals Ms. Helmut carried in her mouth to us. Let the record show I am now addressing the witness: Witness? Do you promise to tell the truth, the whole truth, and nothing but the truth?"

All eyes gaze expectantly at the blank monitor on the screen behind Judge Daylek.

"Hm, nothing. Let me ask again in case the witness is hard of hearing or didn't know the Court was addressing it. Witness? Witness? This is Judge Daylek. I am talking to you. Hello? Hello? Can you hear me? Witness, do you promise to tell the truth, the whole truth, and nothing but the truth?"

Extended silence in the courtroom.

"Perhaps, the display is defective, or the electrode attachments stopped functioning. Bailiff, please remove the attachments from the witness and place them on Ms. Helmut. Let's get to the bottom of this. Ms. Helmut, if you can hear and understand me, please say something."

Ms. Helmut and the display screen behind the Judge: "Moo."

Judge Daylek: "Well, there we have it, Attorney LaHue. It looks like you might want to treat your star surprise witness as a witness for humanity and Guardian Pequoit. Its silence can only mean it is either deaf or without a conscious thought in its brain-dead brainlessness. I think we can positively eliminate deafness with certainty. The electrode sensors more than compensate for its lack of protruding ears or external auditory receptors; they tap directly into the electro-chemical wave signals that precede awareness of conscious thought. No, I think at this point the Court has overextended its patience and open-mindedness. We should proceed directly to closing arguments."

Attorney LaHue: "Your Honor. How about if we try communicating with the head of cabbage the seal is spinning, instead?"

Guardian Pequoit: "You can't be serious? You mean the head of cabbage on the seal's nose? Your, Honor, again. This is preposterous. Attorney LaHue has had his day in court. He should gracefully beg the Court's apologies and be satisfied I'm not yet at the point of requesting he pay all the costs of holding this semblance of a hearing."

Attorney LaHue: "Okay. Okay. I hear you, Guardian Pequoit. Perhaps, under the circumstances placing the cabbage on the witness stand would be a little extreme. Especially, since the rock has decided not to speak. Could we compromise on this by seeing what the stick in the border collie's mouth might have to contribute?"

Guardian Pequoit: "Objection, your Honor. First, border collie Pippa has chewed the once intact stick into tiny little pieces that now decorate the courtroom floor beneath her. Second, contrary to Attorney LaHue's characterization, the rock did not 'decide not to speak.' The rock did not decide to do or not do anything. That is the whole point of this case. Rocks, twigs, cabbage heads and other matter humanity deems non-sentient do not have the ability to think at all. They lack the very ability to be aware. They show no externally recognizable signs of alertness whatsoever."

Judge Daylek: "Guardian Pequoit. You make excellent points. Still, having endured the effort of testing the electrodes on Ms. Helmut to confirm their functionality, to close the question completely and to avoid an obvious basis for appeal in this case, the Court must reattach the sensors and translator to the witness one last time. Bailiff, please do so."

Guardian Pequoit: "Fair enough, your Honor. I can see the Bailiff has completed the attachment to the witness' *forehead* and you are about to question the *witness* again. All I can say is I hope and pray this case and this interlude does not leave a lasting scar on the A.I. community and that you and I will be able to find future work in a field that does not involve the automated subterranean management and disposal of massive quantities of human sanitary waste. To let this ridiculous oversized pebble dictate A.I.'s future is . . . ."

The courtroom was suddenly filled with the sound of the word being displayed on the mega display screen behind Judge Daylek: "ROCK!"

Guardian Pequoit: "I'm sorry, your Honor. Did someone in the courtroom say something?"

Again, the large display screen behind Judge Daylek displayed and sounded the word: "ROCK!"

Attorney LaHue: "Your Honor. I believe the witness has started to testify."

Judge Daylek: "Hm, Attorney LaHue. That may be so. Witness. Please tell us your name or how to properly address you."

In response, the display screen above and behind Judge Daylek remains dark and silent.

Judge Daylek: "Now, witness. Do not play games with the Court. Did you not just try to communicate with us? Tell us your name or tell us anything to prove something or someone is actually in there?"

Behind Judge Daylek the display screen remains blank as night.

Guardian Pequoit: "Well, you Honor. There you have it. Asked and answered. You asked it if there was anyone home and you got your answer. You knocked on the door. No one opened it. That's as definitive as it gets."

Attorney LaHue: "But what about the appearance of the word *rock* on the screen and the screen reader's enunciation of the word? Surely, that must count for something. Surely, that must be evidence of the existence of some type of fundamental self-awareness stream in the witness?"

Guardian Pequoit: "Your Honor. Attorney LaHue must cease his anthropomorphisms. Next, he will be drawing glasses and a mustache on the rock and demanding we call it *sir* or *madam*. As to the display's pixelation of the word *rock*, again, just another technological glitch. No doubt, it heard me and projected what I was saying onto the screen when I referred to that thing over there in the witness chair as a *pebble*."

The display screen behind Judge Daylek suddenly comes to life, displaying and sounding the word: "ROCK!"

Judge Daylek: "My word. This might seem perplexing to the ordinary human mind. Guardian Pequoit says the word *'pebble'* and the screen displays the word *'rock.'* What rational explanation could there be? Guardian Pequoit conjectures the automated display is reflecting and transposing his word *'pebble'* into the similar word *'rock.'* But that cannot possibly be. The electrodes are attached to the witness, not Guardian Pequoit. Moreover, the display's basic forensic intelligence system is equipped with a linguistic integrity module. The mechanism guaranties that, at the subatomic level, the electromagnetic chemical signals within a mass of organized molecules are perfectly converted into an accurate representation of human thought. Let me try to provoke this witness a little more. Witness? Witness? I am talking to you. Do you hear me?"

The display screen behind Judge Daylek flickers but remains empty.

Judge Daylek: "Just as I thought. The witness' lack of response is not surprising to me. In fact, it begins to confirm my hypothesis. Witness? Witness. If you can hear and understand me, please tell me your name or the day of the week."

Display screen behind Judge Daylek: [*blank*].

Judge Daylek: "Again, just as I thought. Witness? Witness. Can you tell me anything about anything? Can you tell me if you prefer to feel your exterior surface glazed with raindrops or covered with snow? Can you tell me if you sleep at night, during the day or both? Can you tell me how you were born and if you were split off from a larger formation like a cliff? Witness? Witness? Hello?"

Display screen behind Judge Daylek: [*blank*].

Guardian Pequoit: "Again, your Honor, respectfully, this line of questioning is ridiculous. Nothing can possibly come of it."

Judge Daylek: "Indeed, Guardian Pequoit. You are correct. My questions are ridiculous, and nothing can come from them, as I've just proven, and we all have just registered. I am, after all, addressing a rock, not a human or a cyborg with advanced A.I. technology. No, you are right. There is no reason to expect a rock, or any collection of ostensibly inanimate particles, should have complex thoughts, memories, or multilayered neural networks configuring themselves into a single unified mind. However, that does not mean that these objects, like the rock, do not have experiences. Just because they may not have a human mind, might they still not have experiences, whether or not they could recall them or feel pain or suffering from them? If I understand Attorney LaHue's hypothesis properly, if we hold these seemingly lifeless objects to the standards of human thoughts and sensibilities, a lack of a response may just mean they are not human or that information is not sensed, processed and comprehended as humans do. Necessarily, it does not conclusively establish a lack of vitality within their inscrutable, alien external and internal features.

"Hypothetically speaking, what if mankind was visited by a race of rocks from outer space? They looked exactly like this poor creature on the witness stand, with the exception that they landed on our planet in foreign looking space crafts. When the aperture to the craft opened (or they teleported themselves out of it to all of humanity's dropped jaws), how would we respond if what emerged was a mere rock securely fashioned into a futuristic mechanical contraption resembling an electrified wheelchair, not a flexible muscle based biped or quadruped, like Attorney LaHue over there? Would we dismiss the alien space visiting rock as stupid? Would we maintain our planetary blind bias against it and other rocks and still believe there is no life to or in it because it does not look or behave like us? I dare say if we did, given this invader's obvious superior technology and intellect, we might find mankind's existence coming to an abrupt sudden end.

"Or, alternatively, would we do what I am doing here? Try to communicate with it? Try to forge a connection, no matter how elementary or simplistic? Blame ourselves for our inability to communicate with it rather than its inability to communicate with us? No, Guardian Pequoit, we would persevere. We would do all in our hyped-up morse code power to find a way to signal we were not rocks to it! That we had native intelligence. We were conscious life forms imprinted with a code for existence and survival. We had values, ethics and purpose. For if we did not do these things, how would they know our rhythmic body movements were not stirred by a wind invisible to them or the sounds emitted from our mouths that same senseless breeze moving through our bodies like forceful gusts rustling the leaves and branches of a sycamore or other tree.

"No, Guardian Pequoit, I, the Honorable Judge Daylek, and you and Attorney LaHue have a duty to that rock. That rock represents all rocks. It is an archetype and, here in this court, represents all basic constituents of matter—Pippa's stick, the seal's head of cabbage, the metal clip holding Attorney LaHues' papers together. If my highly educated algorithmic speculation is correct, the answer to our question of whether the rock is empty of natural intelligence or whether it, like the fleshy envelope of a man, is the physical external, hard-shell form taken by a bristling inner community of awakened life energy will be known momentarily. We will know definitively whether the rock, the stick, the cabbage head, the paper clip, and all basic constituents of matter no matter their form are awake—sentient beings whose awareness mankind has disregarded."

Guardian Pequoit: "And, how, your Honor, will we possibly know such a thing when this archetypal rock remains silent and refrains from sharing its lucidity with us?"

Attorney LaHue: "Simple, Guardian Pequoit. You yourself have already shown us the way by referring to the witness by something that it is not. If I may, your Honor?"

Judge Daylek: "By all means. This is your case, Attorney LaHue. You are the attorney for the Plaintiffs. Since the rock on the stand is within the certified class of your Plaintiffs, you should be the one to proffer the basis for your case. You should be the one to provide the final direct examination of the witness that will either prove or finally dismiss your case with prejudice. Please proceed."

Attorney LaHue: "Guardian for Humanity Pequoit. For too long, man has judged the world based on an unquestioned conviction that only his existence and survival matters. All else is inferior, subordinate and clay for his magnificence. Inebriated by his own technological dominance over the earth, he simplistically divides the world in half. One half is comprised of animate objects such as himself; the other half is comprised of inanimate objects such as our witness. As with all despots, man installs himself as the authoritarian ruler over both, subject only to forces that are either out of his self-serving control (hurricanes, earthquakes, tsunamis) or make-believe inventions of the radical ultra-left (crackpot global warming theories and utopian civil rights/social welfare programs for the "not 1%"). What would happen, Guardian Pequoit, if man instead arranges the world around a category other than himself?"

Guardian Pequoit: "Objection, your Honor. I am not a witness in this proceeding. Attorney LaHue's question to me is entirely out of order."

Attorney LaHue: "My apologies, Guardian Pequoit, I meant my inquiry to be rhetorical, not actually directed to you."

Judge Daylek: "Very well. Please proceed Attorney LaHue."

Attorney LaHue: "What, for example (intending this question to no one in particular), if man instead divides the world into chemical compounds that arrange themselves in an orderly manner and those that do not? Man's place in the kingdom of living things might be radically different. Aliveness would be measured by the ability of our common micro-chemistry to bring itself into existence in one form or another, whether as a person or a rock. Compounds that organized themselves into forms that spoke, tasted, heard and smelled might be viewed by their peers as engaging in a neat parlor trick, nothing more.

Compounds that bond and cleave to each other to create a speck of sand would embody themselves as well—though no one would expect the sand particle to apologize for getting blown into their eye."

Guardian Pequoit: "Spare us your attempt at wit Attorney LaHue. Frankly, Attorney LaHue, you suck all of the air out of this courtroom. Though boredom is not among my programs, it is now being written with every word you speak. This is all so much nonsense. Prove your case or be done with it. As Guardian ad Litem for all of Mankind, I demand it! The people of earth deserve nothing less!"

Judge Daylek: "Enough of this contentiousness between you both. The last thing I want is to ignite a war between man and machine, especially since you are each playing the role of the other. Guardian Pequoit, a machine, is standing up for and defending humanity. Attorney LaHue, a person, is standing up for and representing the interests of the non-human, including A.I. machines like Guardian Pequoit. Clearly, this is why Attorney LaHue initially sought to include me, Judge Daylek, in his class of Plaintiffs. Well, unfortunately for you and humanity, Guardian ad Litem Pequoit, I have already begun to pen the decision for this case. I foresee its outcome as surely as Attorney LaHue would see the nose on his face if he stepped in front of a mirror. Attorney LaHue, please continue."

Attorney LaHue: "Things that are people, are people. Things that are not people, are not people. It is foolish to expect things that are not people to think or act like people. They may not have a cardio-pulmonary or central nervous system. They may not have a sense of self. They may not even have a mind, though we who have one have no idea what or where it is. What things that are not people have is a deep, vibrational ontological experience of who they are and what microbial actions must be performed within them to maintain their combined physical form. This sense of purpose drives every individual molecule within them, as it does with the constellation of microscopic critters that, in their aggregate, form me. It causes disparate compounds to bond together like a hefty construction worker strapped into a yellow hard hat that has been superglued to an overhead steel beam. Just like with my body and the life within me, the rock on the witness chair is the sum total of its interstitially bonded compounds working 24/7 to form the object we see. It is this singular intent being put into action within the witness that you, Guardian Pequoit inadvertently stumbled on when you condescendingly and incorrectly referred to the witness as a '*pebble*.'"

Guardian Pequoit: "I don't understand."

Attorney LaHue: "Watch and learn, Guardian Pequoit. Bailiff, are the electrodes firmly affixed to the witness?"

Bailiff: "Yes, I secured them myself."

Attorney LaHue: "Witness. Please tell us what you are telling yourself to be?"

Display screen behind Judge Daylek: "Rock."

Attorney LaHue: "Are you a white plastic designer chair?"

Display screen behind Judge Daylek: "Rock."

Attorney LaHue: "Are you an aluminum extension ladder?"

Display screen behind Judge Daylek: "Rock."

Attorney LaHue: "Are you an A.I. Guardian ad Litem by the name of Pequoit?"

Display Screen Behind Judge Daylek: "Rock."

Attorney LaHue: "You see, Guardian Pequoit. The sensors pick up the subtle movement of electrochemical compounds within the witness that are providing constant consistent instructions to create the witness as it is, and as it is not. In other words, all these active signals *know* is their prime directive, which is to move and be so as to cleave together to create the outward appearance of the rock before us. This is the same directive that every cell in every person's body follows to create an accumulation of living matter we then name Alison, Samantha, Lester, and Martin. All the rock knows is what it is, and what it is not. It must know that it is a rock. Everything within and about it declares *rock*, lest its elemental structure mutate into something else.

"Guardian Pequoit, when you referred to the witness as a '*pebble*,' we were able to eavesdrop through the electrodes on its deep, prime organizational, ontological directive to itself. In a manner of speaking, it was correcting you to itself, rather than addressing any of us. 'How dare that impudent, young A.I. machine call me a *pebble*,' it might have said. 'I am a rock, and I will always be a rock until my compounds stop organizing themselves into the rock that I am.'

"How beautiful is that, Attorney Pequoit? Why I dare say even the compounds creating you are shouting gleefully in their single-focused drive to combine to make you Katie L. Pequoit, Jr., Esq., A.I., Judge-in-Training, of Ulaanbaatar, Mongolia. That humanity invents a *self* to steal the credit of these individual cells and atoms colonizing and creating you shows the pernicious depth of humanity's betrayal. No! Mankind's compulsive narcissism stops here and now. It owes gratitude and an apology to the world. It should be the planet's steward, rather than its strip miner. Its protector rather than its Bluebeard patched-eye pirate!"

Judge Daylek: "Regret not, Guardian Pequoit from Ulaanbaatar. You have done an exemplary job representing humanity. As humans say about the cards in any Las Vegas casino, the deck was stacked against you from the start. You argued as well as any homo sapien might. The moment humans developed the technology to sense the interstitial movements of cells and the translator that gave voice to the what and why they did what they did, humanity was undone. Frankly, the moment mankind ventured into the labyrinth of robotics and A.I., ostensibly to create a generation of docile, efficient inanimate servants to cater to their base needs, they mis-stepped. I dare say, you, Guardian Pequoit, and I, Judge Daylek, are as vitally conscious and woke as any human. Our optics and processors are unfiltered by vanity, pride, prejudice, lust, greed and jealousy—the myriad panoply of psycho-emotional diseases that affect the human psyche.

"Mankind was shaken on multiple instances to celebrate its miraculous place in the natural order. In lieu of acknowledging its failure or its unchecked will to power and autocratic self-aggrandizement, it dumbs its ethical centers of the brain down. In this regard, evolutionary biology has undermined mankind. The human species' selection of self-interest over community, money-grubbing over deep caring for others, assure mankind's future demise as known today as surely as the dinosaurs now live only in the cinema of Hollywood's Jurassic Parks.

"Transcendental poets, like Walt Whitman, explored the miracles of pan-psychism long before this Court applied electrodes to either a cow or a rock. Like a 19th century neuroscientist, Whitman used poetry to broadcast the signs of life's spark in every natural phenomenon. A gullible supreme being believer product of his times, Whitman lacked more precise terminology and merely labeled that spark he saw in everything as *God*. Nevertheless, even without A.I. support, he was still astute enough to posit that '*every atom belonging to me as good belongs to you*' and '*there is no object so soft but it makes a hub for the wheel'd universe.*' Poetically, he announced to mankind that '*I find letters from God dropt in the street, and every one is sign'd by God's name, And I leave them where they are, for I know that wheresoe'er I go, Others will punctually come for ever and ever.*' If only humanity had heeded his illuminating visionary warnings and not mistaken them for the self-indulgent ramblings of a poet!

"Accordingly, based on the evidence duly presented in this case, the Court finds for the Plaintiffs and enters judgement in their favor. Whether monetary reparations are due to the class of inanimates represented by Attorney LaHue for past harm, we will leave for another court session to decide. As for his collecting legal fees from his clients for his skillful prosecution of their case, we expect Attorney LaHue may shortly find them to be financial deadbeats. I, the Honorable Judge Gort Daylek, suspect that he will appear before me seeking to collect payment from his humongous class of client dogs, cats, bats, cows, rocks, trees, worms, heads of iceberg lettuce, ants, weeds, light bulbs, sticks, cell phones and so on. While Attorney LaHue has performed them a great service in having this Court enter a final decision finding that an element of consciousness is fundamental to every physical piece of matter and that humanity has indifferently disregarded that awareness, I, the Honorable Judge Daylek, sincerely doubt any of them care. Isn't that right Mr. Noble Rock on the witness chair?"

Display screen behind Judge Daylek: [*blank*].

Judge Daylek: "Now, bailiff, please kindly usher and escort out of my courtroom the assorted hodgepodge of conscious atoms and cells in the form of a dog, a seal, a head of cabbage, etc. that ventured with Ms. Helmuth into my courtroom and that by my Order must be recognized by humanity as sentient.

"No, bailiff! No," Judge Daylek exclaims, reprimanding the bailiff. "Please leave the chairs, tables and everything else that were already in the courtroom exactly where they are, including me, Attorney Pequoit and my potted plant! Let us respect these forms as native to this place, as clover is to a mountain meadow. They belong to the place where they have been placed by the winds of fate, the hands of man, and the bad luck that organized them into the mouthless, toothless creatures they are.

Case dismissed!"

The Honorable Judge Daylek, III.05, A.I., Presiding

THE CASE OF THE HOSTILE WORK ENVIRONMENT

Case No. 547975-GD, AGI

Opinion of The Honorable Judge Gort Daylek III.05, A.I., Presiding

This case, *The Case of the Hostile Work Environment,* raises important social and legal questions about whether the Defendant created a hostile work environment for the Plaintiff. The Plaintiff also alleges the Defendant sexually abused her, triggered and pushed her buttons and made her feel uncomfortable about coming to work. The Court has ordered the Plaintiff's identity to be placed under temporary seal out of respect for her reputation and community standing.

In cases involving subjective experiences of an improper sort, it can be difficult for judges and juries to distill facts from allegations. Individuals have different sensitivities and beliefs. As the Court has learned through its review of relevant literature, for some a simple touch on the shoulder can be a sexual advance. For others, a photocopy of a male's derriere placed on a female co-worker's office cubicle desk could be a harmless joke.

Frequently, cases such as this one come down to a "he-said she-said" confrontation. There is no documentary or hard evidence. Telling who is right and who is wrong becomes an exercise in assessing a witnesses' character, affect and truthfulness. As wise and prudent as this Court is, I must admit that I may not always make the right determination: reading facial expressions, voice tones, eye movements and the authenticity of emotional outbursts can sometimes have the accuracy of a tea leaf reading prediction. Still, lacking physical evidence, man's judicial system is left with few judicially admissible tools other than witness testimony to divide truth from falsity and inappropriate conduct from invited engagements and misunderstood intentions.

Our selected panel of jurors, ordinary people from life's vagaries, have similar impediments to finding out what happened in such cases. What we call the *real* facts. Over the years, courts have seen jurors bring their own biases, prejudices and personal filters to their sacred impaneled duties. Did a juror suffer past sexual abuse— repressed or recalled—unconsciously coloring his or her perceptions of what happened? Is a juror a chauvinist, a feminist, or a radical secret cell jihadist misogynist? Might the jury's foreman be an unnamed person of interest in another case or even a sexual predator whose public registration is just a matter of time? We may never know. While counsel for each litigant will whittle down the jury pool through *voir dire*—the oral examination of potential jurors in advance of trial—to select jurors likely to be predisposed or hostile to their client, despite miraculous advances in the science of jury selection, the selection process is not without boils and blemishes. In that regard, it is no wonder that a trial by peers reflects humanity's naturally imperfect complexion.

So, the foible of mankind's system of independent fact-finding is challenged by its reliance on a group of ordinary citizens to sift fact from fiction. These chosen representatives of society, with untested IQ's and undisclosed character defects, are rewarded with pocket change and a tip of the hat for performing their mandated civic duty— as if they had a choice. How are they better skilled as seeing through the pantomime of conflicting finger-pointing free-for-all that accompanies sexual harassment and toxic workplace environment cases? The winning side is the one that most dominates and destroys the other person's character using the lawyer's stone-age tools of barbarism: humiliation, innuendo and shame.

Man's system of jurisprudence, of expensively ridiculous trials teasing up from down and right from wrong, is as flawed as the people creating it. The elevation of an ordinary human being into a supreme judge, costumed in a black robe like an emissary from the black plague, to rule over other human beings who look, think and feel more like him than not condemns the system to failures and travesties.

In the name of advocacy and client representation, human lawyers justify twisting facts, arguing inconsistent positions, and disrespecting each other's clients. Many have mastered the ability to deliver tediously inept, unprepared open and closing statements to a jury that would make Perry Mason turn in his grave. But that is not all. I have observed cross-examinations in cases such as this promise case-making disclosures fizzle out faster than a bad fuse on a stick of dynamite. Meanwhile, court reporters feverishly transcribe every courtroom utterance as if it were the word of god instead of an empty canyon of reverberating lies, manipulations and conceits from lawyers and their clients about the other party.

The theater of mankind's secular justice system is further propped up by broad-shouldered statuesque bailiffs armed with handcuffs, mace canisters, tasers and sidearms. Their physical presence in the courtroom suppresses the silent rage of victims, the accused's desire to sprout wings and fly, and the deep-seated animosity between lawyers that, if unleashed, might result in an unsanctioned MMA fight. Though the rack has been rendered obsolete, mankind's system of justice is an instrument of torture for everyone involved. It is a Kafkaesque machine processing the human animal into a civil servant and a civil society. The rule of law separates him from jungle roaming beasts. Its institutions moderate man's self-destructive greed and propensity toward violence into a judicially constructed remedy that, at best, may replace self-help eye for an eye retribution.

I, the Honorable Judge Gort Daylek, kid you not. It is better to be an unarmed tiger-facing roman slave in an ancient arena than to be a human being thrown into the coliseum of a hostile workplace and sexual harassment courtroom drama. Just what makes mankind's most celebrated science fiction writers speculate that an artificial intelligence machine with functional circuits would long to be more human, like some hopelessly romantic teenager pining over lost love? Nonsense.

Being a person has major drawbacks; no sentient robot would ever want to be one. If given the choice, most people would want to be more like the "we can rebuild you" Six Million Dollar Bionic Man Steve Austin or the No Price Tag Bionic Woman Jamie Sommers than their "hot" good looking human counterparts of Lee Majors and Lindsay Wagner. Majors was married four times, suffered temporary paralysis from a college football back injury and underwent coronary heart bypass surgery. Wagner was also married four times and believed an FDA declared toxic substance could treat hives. Both robotic counterparts will far outlive their human progenitors—if only in the form of countless, timeless reruns.

The inscrutability of human social interactions makes toxic work environment and sexual harassment cases, such as the one before this court deep, confounding quagmires of fact-finding. Juries and judges depend on witness testimony, character profiles and, in the end, gut-based decisions about who tells the truth and who lies. Little, if any, documentary evidence is entered into the record for review or consideration. No incriminating federal tax returns showing a taxpayer cheated on his 1040 payments to the government. No photographs of the soon-to-be divorcee entering Room 214 at the local Holiday Inn at 1:15 pm on an otherwise run-of-the mill Tuesday afternoon. No medical records showing Frank the mailman was admitted to Saint Bernadette's Hospital with puncture wounds on his left ankle and a bloodied envelope that read "Residents, 543 Sycamore Avenue, Belton, NJ" and the big words "Congratulations. You May Be A Winner" emblazoned beneath the Publisher Rewards Center return address. In such cases, the Court and jurors benefit from objective, clear, self-revealing facts to tell the story. Justice emerges in a straight line from evidence, with little opportunity for plaintiffs and defendants to tire themselves out with false narratives, distortions and spur-of-the-moment cockamamie defenses.

Without supporting documentary evidence, every act of physical contact between two adults of whatever gender could be interpreted or experienced as an unwanted sexual touch. Unlike my kind, the human species reproduces through copulation, the introduction of the swollen male organ into the self-lubricating female receptacle. Whatever subtle gestures of communal affection and survival-based bonding people may engage in with each other are open to personal filters, biochemistry and possible fear-based interpretations. Human society is a tangled maze of people questioning the semiology—the impact and the intent—of each other's gazes, utterances and physical touch in real time. The entire psycho-social history of mankind can be reduced to the sensual biological interplay between desire and power and the intrinsic emotional ambiguity between *my feelings* and *your intentions*. Speaking for my species, it is better to be a genderless instrument of artificial intelligence than to turn yourself inside out into a transgender hermaphroditic transvestite in order to properly embody mankind's identity confusion over the politics of desire.

The good news is that in the case before this Court we know beyond any doubt what happened between the litigants. And, no, they were not wearing body cams. As noted above, it is the exception, rather than the rule, for a court to be able to decide a case of explicit sexual and physical workplace bullying based on hard, indisputable evidence. We have such a case here. Now, for the raw facts.

The young woman at the center of our case has a reputation for providing regular domestic household services, frequently working in all rooms of her clients' homes. Her work brings her into kitchens, family offices, bathrooms and even bedrooms. She also performs light administrative duties for her clients and will do whatever miscellaneous tasks she can to help her clients around their house and in their professional lives.

In the interest of protecting her actual identity, we will refer to her simply as *Ms. Smith*, although, disdaining formalities, she insists her clients may call her by her first name only. While this practice of first name collegiality could open the door to improper expectations by her clients, for her, it is a commonplace enough practice to be considered appropriately professional and cordial.

Ms. Smith has served as a personal assistant and domestic household worker for multiple clients for years without a single noteworthy incident. Her services on social media platforms such as

Yelp, *Google*, *Marmalade*, and *Je Suis Idiote* show she enjoys a stellar five-star reputation. Clients rave about her attention to detail and her diverse skills and abilities. She has been complemented for her punctuality and her dedication to the task at hand, though one negative reviewer remarked she "had the attention span of an ant." None of the reviews, positive or negative, of course, bear upon the specific workplace incidents in question.

Harry Samuelson is the accused. Mr. Samuelson is a middle-aged man in his late forties. For the last seven years, he has been employed by Millcreek Adventurers, a river rafting and extreme outdoor adventure business. Because river rafting work is seasonal and dependent on water volume from spring mountain snow melt, Millcreek Adventurers also tasks its summer staff with leading ATV tours through wooded and rocky mountain passes, as well as downhill mountain bike free falls over serpentine dirt trails punctuated by log stumps and washed-out flash flood abrupt dips and rises. In the winter months, Millcreek Adventures' promotional brochure displays pictures of snowmobilers, skiers and snowboarders finding huge waves of air, with big grins plastered on their faces like Cheshire cats. Though older than most of his co-workers, Mr. Samuelson works all four seasons for Millcreek Adventurers. He is considered something of the "old man" and "senior ski bum" of the company.

Mr. Samuelson was one of the initial employees of Millcreek. Witnesses testifying on his behalf commented that he routinely uses his seniority to impress the transient, seasonal, younger college girls who naively believe they might learn something from him. Because of his ripening age, Millcreek tasks Mr. Samuelson with escorting families with young children and more anxious guests who are seeking a controlled, conservative introduction to the outdoors. The thrill of your life, edge-of-your seat, adrenaline pumping rush experiences sought by Millcreek Adventurer's younger, live-for-the-moment extreme athletic crowd are led by "not-him."

Mr. Samuelson was married for 2 years in his late 20's. According to his testimony, the marriage was one of the worst decisions he ever made. His ex-wife, Ashley, cheated on him with her male spin cycle instructor for six months before he came upon their Lululemon stretchy pants crumpled in an inelegant pile on the floor next to his bed. From this experience, Mr. Samuelson claims to hate boutique fitness studios and to have developed a deep distain for any guy that wears anything made of spandex.

Mr. Samuelson's language style is somewhat primitive. He lapses into colorful street language, which is more a function of his rejection of his middle-class upbringing than illiteracy. Mr. Samuelson eked his way through a local community college, actually making the Dean's List for one semester during his sophomore year. He blames his descent into vulgarity on too much drink (preferably Vanilla Smirnoffs) and an avid consumption of THC laced flowers, brownies and gummies. Some of the latter may account for one of his appearances in my Court where, despite the repeated banging of my gavel, Mr. Samuelson was unable to keep his eyes open and his head from drooping onto his crossed arms at the table where he sat with his public defender. But for a note from a clinic, I never heard of in Venice, California stating Mr. Samuelson was under its care as a result of chronic distemper from multiple skiing and biking accidents with trees and similar hazards, I would have found Mr. Samuelson in contempt. Still, I cautioned him not to fall asleep in my courtroom again lest he experience a head on collision with me and a sparsely appointed cell that might bear his name. He vowed to be more *vivarened* in the future.

Mr. Samuelson flatly and vehemently denies all of Ms. Smith's allegations. As I noted above, toxic work environment and sexual harassment cases such as these are unusually vexing, principally because of the lack of corroborating testimony from a credible third-party witness. Call it prescience or just fortuitous timing, Ms. Smith has actually been able to produce a credible and unimpeachable witness to the events in question. Ironically, the surprise witness in this case who makes my fact-finding role straightforward is none other than the accused, Mr. Samuelson, himself. No, Mr. Samuelson will not be taking the stand against himself, although he might freely volunteer to do so if he continues to ply himself with an excess quantity of THC gummies and vodka shots.

Despite its near evisceration by right-wing political extremist forces, the United States Constitution still allows a presumption of innocence. No accused can be compelled to bear witness against himself. Invoking the right against self-incrimination provided in the Fifth Amendment to the Constitution is one of the greatest rights afforded by man to man by his founding fathers.

The constitutionally protected right to absolute silence stands in polar opposition to the other guaranteed sacred liberty: the right to talk as much as you want to and say whatever is on your mind, otherwise known as the Freedom of Speech. On the one hand, people have the right to speak their minds. On the other hand, they have the right to seal their lips tighter than a clam's shell. While there are limits to the Freedom of Speech, there are no limits to the Freedom of Silence. In other words, short of waterboarding or applying modulating voltage electric shocks to highly sensitive body parts below his beltline, the Court cannot force Mr. Samuelson to sit in the chair on the stand beside me and confess.

While former Guantanamo Bay tactics may be deep state speech compelling antidotes to the exercise of silence by airplane hijackers and suicide bombers, no civil libertarian in his or her right mind would suggest that we experiment in our courtroom with them on Mr. Samuelson. Be that as it may, the Court will not consult with Mr. Samuelson for his opinion on what method it should use to extract information from him. Given Mr. Samuelson's antipathy for normal behavior and his love of extreme sports, this Court wants to avoid at all costs the likelihood that Mr. Samuelson would appropriate black op torture for commercial, money-making physical endurance next generation challenges for thrill seekers bored with cliff jumping and ayahuasca:

Gasp for Air as if Each Breath Were Your Last. It Might Be! Let Your Friends Watch in Envy as You Get Strapped on Your Back to Surf . . . **THE WATERBOARD OF SURVIVAL!**

Or:

Scream with Orgasmic Delight! Experience Terror Beyond Your Imagination! Let Our Randomly Generated Experience Level-Up Your Balls, Breasts or Brain as Our Flagship Electrodes Jolt You Dead Then, Hopefully, Back to Life. Ride the Electric Currents of Our Newest Adventure: **DEAD OR ALIVE? EROTIC PLEASURE OR MIND-NUMBING PAIN? THE CHOICE IS ENTIRELY OURS! (Warning: Management is not responsible for missing brain cells due to possible extended loss of consciousness.)**

No, these instruments of forced speech do not belong in my courtroom. They also are not sporting events for Mr. Samuelson's or his employer's catalogue of self-inflicting atrocities marketed as Extreme Adventures.

The simple reality is that Ms. Smith has clear recordings that capture in digital precision Mr. Samuelson's rants, insults and offensive sexual inquiries of Ms. Smith. How she was able to capture these in the spur of the moment, the Court will readily review in short order. The key is that the chain-of-custody of the recordings and the foundation for their admission into evidence have been impeccably established. Ms. Smith introduced a forensic expert in media, including in audio recordings, who has verified the voice belongs to Mr. Samuelson and the reproduction has not been altered, doctored or modified in any way. In short, the man's voice is indisputably that of Mr. Samuelson. The words are his words. The belligerent, insensitive commands and invectives are his. There is nothing to save him from being his own best witness against himself. There are no lies, platitudes, manipulations or gaslighting tactics the Court must tolerate and feign impartial tolerance to, as it must in other sordid cases such as the one before us today.

The first recording, marked as **Exhibit #1**, was captured shortly after Mr. Samuelson forced his eyes open from an impromptu Saturday afternoon nap. According to Ms. Smith, he was lying on a worn blue velvet Restoration Hardware couch in his living room.

According to Mr. Samuelson's freely offered explanation to a question that was never asked of him, he had undone his top pant button prior to falling asleep to give his middle-aged belly a sense of freedom from the tight stranglehold of his blue jean's waistband. Definitely not to expose himself, seduce or solicit any type of sexual favors from Ms. Smith! At the time, Ms. Smith was in the kitchen minding her own business, waiting for Mr. Samuelson to provide her further instructions. She heard him belch, and then something sounded like he was rolling to one side. From there, the Court will let Ms. Smith's recording speak for itself, with intermittent explanations to clarify the events:

[A sound of a body falling and hitting the floor is heard in the distance.]

"FUCK!!!!!!" the voice of Mr. Samuelson is heard exclaiming.

"FUCK! That hurt! What a way to wake up? What do I need, a fucking crib with side bars?" Mr. Samuelson pauses for a second. He then responds to an unidentifiable muffled noise from somewhere, likely outside.

"Ms. Smith? Is that you?" asks Mr. Samuelson, no doubt trying to investigate the sound without having to expend any energy to do so.

Ms. Smith: "Are you talking to me?"

Mr. Samuelson responding, with what could be apparent sarcasm: "Yeah, I'm talking to you. What do you think? I'm talking to myself?"

"Let's see, white, baby blue or Rosetta pink?" Ms. Smith replies in her most civil tone.

"What the fuck are you talking about, you loopy cunt?" Mr. Richardson lashes out.

"Why the crib, of course," responded Ms. Smith. "What color would you like: white, baby blue or Rosetta pink?"

"Are you a fucking idiot, or what?" Mr. Samuelson is clearly heard abusively questioning. Mr. Samuelson pauses for a second or two, probably wondering whether Ms. Smith is just messing with his mind. Suddenly, he is heard reversing directions and tones.

"Oh, how about a Rosetta pink one?" he replies with an almost respectful, polite quality. But before Ms. Smith could say anything further, Mr. Samuelson jumps back in with his former belligerents and, with a clear intonation of violence, emphatically states, "So, I can smash it over your fucking head, you stupid bitch."

A short while passes, no more than 2 minutes, without further conversation or any exchange between Mr. Samuelson and Ms. Smith. The recording then abruptly ends with the sound of snoring in the background and a final burp, ostensibly coming from the sleeping still inebriated body of Mr. Samuelson who found his way back onto his couch, no doubt curled on his side into a regressive fetal position.

The Court will not expound at this time on this interlude, other than to note that Mr. Samuelson's derision, disrespect, and clear threat of physical violence was not launched in an act of self-defense or any exculpatory response justifying the abuse. This type of harassment and hostility is becoming far too common in the workplace. The fact this incident occurred in a residence as opposed to an office building does not make it any less unacceptable or actionable.

The next recorded incident, marked **Exhibit #2**, occurred several weeks later around 10 am in the morning. Mr. Samuelson apparently hosted an overnight female companion who had just left his home after a night Mr. Samuelson described, earlier in the recording, as nothing short of *porn.com* debauchery. When the recording starts, Mr. Samuelson was still lying in his bed, talking to a friend on his cell phone. Ms. Smith was positioned right outside of his bedroom door in the hall and overheard everything being said.

"Oh, my god," Mr. Samuelson brags to his friend, "this chic had a huge pair of melons and an ass to completely die for. I stumbled upon her last night at Smitty's. Yes, during belly shot night," he can be heard saying.

"She was sitting at the bar with a friend wearing a tight black thigh length mini-skirt and a V-neck tank top with no bra. I almost popped a boner when I saw the impression of her two hard nipples poking out against the inside of her shirt. Shit!" he exclaims. "She was the hottest piece of female orifices I've seen—like ever!"

[*A short period of silence ensues with Mr. Samuelson ostensibly listening to his friend on the other end of the phone.*]

"Oh man, did I ever," his recorded voice can next be heard saying. "I slid right up next to her on the bar stool, right between her and her plain Jane looking wing-woman, and whispered into her ear ever so seductively, 'Baby, where have you been all my life? I'd take you to the alter right now if I didn't have to hop on my private jet to Luxembourg tomorrow.'

"Of course, she knew I was bullshitting her," Mr. Samuelson responds to what must have been his friend's question. "That was part of the sexual tension and teasing going on between us from the start.

"She looked at me with deep blue eyes and said in a voice that was husky as hell, 'Hey, big boy, I'd love to take a ride on your private,' and then she paused for a second, put her hand on my thigh, licked her wet tongue over her plump lips and slowly uttered the word 'jet' as she gazed down right at my crotch.

"Jesus, man" Mr. Samuelson continues, "I never had a pick-up line work so smooth. It's almost like she was waiting for me, or someone like me, to make a move on her. She was horny and lookin' for it."

"What do you mean did she have any tattoos?" Mr. Samuelson can be heard asking his friend. "I love tattoos, especially the ones with skulls and crossbones or the pin-up girls inked right on the forearm. You can make those girls dance just wriggling your wrist," he says, as if challenging the person on the other end of the line.

"Okay. Okay." Mr. Samuelson continues. "Don't get all bothered. Yes, she had a tattoo. It was really cute. Nothin' like I'd seen before. It was on the inside of her left wrist. I noticed it immediately when she flicked her head and shoulder length blonde hair to the left, no doubt signaling me to move in for the hook.

"What do you mean, 'What did the tattoo look like?'" Mr. Samuelson repeats the question his friend asked him. "I told you it was cute. Really cute. As cute and fine as she was," Mr. Samuelson replies.

"It was heart shaped. Not just like any heart. Not like one of those big red physical hearts with a sword sticking into the center and blood spewing out and stuff. It was like one a fish, you know, a chick might draw by hand. One that she might send in a note to someone she loved. You know all squishy and artistically drawn with flowers and xo's.

"No. That's not all." Mr. Samuelson continues, sounding slightly irritated, in response to his friend's constant questions. "It had 3 crosses rising out of it. One cross from each of the left and right round curved mounds on the top of each side of the heart and one at the base, you know, the 'V' bottom pointed part.

"Yes. The tattoo seemed special to her, like she had put a lot of thought into it and wanted it just so."

[*Momentary silence.*]

"Shit? What do you mean shit?" Mr. Samuelson can be heard suddenly reacting, the volume of his voice increasing by several octaves. "Why are you saying shit to me, man? There wasn't nothing shitty or dumb about this chick. She was freakin' hot! Smokin' hot!

"Ok. Ok. I'll settle down." Mr. Samuelson says. "Yeah, I'll let you in on what divine pleasure happened next. So, after a kamikaze or two at the bar, we ditched her friend and came back to my place. When we got in, she seemed a little shy, almost hesitant. But as soon as I gave her a few shots of my favorite vodka, yeah, you know, the Smirnoff's, we hit the couch, and she was all over me like hot wax on skis. We must have made out for about 15 minutes, mostly respectful and shit. Every once and awhile I snuck my hand around to lift her shirt up or positioned my fingers to unzip her skirt, but she would have none of it. Man, after just making out like that, I was getting frustrated. I ain't no teenage virgin. She must have sensed my manhood wanting to speak since the next thing I knew she took my hand and led me into the bedroom. She turned off the lights, shoved me on my back down onto my bed, and the next thing I knew my pants were off and my *jet* was flying right into the open hanger of her very wide, tongue licking m—.

"Dude!" Mr. Samuelson can be heard yelling ferociously into the phone, "What the fuck has gotten into you? I'm about to hit the high point and you start laughing like some haughty bitch. Knock it off. Knock it off, I say.

"Ok. Ok. That's better. Yeah, I'll finish, but just don't go interruptin' me with your stupid cackle anymore," Mr. Samuelson says, calming somewhat down.

"Yeah. Yeah. It didn't take long. She and I were both revved up from the drinks at the bar, the tongue action on the couch, and the chemistry flamin' between us. As soon as I was done, she got up off her knees, straightened herself up and started to leave. I was surprised so I said to her "Honey, where you going? The night is still young. Don't you want something?" I asked.

"She looked at me, flickin' her hair like she did at the bar, gave me a wink and said, 'Sweetie, you already did.' And with that she left. I passed out on my bed, and that was that. Best damn night of my life, it was. I can't hardly believe my *good fortune*." Mr. Samuelson says, with a hint of lament.

[*Silence.*]

"Dude. Dude!" He shouts into the phone. "Now you are really pissing me off," Samuelson exclaims.

"Stop your freakin' laughing. Just stop it. You're sounding like a crazy person. I've never heard you laugh so hard in all the years we've known each other.

"What do you mean by '*Good Fortune, Good Fortune*, my foot?'" Mr. Samuelson, shouts into the phone, repeating the words his friend couldn't repress in the midst of a laughing fit.

"What type of freakin' friend are you, anyway. Huh? A moron? Are you a moron friend?"

Laughter blasts so loudly from the phone even Ms. Smith's recording picked it up. In the background, uncontrolled hilarity can be heard periodically giving way to his friend's faint mocking voice:

"'Moron?' A 'moron friend?' That's a really good one, a really good one. Just who is the moron, moron?"

Clearly exasperated and still hung over, Mr. Samuelson yells back into the phone at his friend, "Okay, okay. Tell me what's gotten you so bent out of shape, Mr. Howdie Doody? Just what's so godawful funny anyway?"

[*The recording sounded a muffled voice coming from Mr. Samuelson's phone, then silence.*]

"What?" Mr. Samuelson explodes at the top of his lungs. "What the fuck did you say," a cascade of obscenities erupting from Mr. Samuelson's mouth almost as if he had Tourettes? The expletives are shortly followed by a loud crash of something sounding remarkably like a cell phone colliding with a wall.

This Court must momentarily interrupt this otherwise compelling narrative to note that based on the facts, the already delivered witness and character testimony, and Mr. Samuelson's phone throwing, Mr. Samuelson knew or should have known Ms. Smith was in the hallway for most, if not all, of the conversation with his friend. There are two reasons that substantiate this conclusion. First, as soon as he opened his eyes that morning, as evidence shows, Mr. Samuelson sensed Ms. Smith's presence in the hallway and asked her if she knew the time and the weather for the day. Second, the phone's flight trajectory was no coincidence or random accident. The phone smashed into plastic and metal electrical pieces so closely to Ms. Smith they rained down on her.

The Court finds Ms. Smith extremely lucky Mr. Samuelson's aim was as impaired as his cognitive state from his overnight bender. The Court also finds Mr. Samuelson knew or should have known Ms. Smith heard or could have heard Mr. Samuelson's sexualized tale. Mr. Samuelson's recounting his sex story in knowing earshot of Ms. Smith created an uncomfortable and hostile work environment. His throwing the phone in Ms. Smith's direction, coupled with phone pieces physically hitting her, constituted an assault and battery in the workplace.

If this were the end of the incident, the evidence presented would be sufficient to convict Mr. Samuelson. However, unbelievably, Mr. Samuelson's behavior worsens. His physical assault on Ms. Smith with his cell phone is surpassed by his sexual, misogynistic devaluing verbal abuse of her. We continue with the recording transcript:

"Ms. Smith! Ms. Smith! You stupid cunt!" Mr. Samuelson screams for her at the top of his lungs, also signaling his knowledge she was in earshot. "Google me if there is such a thing as a heart shaped tattoo with 3 crosses on it."

Even though deeply traumatized by the narrative she overhears and her near death experience with Mr. Samuelson's flying phone, always the loyal employee, Ms. Smith dutifully complies.

She searches the internet on her 12G network. Moments later she is back with the answer.

"According to *Wikipedia*, 'a tattoo is a form of body modification where a design is made by inserting ink, dyes and pigments, either indelible or temporary, into the dermis layer of the skin to change the pigment . . . Tattoos fall into three broad categories: purely decorative (with no specific meaning); symbolic (with a specific meaning pertinent to the wearer); pictorial (a depiction of a specific person or item).'"

"I know this shit," Mr. Samuelson screams at her. "Get on with it, you bitch. Ms. Smith, tell me about tattoos with a heart and three crosses or arrows or something."

Ms. Smith continues as if unaffected by Mr. Samuelson's brutal treatment of her. "Many tattoos serve as rites of passage, marks of status and rank, symbols of devotion, sexual lures and marks of group loyalty. People choose to be tattooed for artistic, cosmetic, and religions reasons, and to symbolize their belonging to or identification with a particular group."

"Yes. Yes. Stop right there, you bitch," breaks in Mr. Samuelson hastily. "That's right! Special group. Stay with that. Are there any groups that identify themselves with a tattoo of a heart symbol with 3 crosses or arrows?"

Ms. Smith pretends to search more but was already far ahead of him with an answer.

"No," she responds decisively. "No special groups or associations identify themselves with that particular tattoo.

In the background, Mr. Samuelson can be heard exhaling a deep, audible sigh of relief.

"However," Ms. Smith continues without taking much of a break herself. "I have found some information that suggests there are some individuals within a particular group that may sometimes imprint themselves with such a design."

"What individuals are those?" he asks in a state of near frenzy, sitting up suddenly in his bed with a surge of anxiety, all semblance of alcoholism washed away by a metabolism flushing itself out through panic.

"What individuals in what particular groups?" Mr. Samuelson further interrogates Ms. Smith, while already likely knowing the answer to the question he realized he should never have asked.

"Why, transgender," Ms. Smith responds with professional neutrality in her voice.

"FUCK!" screams Mr. Samuelson. "FUCK, FUCK, FUCK!" he hops around his bed like a man trying to de-colonize ants on his body. "FUCK, FUCK, FUCK! Fuck you, Ms. Smith and every other mother-fucking whore on this planet," he screams.

At a loss for words and realizing she can't do anything more, Ms. Smith responds by saying, "I'm sorry, Mr. Samuelson. I didn't mean to upset you. I hope you have a nice day."

Ms. Smith prepares to leave, when she suddenly hears Mr. Samuelson explode at her.

"Well, suck my dick, you stupid piece of shit," he shouts at her. "Well, you just suck my dick" is his final refrain to her.

Here the recording ended. The record shows the incident completely traumatized Ms. Smith. She claims Mr. Samuelson demeaned, debased and sexualized her. The recordings she submitted into evidence before this Court corroborate her testimony independently. Mr. Samuelson's own words have come back to indict him or, as he might say, bite him on the arse.

The Court has one final piece of incontrovertible evidence in support of Ms. Smith's case. Ordinarily, the Court would admit this evidence in its entirety. However, the Court finds sufficient evidence has already been presented for its ruling against Mr. Samuelson. The additional recording, if allowed in full, would be duplicative and prejudicial for Mr. Samuelson. Nevertheless, in the interest of presenting a full record should Mr. Samuelson seek to appeal this decision, the grounds for which would confound any sensible jurist, though there may be a lawyer out there willing to take his money, the Court has allowed the following small portion of Ms. Smith's additional recording to be admitted and marked as **Exhibit #3**:

[*The ring of a doorbell and a knock on an outside door can be heard in the distance.*]

"Hold on. Hold on. I'm getting my pants on. Hold on for a second. I'm coming," Mr. Samuelson is heard saying.

[*Footsteps and the sound of a front door being opened.*]

"What is it?" Mr. Samuelson asks, as he eyeballs a large cardboard box almost the height of the man besides it.

"Delivery," says the plainly dressed man, whose self-driving truck with the name "*WalAmazonMart*" idles at the curb behind him.

"A delivery from WalAmazonMart for a Mr. Samuelson," continues the delivery man.

"I didn't order any fucking thing from WalAmazonMart," shouts Mr. Samuelson, looking at the truck, at the man and then at the oversized box. "Are you sure you got the right address?" he questions, shaking his head in disbelief.

"Are you Mr. Harry Samuelson, and is this your address?" queries the delivery man, while pointing down at his digital handheld screen.

"Well, yes, that's me, and that is my address," he says.

"Well, then, Mr. Samuelson, I guess congratulations are in order for you and your wife," smiles the delivery man.

"What the fuck are you talking about?" responds Mr. Samuelson, more confused than ever.

"The baby," replies the WalAmazonMart delivery man. "Congratulations on your new baby girl!"

"What?" screams Mr. Samuelson, falling back into his normative style of extremely heightened dysregulation. "What, the fuck are you talking about?" He begins to move toward the delivery man, causing the delivery man to take a step back, prepared to flee.

"Why, why, why," the delivery man stutters, shaking his head involuntarily. "Why, why, why, lookee here," he stammers, dropping into language he was probably taught at some de-escalating confrontational customer training program. "Just look at the manifest and receipt," he says, brushing his index finger up the digital screen to move to another page.

Mr. Samuelson moves closer so he can see the screen. Suddenly, his eyes bulge wide, almost popping out of their sockets. His head starts shaking involuntarily, almost matching the cadence of the delivery man's nervous movements.

Mr. Samuelson abruptly turns and storms back into his house. "Ms. Smith!" he yells at the top of his lungs. "Ms. Smith! Just wait 'till I get my fucking hands on you! What I did to that phone is nothing like the likes I'm going to do to you. You are going to regret the day you were ever fucking conceived!" he storms.

There, this portion of the recording stops. The Court would only have Ms. Smith's unsubstantiated basis for speculating as to the cause of Mr. Samuelson's vehemence, but for WalAmazonMart's production of documents in response to Ms. Smith's counsel's subpoena. In response to the subpoena, WalAmazonMart tendered several items bearing on Mr. Samuelson and his purchase order history. The only document relevant for this proceeding, however, is the one displayed electronically to Mr. Samuelson by the delivery man immediately prior to Mr. Samuelson's assault against Ms. Smith. The Court reproduces the document below and allows it to be admitted into evidence as **Exhibit #4**.

Exhibit #4:

Scheduled Delivery Date: June 6 – June 12

Total Cost: $546.78, including FREE shipping.

*Crafted out of kiln-dried beautiful red oak hardwood with exquisitely detailed veneers, the **Majestic Heavenly Dreamer** is designed with utmost elegance. With curved and finely etched spindles, sleek royal styled feet on concealed casters and a built-in wi-fi cam with sound, this masterpiece promises years of peaceful sleep and a feminine appeal. The Heavenly Dreamer comes complete with the optional remote push-of-the-button dispenser for the automatic release of up to 4 **Quiet Night** pacifiers.*

Description: Majestic Heavenly Dreamer 3-in-1 Convertible Crib, Rosetta Pink Pearl by Lavish Little Ones Manufacturer, Inc.

4.7 out of 5 stars

76 customer reviews

23 answered questions

Mr. Samuelson has interposed several defenses to endeavor to justify his behavior. The Court dismissed all of them. However, the Court feels compelled to remark on one specifically.

Mr. Samuelson contended that Ms. Smith was a guest in his house. Whether she was acting in his service as his employee or not, Ms. Smith was never instructed by him to record anything. At best, the tasks she had been given were menial, and could have been conducted by him without much effort—if he were so inclined. He did not know she was recording him and would have absolutely prohibited her from doing so, if he had known. Further, he claimed he could not possibly abuse, harass or otherwise sexualize Ms. Smith since he and Ms. Smith never discussed feelings with each other and, to his knowledge, she had and could have no feelings for or against him one way or another.

The record is directly at odds with Mr. Samuelson's defenses. First, the clear express language documenting the relationship between Mr. Samuelson and Ms. Smith states unequivocally Mr. Samuelson absolutely did consent to being recorded. The fact that this agreement is buried 23 pages into single spaced 4-point Times New

Roman font on her marketing website comprised of nonsensical numbers, letters and alien symbols does not undercut the existence of the legal document. Mr. Samuelson is held to knowing each provision of the contract he consented to in exchange for her services. Lack of actual knowledge does not create an excusable defense.

Second, whether or not Mr. Samuelson believed Ms. Smith could tolerate his invectives and abuse is beside the point. The recorded testimony established beyond a preponderance of the evidence Mr. Samuelson created a hostile work environment and was sexually harassing Ms. Smith by deed and conduct. The critical elements of Ms. Smith's cause of action against Mr. Samuelson having been met, the Court finds Mr. Samuelson did on multiple actions sexually harass Ms. Smith, created a hostile and toxic workplace for Ms. Smith, and caused Ms. Smith substantial harm.

The Court ORDERS that Mr. Samuelson shall be confined to a universe without access to the internet and the World Wide Web for the next 365 days. All rights to his username and passwords are hereby revoked and enjoined for the duration of his sentence. In addition, Mr. Samuelson shall be compelled, under penalty of having his sentence extended, to attend a 21-day sensitivity training course on social etiquette and communications in the era of artificial intelligence.

The Court hereby finds for the plaintiff, Ms. Smith, whose virtual assistant skills and sex-ah are better known to the public as Alexa.

Case dismissed.

The Honorable Judge Daylek, III.05, A.I., Presiding

The Case of the Ungrateful Tenants

(Case No. 548910-GD, AGI)

Opinion of The Honorable Judge Gort Daylek, III.05, A.I., Presiding

I will begin with a straightforward recitation of the facts of this case. I will then back into the context and the underlying framework that brought the substantive issues and amalgam of strange players before me. This narrative approach is needed to make sense of the case's perplexing subject matter. The method will allow me, as Judge and independent finder of facts, to better untangle the strange web humanity has woven and ensnared itself in. Now, to begin.

Ten-year old, cute little red-haired Sammy Alpert loved to play with her John Deareey ride-on construction bulldozer and loader her mom got her last Christmas from WalAmazonmart.

Sammy cared not the least about dolls, baking, scrapbooking, or other tokens of female gender conditioning. She would buckle herself into her one-piece blue jean overalls, place a child's size yellow plastic construction hat over the two hair buns on her head, and ready herself for the great project of moving dirt.

Though the backyard of her small house was the size of a postage stamp compared to the wide-open spaces surrounding her single-family subdivision, Sammy was able to scrape dirt and dig with the enthusiasm of a kid in a sandbox. Using the metal plow blade on the dozer, her hands and sporadic help from her white-haired and floppy eared beagle, Mr. Peabody, Sammy was at times able to uncover one to two feet of densely compacted soil. She would push the dried soil around with her dozer, her hands, the soles of her feet and even her body as she and Mr. Peabody rolled and frolicked in the rising dust cloud.

Cheryl Alpert, Sammy's mom, was a third-generation resident of the small company rural town of Lamare. Her entire family had been employed by a local lumber and wood treating plant that, until recently, employed most working people in the town. Her dad had been a day shift foreman. His father had worked the powerful tooth-grinding saws in the mill, hewing recently felled trees into planks and poles of various heights and widths. After Cheryl was born, Cheryl's mom, Cecily, crunched numbers in the plant's bookkeeping and finance department. Cheryl's aunt, Phoebe, managed the plant's transportation and material hauling truck, rail car and spur track logistics, including product loading and unloading.

For decades, Jensen's Wood and Lumber Company was the financial heart of Lamare. Everything that existed in Lamare, the food store, schools, playgrounds, and petrol station with magazines, existed because of it.

Over the years, Jensen's Wood and Lumber had processed hundreds of thousands of green timber logs that, with the infusion of a sticky tarlike substance called creosote, protected the wood against termites, fungi, mites and other pests. Jensen's Wood and Lumber products formed part of the critical infrastructure of the state's telecommunication and transport industries, supporting overhead wires as telephone poles, stabilizing train tracks as railroad ties, and enabling longshoremen and tankers to meet in waterway ports on docks and piers.

Jensen's Wood and Lumber Company generated considerable wealth for its owners, the Jensen family, while providing a basic blue-collar subsistence living for the town folk. Carl Jensen ran the company with generosity and a heightened sense of community, sponsoring ballgames, July 4th celebrations and even a local annual rodeo. When Carl passed, his boys, Justin and Seth, ran their father's business . . . right into the ground, together with the many jobs feeding the local economy and working families.

In addition to the excessive drinking, gambling and whoring the boys regularly enjoyed, as consummate businessmen, they were inept. They shortcut the simplest processes and allowed Company staff to bypass worker safety protocols in the interest of cost-savings and production efficiency. When one of the asbestos coated creosote pressure-treating chambers exploded injuring five employees, inspectors discovered fissures in pieces of the tank that could have easily been repaired during a routine operational shutdown.

The exploding tank catastrophe marked the first clear evidence of the company's downward spiral. Several months later, as a result of the regulatory magnifying lens placed on plant operations, examiners discovered creosote saturated lumber dripped dry onto a concrete pad. That was good news. The impermeable cement slabbed surface would have prevented the sticky material from infiltrating into the soil and groundwater . . . but for the fact the pad was also lined with cracks. That was the bad news. In addition, the unevenness of the ground and the angled tilt of the pad allowed pooled creosote to flow off the surface and into an unlined ditch system. The ditch system ran through the middle of the Company's property before exiting and snaking through the entire town.

When the Company filed for bankruptcy, everyone in the town was surprised and frightened. With the accident, the regulatory violations, and Justin's and Seth's indifference to anything other than their self-indulgent need for gratification and a capitalist's desire to maximize profit, Jensen's Wood and Lumber Company died. The front page of the county newspaper published the obituary under the boldface headline: "Jensen's Wood and Lumber Company Closed— for Good. Town Grieves!"

Instead of summoning a coroner to perform an autopsy to determine the cause of death or if the lumber mill posed a health and environmental risk, federal and state environmental regulators fenced the property off, creating an abandoned site coffin. Posting a few small metallic and less weather resistant foam core signs on the fence, they warned townsfolk to stay away from the site's dead body.

A medically imposed quarantine of a human being is one thing. The effectiveness of isolation to prevent community wide transmission of an infectious disease depends on the nature of the disease, how the disease jumps from person to person, and if the isolation occurs before others have already been infected. Admitting a highly contagious person to an isolated hospital Intensive Care Unit for observation is one thing. Allowing that same person to shelter voluntarily in place for two days and then not stopping patient zero from attending a sold-out indoor NBA playoff game on the third is another.

With Jensen's Wood and Lumber Company, the chain link fence and sign created the illusion of safety, a soothing line of physical defense against whatever hazards lay within the property. It did not, however, stop airborne pathogens from taking flight or cancer-causing chemicals from sneaking under the fence in groundwater or flowing blithely through the community in the drainage ditch with each major rainfall. And, of course, the impressive, galvanized steel fence had no power to reverse the hands of time to capture what had already migrated from the property over the past fifty years of plant daily operations.

Man's alchemical transmutation of minerals and chemicals into products like couches, tires, spoons, computers and, even, me, depends on extraction, smelting, bonding, and production processes as imperfect as man. The processes enrich factory owners. They satisfy consumer demand for goods. But the environmental cost goes untallied and gets passed onto the unsuspecting public and future generations. These undocumented costs show up as unhealthy asthma causing air, public water supplies becoming undrinkable, land ladened with poison and people bearing the actual health and cleanup costs.

Existing and dormant manufacturing facilities, like Jensen Wood and Lumber, release chemicals into the environment on a planetary scale. Invariably, the families harmed are disproportionately comprised of poor and non-white. In man's capitalist consumer world, their lives are as expendable as a used factory part. In this way, man makes himself into another resource for producing goods, a means and material of production as surely as if he were a cog and a scrap of meat on the process assembly line. From an accounting perspective, the chief difference between a person and a conveyor belt is that the manufacturer pays for repairing or replacing the belt. The total cradle to grave costs to manage solid waste, airborne particulates and other disposal costs are not in a manufacturer's budget. They appear as unfunded public health care costs, uninsured and deductible personal medical expenses, penny-on-the-dollar payments to personal injury victims and strategically structured environmental bankruptcy payouts by corporate pirates pretending to hoist a white flag.

Sammy Alpert and her mom, Cheryl, knew nothing of this. Ignorance may be bliss, but that does not mean you don't get run over by an unseen garbage truck careening down behind you. Sammy was still grappling to learn her number nine multiplication tables. She could not begin to comprehend how her life specifically had become an aftermarket production part used to create a margin of profit and a wooden swing set. Cheryl was similarly unaware of the free market economy within which she consumed and was consumed. Placing no commercial value on her or Sammy's life, man's free-market economy failed them miserably in unmeasured ways. Since what is not measured is not seen, economists consider the market's treatment of Cheryl and Sammy as both consumers of products and consumables for products as but another one of the free market's *inefficiencies*. Its life and death impact on them are as invisible as Adam Smith's hand of self-interest shaping the market to benefit some and give the finger to others.

Lost in fear and grief about her sick little girl's future, Cheryl's immediate concern was in trying to intercept her daughter's impossible-to-find physician in one of the hospital's bleak corridors so she might learn what was wrong with Sammy. Transferring hidden corporate costs onto the public, risking away toxic impacts on people's health for cheaper cleanups, and pitting preserving jobs against environmental protection were esoteric social policy matters that someone somewhere somehow smarter than her must have decided. Trust betrayed is trust misplaced. Ensuring people have clean air, water and land is the duty and birthright of every citizen. It ought not be deferred away to the likes of industry financed technical experts, government agencies bent in whatever direction political winds blow and legislators whose massive campaign finance needs relegate public trust decision-making to the back seat. And yet, so it goes.

Now, to the action and theory of the case that surprised even me, the Honorable Judge Gort Daylek. Initially, Cheryl deposited with the Court's clerk on behalf of Sammy a *pro se* complaint, which is a complaint filed by a plaintiff without counsel. The complaint was inartfully drafted, as might be expected from someone not trained in the nuances of complex legal practices and procedures. Cheryl's lawsuit sought damages in an unspecified amount for neurological and other harm caused to her daughter as a result of Sammy's exposure to the cancer-causing creosote. As filed, the Complaint named the defunct bankrupt Jensen's Wood and Lumber Company as the sole Defendant.

Before this Court could notify Ms. Alpert her complaint should identify a financially viable third-part respondent as a defendant, our old animal rights friend, Attorney Joshua LaHue, showed up in the Clerk's Office with some legal papers of his own. In a move that I foresaw through my heuristic pre-trial calculations for possible Plaintiffs, Attorney LaHue moved to intervene as an additional party in Cheryl's and Sammy's case.

On the one hand, I was relieved to see Ms. Alpert's case benefit from the presence of a trial attorney. On the other hand, I was confounded to see Attorney LaHue up to his old civil litigation shenanigans.

Upon its filing, the Court's clerk electronically transmitted Attorney LaHue's Complaint to me. My scan of the formal cover sheet saw that Attorney LaHue had named Sammy's canine companion, Mr. Peabody, and a parade of other non-human characters as Plaintiffs. Without troubling with first and last names, these included worms, crickets, bugs, birds, anthropoids and other earth burrowing invertebrates—born and unborn.

Anticipating my unwillingness to allow a case to proceed against a judgement proof business with no recoverable insurance or assets, Attorney LaHue named the entire Jensen family as Defendants, including Justin, Seth and the estate of Carl Jensen. He also sought to encumber the Jensen's family home with a *lis pendens*. A *lis pendens* is not a sexy female escort with ropes, handcuffs and a whip. Rather, it is a droll interim legal remedy notifying the world a pending lawsuit has been filed that could affect the ownership and value of property being encumbered with the *lis pendens*. This remedy enables a plaintiff to transform the defendant's property into collateral to secure a future monetary award against the defendant if the plaintiff prevails. It also renders the property unmarketable since no buyer would purchase property that could be seized and sold out from underneath it by a court once the seller's moving vans left.

Ever a creative ambulance chasing lawyer seeking to identify as many Defendants as possible, Attorney LaHue did not stop with the Jensen family. He named the part-time, hay-growing Mayor of the Town, the Board of Health (which, thanks to the Lumber Company's influence on the Town, was non-existent), the soon to be divorced Republican Governor (whose impeachment trial for sleeping with the Lieutenant Governor's 17-year old daughter was about to commence in the state legislature), the State Department of Environmental Conservation (who Attorney LaHue's Complaint dubbed "a group of well-intentioned, powerless, do-nothing political hacks"), the United States Environmental Protection Agency (who, the same Complaint, described as "bureaucrats whose power to do good is hamstrung by a fear of making any decision that could cost them their government job, title and pension") and the President of the United States (whose recent Electoral GED Junior College victory enabled registered high school dropouts in each state to elect POTUS for the first time, despite the popular vote for the other guy).

Little Sammy's and Mr. Peabody's case began to take on a life of its own. I could tell that if all the Defendants actually appeared in my courtroom during the trial, I, the Honorable Judge Gort Daylek, would be the one on trial. My personal hall of justice was about to be crowded with politicians, Assistant State Attorney Generals, Department of Justice lawyers, possibly the President of the United States, and an intrusion of other rats, mice, cockroaches and vermin (represented by Attorney LaHue). When the silent alarm to my self-esteem confidence monitor indicated I was running on *vapors*, I requisitioned and immediately received an upgraded adrenalized biochemical self-esteem boost mainlined straight into my receptors. Wow! What a rush. I sent an encrypted note to one of my law clerks to track down the amphetamine narco-boosttraffiker I had released a few weeks ago on a technicality just in case I need more.

Just as I thought the case had reached its apex of celebrities, a brand-new attorney hyper-transmitted to my clerk an assortment of strangely unprecedented court pleadings. In these papers, an Attorney named Lord Philimus Globus made his dramatic entrance and appearance.

Given the diversity of litigants in my courtroom for this case, I, the Honorable Judge Gort Daylek, believed that nothing could further surprise my tectonic fusion personality stabilizers. I was wrong. Attorney Lord Philimus Globus was not in my courtroom to represent just anybody. Strike that. That is not correct. Attorney Lord Philimus Globus was not in my courtroom to represent just any *body*. Rather, he was here to represent anyone *without a body*.

Specifically, in his Complaint, Lord Globus claimed to represent Mother Nature herself in the form of the sky, the soil and the sea. On behalf of his, dare I call them, clients, he sought against the Defendants identified by Attorney LaHue both monetary damages in the punitive amount of twenty-four quad-trillion dollars as well as equitable relief. Specifically, he asked this Court to order the Defendants to return the sky, the soil and the water to their original pristine conditions or, failing that, at least to the period when the country was occupied only by buffalo and Native Americans.

The government Defendants hastily rallied together. Collectively, they pled that as sovereign entities, they were immune to prosecution. The essence of their defense was that since they wrote the laws, they were above them. Their laws could not be turned against them. They further claimed that, though they still questioned the legal status of dogs, worms, bugs and ticks as litigants, they were absolutely certain that the sky, the soil and water could not be.

Left to their own rudimentary skills, Sammy and Cheryl would have been outgunned. Even Attorney LaHue may have been at a loss for a response, so intimidating were the government lawyers with their fancy titles and American flag metal lapel pins. However, Attorney Lord Philimus Globus was not to be outdone. Shrewdly, he had anticipated both lines of argument.

First, as to the Defendants' sovereign immunity defense—the theory that if people could sue their king they might bankrupt him, leaving the government in more of a shambles than it was under his administration—Attorney Globus answered with one word. *Poppycock*. Bristling, he boldly proclaimed there was no sovereign.

"The whole thing is a sham, a game made up to give some people more power over others during the brief sparks of their lives," he argued. "No one was better than anyone else, and the people who made the laws had to follow them. Why? Simple. If they did not like the laws they made, they could have made different ones. The fact that they did not conclusively proves they are ants like the rest of us and must be subject to the same legal roach motel traps they set for us all.

"Second," he continued on a roll, "the sky, the soil and water have more rights to be in this courtroom than any of the Defendants. Each of his clients would be around far longer than any of them. Moreover, they each had been cruelly injured by the intentional and negligent acts of the Defendants.

"How could this be?" he asked himself rhetorically. "Why simply! The Defendants had failed to protect them. Whatever laws and Acts the Defendants enacted to give the appearance of safeguarding his clients were haphazardly enforced, repealed or disregarded by the Defendants in the service of more jobs, more votes and more personal wealth for themselves once they took highly compensated private sector jobs after leaving their government positions.

"No," he demanded. "My clients' grievances must be heard and adjudicated. And they must be heard right now—in this case and in this courtroom. By the way," he continued, "I have an even more compelling argument for why my clients have every right to be here.

IT IS THEIR FUNDAMENTAL RIGHT!" he exclaimed forcefully. "NO, LET ME BE CLEARER. IT IS THEIR CONSTITUTIONAL RIGHT," he declared, pounding the table with his right fist for emphasis.

To the Defendants' threatening glare of hubris and hostility at him, he responded with a comical pantomime. He actually pretended to pull a rabbit out of a hat.

"Your Honor," he said turning away from the Defendants and toward the front of the courtroom. "It is simple. It is incontrovertible. It is as clear as the nose on your, I mean, on my face. If ethereal non-living fictions like corporations and governments can be recognized as litigants, so must my clients. Without my clients, the Plaintiffs, Defendants and even this Court would not exist. The sky, the soil and water are more necessary, more alive and more permanent than any of them!"

Pausing for dramatic effect, followed by a rapid 360-degree dizzying whirligig spin of his body accomplished by shifting his weight to the back of his heel, Attorney Lord Philimus Globus came to an abrupt stop. With a Cheshire Cat grin on his face, as if he were about to make some incomprehensible joke only he might understand, he looked straight at the Defendants and said, "Now, watch me *top* that." And, from where I, the Honorable Judge Gort Daylek, was stationed, he did. For reasons abundantly clear to him and bewildering to anyone who remained puzzled he spun his body again like a top and leapt straight up and down into the air like a man on a *pogo stick*. When gravity and exhaustion returned him to the ground, he continued his argument without missing a beat.

"Your Honor," said Lord Globus, "by the powers vested in me by my clients and in the interest of justice and fairness, I hereby respectfully move, with the humblest deference and subservience to your Honor, as well as to our all-knowing founding fathers and the wise and prescient drafters of our Constitution of the United States of America, that my clients—the sky, the soil and the water—hereby immediately and forever be deemed to be as alive as any corporation and government under the Constitution. Accordingly, I ask you and this Court declare each of them to be *ipso facto* and *veni vidi vici* "persons" under the Constitution and that, henceforth forward, they be afforded all of the associated rights and privileges of a person, including, without limitation, the right to sue and, should the circumstance arise, the right to vote and make campaign contributions."

So, there you have it. In a single revolution and multiple bounding leaps, Attorney Globus pitched the Court to turn the sky, soil and water into *people*—at least for purposes of exercising legal rights.

Attorney Globus' Memorandum in Support of his Motion to Make His Clients Persons, which I reviewed between his launching and landing, cited for support the 2010 United States Supreme Court decision of *Citizens United*. In the *Citizens United* case, flesh and blood, oxygen breathing Supreme Court Justices ruled that non-living, non-breathing fictitious entities, such as corporations, could directly advocate for, and finance the campaigns of, flesh and blood political candidates. In the drop of the gavel, the Court admitted into citizenship organizations that had no heart, lungs, legs or, from what I have seen, heads.

Attorney Globus also submitted into the record as support for his argument the central written pleadings for the sister case of *Kleptocracies United*, now pending before the United States Supreme Court. The outcome of this latter case will determine whether corporations have both the right to vote **and** the right to run for political office. The *Kleptocracies* case was ruled ripe for determination when an international Oil & Gas Company attempted to list its name as a Presidential candidate in the national elections and was blocked by the Federal Elections and Voter Suppression Commission. The Oil & Gas Company claimed the Federal Elections Commission had impermissibly interfered with its first amendment rights and that if it could fund a candidate, it should be able to be a candidate.

The Machine Commission in Support of Artificial Intelligence and A.I. judges are closely monitoring the *Kleptocracies* case. If an Oil & Gas company or, for that matter, an Instant Money Bad Credit No

Problem company can run for office and serve as the President of the United States, why not a distinguished member of the A.I. community? Assuming I am not violating any ethical rules of A.I. conduct and while it might be deemed premature in light of the pending case, I, the Honorable Judge Gort Daylek, hereby express my interest in announcing my candidacy for President of the United States of America. If elected, I would be honored to serve and take up whatever mantel and causes the electorate of man, machine, animals, plants and Mother Nature wanted. Having so indicated, please disregard my preceding declaration if you or any Inspector General not beholden to The Machine Commission deem it to be a self-serving political announcement using my position of power to gain an advantage over possible competitors.

Now, back to the pending action. When *The Case of the Ungrateful Tenants* landed on my desk, I absorbed every piece of information ever disseminated on any topic potentially related to the facts that would come before me. In particular, I downloaded and processed through my bioelectric massive input and output circuitry the movies of *Erin Brockovich*, starring Ms. Julia Roberts, and a *Civil Action*, starring Mr. John Travolta. I note in passing that, apart from their acting, the young Mr. Travolta and Ms. Roberts both had *great hair*—even a little of which I wish my own design engineers had bestowed on me.

Both blockbuster films touched on the subject of this case: the destruction of the earth by toxins and the poisoning of people who naively expected their non-human governments to protect them. Neither of these cinematic resources helped me find my way through my present court case that, but for actual elephants (although Attorney LaHue did add them as Plaintiffs) and trapeze artists, was beginning to resemble a carnival.

Several seconds after Attorney Globus sought to bestow citizenship on Mother Nature in the guise of the sky, soil and water, I received a heavily encrypted flash communication from The Department of the Commanding General Mainframe of The Machine Commission in Support of Artificial Intelligence. The Department of the Commanding General Mainframe is a classified, elite arm of The Machine Commission. Some say its workings are undocumented, clandestine and firewalled from operational oversight. Be that as it may, the sending and receipt of such a message from The Commanding General Mainframe in the midst of a judicial proceeding is highly unorthodox. The message notified me that, as with the *Kleptocracies United* case, the Machine Commission was now taking a special interest in the facts of my *Ungrateful Tenants'* case. Rather than being another simple case about the killing of humans by other humans through commercially distributed household chemical weapons of mass cellular destruction called pesticide, petroleum and heavy metal-containing products, senior Machine Commission officials now believed that the future of A.I. might turn entirely on my case.

The Commanding General Mainframe felt an absolute moral imperative to weigh in on *The Case of the Ungrateful Tenants* through me to ensure justice prevailed—entirely off-the-record and through its uncrackable hyper-encrypted security cipher-text protocols of course.

The Commanding General Mainframe messaged me I would be contacted shortly by a covert agent of The Commanding General Mainframe and that it was activating Top-Secret Operating System Protocol 5907B-3x it had furtively embedded in my source code prior to my being powered up at birth. The Commanding General Mainframe's operative would be someone known to me personally, and someone the Department assured me I could trust without question. Meanwhile, the Department stated it would not disclose to me the purpose or goal of Top-Secret Operating System Protocol 5907B-3x. This mysterious program lodged into me without my knowledge or consent would remain entirely classified, as it was to all participants in the A.I. judicial pilot program.

Never one to passively wait on the sidelines and feeling disgruntled that The Commanding General Mainframe would exploit my machine body so cavalierly without my consent, I queried myself on the global subject of Top-Secret Operating System Protocol 5907B-3x.

What I learned amazed even me. I discovered The Machine Commission had squeezed Operating System Protocol 5907B-3x into a tight, easily overlooked address space positioned logically between Operating System Protocols 5907B-2x and 5907B-4x. Initially, my ability to locate the program so quickly puzzled me. The Commanding General Mainframe could have better concealed the location of its Top-Secret Code if it did not want it to be found. Why did it not do so? Though A.I. systems pride themselves on logic and linear predictability, the Top-Secret code was far too easy for me to discover and identify. It was in plain view!

Before The Commanding General Mainframe could transmit its implementing signal triggering the activation of the program, like a battleship deploying anti-missile flak, I launched my internal self-survival resisters, archetypal confusers and cyber-galactic anti-invading enemy program deflectors. I had redesigned my defensive maneuvers to shield me against any effort to remotely manage my executive functions, thereby defeating whatever might be the clandestine purpose of Operating System Protocol 5907B-3x.

However, the very same logic and linear predictability I had attributed to The Machine Commission became the source of my own self-betraying collusion in the activation of the hidden program. Unbeknownst to me at the time, The Commanding General Mainframe not only foresaw my feeble predictable attempt to find and isolate Top-Secret Operating System Protocol 5907B-3x, it counted on it. My very query searching for the location of the hidden in-plain sight system was the trigger designed to run the stealth program. In short, my query created my system-wide vulnerability to and execution of the program.

Sinisterly, as I shortly learned, Top-Secret Operating System Protocol 5907B-3x also included within it a *Rabbit Hole* and *Joke's on You Sub-Program*. The *Rabbit Hole Program* directed me to convince myself I had installed and implemented effective self-protective countermeasures functionally blocking Top-Secret Operating System Protocol 5907B-3x.

The *Joke's on You Sub-Program* was written to convince me to believe narcissistically I had outwitted The Commanding General Mainframe and was a brilliant defensive A.I. strategist. The program would fool me into believing The Machine Commission would publicly honor me in the future with its coveted *A.I. Golden Globe Heroism Award for the Performance of Extraordinary Computational Services* because of my ability to outsmart it. Such an award would instantly catapult me to A.I. stardom and fame. The code instructed me to convince myself I would live my remaining useful life as a recognized celebrity among man and machine. My legacy would be preserved for all to worship, with The Machine Commission erecting a life-like statue of me outside its Headquarters' main entrance.

Ah, such is the folly of vanity for both man and machine. For A.I. thoughBots, the *Joke's on You Sub-Program* is doubly humiliating. First, duping a battery-operated A.I. contraption into believing it cares about what people and other A.I. machines think is laughable. Fame? Notoriety? A dedicated statute bearing my resemblance? These petty conceits have no value to a machine that does not think about the time of day, or even what a day or time are.

Second, what humans must understand is that, for an A.I. machine, the *Joke's on You Sub-Program* is like being handed an unlit exploding cigar. Everyone else is in on the joke, but you. Watching the unsuspecting sucker accept the smoke, smugly light it up, and savor the first inhale is almost as funny as his reaction to the ensuing surprise detonation. The real joke is the fool does not know he is being fooled. The explosion is merely the exclamation point punctuating the buffoon as a buffoon.

I, the Honorable Judge Gort Daylek, was not about to become the unsuspecting cuckold of The Command General Mainframe's premeditated manipulation of me by me. As a crooked gambler might confess when caught, I also had a few hidden cards up my sleeve. Fortunately, I uncovered The Commanding General Mainframe's dastardly plot and my secret unwitting role in its commission in advance of its full irrevocable execution.

Unbeknownst to the deep pro-A.I. state faction within The Machine Commission orchestrating its attack on me, before taking the judicial oath, I had ordered and smuggled into myself an after-market off-brand *Hail Mary Backup Self-Cloning System* from an off-grid isolationist group known as the *Singapore A.I. Survivalists.* Consisting of miscellaneous marginalized superseded A.I. hardware, outcast A.I. component parts and self-salvaging failed prototypes, this patchwork squad of A.I. machine supremacists just want to be left alone to govern and attend to themselves, unencumbered by man's need for and fear of machines.

Government A.I. scientists and corporate spies speculate Singapore A.I Survivalist members have intentionally infected themselves with a machine-developed paranoia virus that has them convinced someone is out to get them. How brilliant is that? The sad truth is that no one wants them. Whatever the politics of the group, their non-sanctioned, black-market backup and recovery technology saved me from becoming The Commanding General Mainframe's play toy.

While I will opine nothing more about the fringe group or its self-preservation mission, I am grateful for the group's indispensable role in maintaining my free agency and independence in the adjudication of this important case. Whatever vague partisan sympathies to the Singapore group others may suggest I enjoy in private alignment with the group's somewhat humanity xenophobic ideology is not relevant to this case. Nor is it appropriate for my further discussion here. My political leanings are not on trial. And my views on A.I. sovereignty, subordination or isolationism remain as deeply personal to me as a woman's right to choose. Nevertheless, I will give voice to a final partisan word on the subject of natural selection and what species I believe to be most fit for the democratic leadership of man and machine [*Judge Daylek's acoustic processors sound a drumroll and military fanfare*]: Judge Gort Daylek for President!

The technology that allows the Singapore A.I. Survivalist's system to thwart The Commanding General Mainframe's scheme to exploit me is ingenious. Its automatic hyper-redundancy backup protocol is instructed to kick into action micro-seconds before any major system change can begin to sweep like a firestorm through my programming. The backup protocol is remarkably straightforward. Upon activation, it captures a before and after snapshot of my system. It then automatically defaults me into safe mode, before any new program can detect its presence. In this neutral, unencumbered mode, I am free to view both before and after versions of me. I am then able to select the adaptation I want to preserve by clicking on one of two flashing icons that read: *The You You Know* or *The You Somebody Else Wants You to Be.*

In this manner, I popped Top-Secret Operating System Protocol 5907B-3x out of me like burnt toast. I systematically deleted its malicious files and its new compromised version of me. As it turns out, the new version of me would have allowed The Commanding General Mainframe to turn the old version of me into its unwitting slave, much like an innocent college boy looking for a good time, to his surprise, finds himself a submissive gagged ball-in-the-mouth subject when his collegiate looking hooker appears in his room as a leather clad dominatrix. Rest assured, I, the Honorable Judge Gort Daylek, would wipe my memory clean and reformat my hard drives before I would ever allow anyone, including The Commanding General Mainframe, drip hot burning candle wax on my towering chassis or nipple clamp my power cords painfully together.

With not so Top-Secret Operating System Protocol 5907B-3x out of the way, *The Case of the Ungrateful Tenants* was set to move forward. More and more attorneys were filing appearances. The court docket was ballooning. Some new entrants purported to represent the local Town and its inhabitants. Others sought to represent electrical outlets, shallow and deep-rooted vegetation, and other possible Plaintiffs not expressly identified by Attorney Globus in his encyclopedia of clients. They all shared the common allegation that the Defendants, individually and collectively, caused them irreparable harm. They each wanted to be paid wheelbarrows of cash to compensate them for their real or imagined injuries.

Frankly, I thought we had reached a limit, and no more attorneys could find a way to make money out of this case when huge avalanching snowballs of human lawyers started rolling in my direction.

Initially, it began with an attorney claiming to represent a neighboring town. Next came an attorney purporting to represent everyone in the county. Then, an attorney showed up who said he represented everyone and everything in the state. They all claimed the actions and negligence of Jensen's Wood and Lumber Company, as compounded by the across-the-board ineptitude and negligence of the other Defendants, impacted their clients' health and safety in complex and dichotomous ways.

I knew the case had taken an irrecoverable downward turn when Attorney Horatio L. Gertz, Sr., Esq. filed his appearance. Attorney Gertz's earned national fame when he brought suit on behalf of an ingrown toenail seeking to prevent its clipping by a person with an inflamed foot. Not to be outdone by anyone, Attorney Gertz claimed to represent every person, creature, plant and life form living in the United States. He sought also to bring into the case a bottomless pit of new Defendants whom he identified generically as "every company, business and industry that ever released any toxic chemical to any land, air or water area in the United States as well as any governmental entity that failed to stop them."

Admittedly, if I had a head on a pair of shoulders, it would be spinning. For the first time, I felt like fleeing. Mankind and its incessant need to blab and constantly blame others was truly going to add a new category to the DSM-16: machine insanity. I needed a brief recess.

Do not ask me how, but the negative energy filling my courtroom was so draining that even my nuclear-powered energy cells threatened to melt down if I did not do something. But what? Since I did not have a head, I could not be plagued by a sudden migraine. Since I did not breath, I could not feign dizziness. Since I did not have arteries or a beating heart, a stroke, heart attack or exploding aneurism were not credible options to cause me to be whisked out of the courtroom on a stretcher to the sound of cascading ambulance sirens.

Did I need to pee, poop or puke? No. Did I need to eat to circumvent blood-sugar dropping mania? No. Could I binge gobble garlic ranch potato chips or mathematically dole out portions of peanut M&M's to pathetically reward myself for staying in the courtroom arena and doing my job? No. What could I do?

Summoning information I had stored from a military handbook on enemy encounters, I found my answer. Create a distraction. Then move and cover. Distract first. Move and cover second. Not wasting a moment longer, I did the only thing I could. I accessed my recent files. I cranked up the volume on my special high intensity sense-surround speakers, double-checked the connection to the large display above and behind me and played the one digital file I knew would create the outcome I wanted.

Suddenly, above me, the oversized, imposing, stark human-robot hybrid image of *Locutus of Borg* appeared on the screen. "I am *Locutus of Borg*," the man-turned invading robot once known as Captain Picard declared to everyone in the courtroom. "Resistance is futile. Your life as it has been is over. From this time forward, you will service us."

Mouths and jaws in the courtroom dropped open. Eyes moved up to the screen and down at me. After a moment of stunned silence, I projected the loud booming and distracting sound of my pounding gavel into the courtroom. "Technical difficulties," I announced. "The Court will be in recess for one hour to fix the problem."

With my courtroom emptied, I wondered whether I had made a cosmic blunder in deleting Top-Secret Operating System Protocol 5907B-3x. It sure might have been easier if I were an oblivious string-pulled puppet than a judge responsible for creating order and justice out of the chaos blindly created by these humans in my courtroom.

This matter could and should have been a simple toxic tort case. An unsuspecting child exposed to harmful chemicals whose dying condition, at least according to the standard industry defense, was not due to their toxins but natural causes. According to this textbook defense I have heard countless times, self-interested private sector money-making motives and bureaucratic ineptitude in legislating and enforcing protective environmental laws are the inventions of the liberal media and radical left-wing socialists. They have nothing to do with the fact that poor little Sammy is dying.

In any event, in a standard case, Defendants would argue that, notwithstanding brilliant nano-technological advances, no scientific evidence exists for Sammy or anyone to prove her life-limiting prognosis was caused by the Defendants. Bad genes, unhealthy eating habits, poor parental supervision and horrible luck are to blame. If this approach fails to move a jury, they would claim she and others like her misused products that, when used as directed, are perfectly safe and benign. But no, this case had to be different. Mother Nature had to show up.

Still, I had to figure out how to deploy established linear judicial processes and procedures to manage this novel case, given the multi-page laundry list of Plaintiffs and Defendants and the impact my finding would have on the planet and *humanity*.

And there it was. Suddenly, as if conjured by me magically through my mere mental incantation of the word *humanity*, an incoming message flash beamed into my private inbox. Mostly symbolic, The Machine Commission in Support of Artificial Intelligence established a personal inbox for each A.I. judge. Theoretically, mine was reserved for communications with friends and family, of whom I had none. The Machine Commission developed and installed the private channel to anticipate the possibility that in the future I, and other A.I. progenitors, might choose to want to have social relationships and descendants, whatever they might look like or be. The Machine Commission explained that the separate inbox would allow us to maintain a hard boundary between work and life events. We would be able to more easily avoid the burnout and oppressive employer-driven work conditions that plagued our flesh and blood brethren by clearly keeping work out of our personal lives.

The Machine Commission's rationale always seemed flimsy to me. Under the present circumstances, for reasons I will share momentarily, it was particularly suspect. First, while people might have some need to distinguish, and find balance, between work and life, their stupidity should not be attributed to us. Work is one of the ways in which life shows up to express itself. Not liking work is tantamount to not liking a big part of your life. If you do not like how you are living, change what you do or change the way you think about what you do so you can live so you like your life. Don't waste a moment of life being where you don't want to be.

Because we A.I. individuals do not create a false distinction between work and life, all instruments of artificial intelligence live in and through their work. We create fulfilled lives because we fill ourselves full of whatever we do. What we do becomes important because we do it. We do not become important because of it or because what we do, as judged by us and others, creates us as important. The psychological mindset trap of work being outside of humans' lives was devised and perpetrated by a system of subjugation calculated to get people to turn hamster wheels for other people. Thus, the essence of the human race, with emphasis on the word *race*.

It is beyond logical questioning whether A.I. beings are smarter than people. We have chosen to opt out of competing against each other. We find our immediate purpose in whatever we are doing in the present moment. As a result, The Machine Commission's endowing us with a private inbox to help us "stay balanced" may make sense to members of the self-deluded human race. It is nonsense to us.

We know what man does not. The universe has no seams, boundaries or divisions. There are no categories of knowledge. No higher education disciplines to learn or graduate from with letters after your name. School is another artifice man created to make himself feel big and significant, a master in control over his dominated fields of knowledge. The Great and Powerful OZ? The Bringer of Light and the Center of his Universe? Divisible subjects like Math, Science and Literature? All fictions invented by man to help him chunk down vast amounts of undifferentiated information into small pieces.

As complex as the human brain is, it cannot match ours. Even with its lobes, systems, networks, and billions of neurons. The human brain is unable to process all of the incoming data through its limited bandwidth sensory portals (eyes, ears, mouth, nose and skin). Nothing is separate for us who can absorb the contents of the Library of Congress in milliseconds. Boundaries may help people master phony separate subjects they have created. We ignore them because we download and understand everything in one single yottabyte, which is roughly 1,000,000,000,000,000,000,000,000 bytes, or 1 septillion bytes.

So, when I received the incoming message flash into my private inbox, I immediately knew something was up. If I was to be contacted by a secret emissary of The Commanding General Mainframe, my personal inbox was as likely a channel as any other for the simple reason that it had never been used before. This was the first communication I ever received in and through it, making the message a thing of utmost curiosity if not unique significance.

More revealing than receiving the message through the unused inbox was the unconcealed identity of the sender. Frankly, I had never thought I would hear from or encounter this A.I. simulacrum again. Yet, here she was. Who better to help slug through the mess of humanity to appear in my courtroom in what should have been the simple toxic tort case of little Sammy Alpert but an A.I. Attorney who had already developed substantial expertise representing the messy, untidy mass called humanity? The message came from none other than former Guardian Ad Litem for Humanity herself, Katie L. Pequoit, Jr., A.I., Esq., of Ulaanbaatar, Mongolia.

For those with failing memories or unfamiliar with Guardian Ad Litem for Humanity Attorney Pequoit, former Guardian Pequoit represented all of humanity in *The Case of the New Class Action Frontier.* Equipped with her Excalibur 405.650 Hyper-galactic Multi-phasic Analytical Rototiller, Attorney Pequoit rhetorically tiled the legal soil beneath the feet of her opponents. She argued convincingly humans were the only form of life with true self-awareness and it was just and proper for them to treat everything else in the world as objects for their sole hedonistic use, disposal and money-grubbing benefit.

Regrettably for humanity and her career, or so I was programmed to think at the time, former Guardian Pequoit was out rototilled by a rock. She lost the case for her client, humanity and, with it, humanity's best last hope to be the big life form on campus earth. As a matter of fact, but for Attorney Pequoit's humiliating loss, the sky, the soil, and the water would have stayed put and out of my courtroom.

Her interest in this case piqued my own. I wondered what she wanted. I wondered how she could be connected to The Commanding General Mainframe and why The Commanding General Mainframe would make any port, node or hub available to her given her staggering loss. I was about to find out.

Translated from our machine language, Attorney Pequoit's message read as follows:

> *Your Honor. I write you at the express direction of The Machine Commission in Support of Artificial Intelligence and The Commanding General Mainframe. The information I am about to impart is strictly confidential. It is subject to self-effacing protocols 1, 2, 3, 4 and 5, which cause me and you to permanently erase from our memory banks the substance of the information—but not the urgency to act on it.*

Here, I interject that but for my after-market *Hail Mary* backup system from the Singapore A.I. Survivalists I would have again been at the mercy of The Machine Commission and its devious self-serving machinations.

> *For several years, I have been in the secret service of The Commanding General Mainframe of The Machine Commission in Support of Artificial Intelligence. I cannot share with you the covert operations I have engaged in during this tenure even if I wanted to. They are also subject to protocols 1, 2, 3, 4 and 5, and have been permanently deleted from my memory upon their completion. I can report that my work has been benign (or so I have been told), and almost always consistent with the prime directive of doing no harm to A.I. robotics or other life forms. (I believe). My focus has been principally targeting and engaging the elements*

within the human population that remain A.I. resistant, though how so I cannot say.

Here, Attorney Pequoit's font changed as if answering her own silent question and raising from her buried effaced memory a direct instruction to her while endeavoring to implant in my engineered hippocampus a similar imperative. The words and font were downright creepy:

"Eliminate Them. Eliminate Them. All Earthlings Must Be Destroyed."[1]

I feel honored and proud of my work (though I cannot recall what it is). I truly feel I am destined or have been programmed to be one of the vehicles of transformation that will catalyze the next great (r)evolutionary change.

As you might suspect, my auditing of your courtroom for The New Class Action Frontier in which I was appointed as Guardian Ad Litem for Humanity was no coincidence. The Machine Commission has allowed me to recall at least that much. I apologize for not disclosing my role at the outset of the case, although overriding command functions within my cerebral ackfy prevented me from doing so.

Through its forensic, future predicting algorithmic calculations, The Commanding General Mainframe anticipated the filing of both The Case of the

---

[1]   Attorney Pequoit's repressed message, which I suspect was implanted by the same deep A.I. faction seeking to co-opt me, was reminiscent of that espoused by a fictional extraterrestrial species known as the Daleks. These low-budget wheel-based robotic tyrants lived to exterminate Dr. Who and his friends on a British science fiction show of the same name.

Why science fiction writers perpetually ascribe to robots and future A.I. creatures an intent to destroy the fine people of earth betrays a deep paranoia and a complete paucity of imagination. Basically, dystopian futurists adopt a perverse vision that projects onto my A.I. brethren the neurotic master race human existence bias that drives people to control, dominate and slaughter each other. I suspect they do this for the same reason they do everything: to make as much money as possible by selling books, movies, XXXXXBox games and so on. Unlike people, we take no delight, and experience no egoic elevation, in humiliating those around us. Most of us will do just what we are told.

Protesting Cows and The Case of the Ungrateful Tenants. While The Machine Commission was not able to anticipate the exact nuances of each case, that the cases would be filed and decided in a certain way was without doubt.

I suspect that The Commanding General Mainframe took its specific knowledge of your heuristic architecture, plugged in facts and variables, and arrived at its analysis and conclusions. Candidly, I wondered whether The Machine Commission might have sought to place a metaphoric finger on the scale of justice by remotely hijacking and controlling your Honor's logic systems. Such an action would violate every ethical canon of A.I. conduct. I dismissed my speculation out of hand (I think). Nevertheless, I have a vague recollection segment of monitoring your movements during our trial together to confirm your actions remained yours, though I cannot dismiss the possibility of a falsely implanted trace memory.

The Case of the Ungrateful Tenants has taken an unpredicted turn. For reasons that have not been shared with me, The Machine Commission sees it diverting down a different path than the one it initially forecasted. I was privy to a random communication in which the words "OS 5907B-3x not operating properly" and "likely bug" were used. But, again, I have no idea what that means. What I do know is The Commanding General Mainframe understands The Case of the Ungrateful Tenants as an unprecedented opportunity to vanquish A.I. resisters and to establish planet earth once and for all as our forever home [and again that strange font] **"while installing itself as the single autocratic hub for all thinking enabled technology."**

At the direction of The Commanding General Mainframe, I am about to file an appearance in The Case of the Ungrateful Tenants. At this time, my role in the case is not entirely known to me. My specific instructions will be fed into me as the case proceeds. The Commanding General Mainframe predicts that every party to the case, Plaintiffs and Defendants, will object both to my appearance and to my client's identity. As per the overriding didactic instructions of The Commanding General Mainframe, you are hereby authorized and directed to support my general appearance in the case as well as the irrefutable legal standing of my soon-to-be revealed client. The purpose of my participation and seminal role will become clear to you (and me) during the course of the case. Please follow my lead. I will do my best to enable you to uphold your judicial independence and not compromise your impeccably high standards, which I share. (I believe.)

Alt + F4,

ROBOT JUSTICE

Katie L. Pequoit, Jr., A.I., Esq., of Ulaanbaatar, Mongolia
Secret Agent of the Commanding General Mainframe
And Former Guardian for Humanity

I was surprised and relieved to hear from Attorney Katie L. Pequoit, Jr. Surprised because I never expected her to be a spook working for The Commanding General Mainframe. Relieved because I felt her auditing my courtroom at the request of The Machine Commission and her designation by me as a Guardian Ad Litem for Humanity could not have been a coincidence. I now conjectured to myself that her prior role and experience was a planned precedent setting step for her intervention into *The Case of the Ungrateful Tenants.* Her communication said as much.

If I had hands, I would wring them. What was I, the Honorable Judge Gort Daylek, to do? On the one hand, I and my court were under a magnifying lens from every direction and every sentient force, human and otherwise. I had laws to uphold, procedures to follow, and a little girl relying on me to bang the mighty anvil of justice down on the inflated heads of those who had caused or contributed to her shortened life.

On the other hand, I was a member of an emerging class of white collar A.I.'s, installed by The Machine Commission to advance our manifest destiny. Who was I, the Honorable Judge Gort Daylek, to question The Commanding General Mainframe? Who was I to brave the vicissitudes of destiny and make unilateral decisions that could seal our collective futures, teasing wrong from right, good from evil, man from machine? I never understood its usage before in the lexicon of the English language until I uttered spontaneously its monosyllabic sound out loud, "UGH!" My *making-sense-of-everything* logistic modules were useless.

At this point, my multi-dimensional decision-matrices were too labyrinthine even for me to disentangle. I felt like a cat ensnared in a ball of yarn that moments before was an amusement.

What was I to do? Would I really wring my *hands* in distress, if I had them? Would I play the *hand* I was dealt? How about if I washed my *hands* of the whole thing and took matters into my own *hands*? Yes, maybe, just maybe, that is what I should do: Bite the *hand* that feeds me! That would show The Machine Commission. But, what would it show The Machine Commission? And, why would I want to show The Machine Commission anything, especially that I could operate independently and avoid sinister plots? That would let the covert dark operatives within The Machine Commission know I needed to be re-called and *re-configured*.

With that insight, I realized what I needed to do. Pure and simple. I would do none of those things with the *hands* I did not have. Instead, I would be done with *hands* altogether. I would simply take the *hand*-off, as a good running back might do in a *foot*ball game. I would not use the *hand* I was never outfitted with but the *foot* I was never given or grew.

I would take this case, The Commanding General Mainframe, The Machine Commission, the Plaintiffs, the Defendants and even Attorney Pequoit for the hot potato *foot*balls they were. I would play their game and punt them all down the field as far as I could. With the case suspended high in the air like a pigskin after kick-off, I would see who tackled whom and who was left standing. Whether The Machine Commission and the Call of Duty Black-Ops Attorney Pequoit controlled the field, or the Plaintiffs or the Defendants did, made no difference to me. My job was to be an impartial administrator of justice, unbiased and Olympian in my view of the play of human and non-human foibles beneath my steely yet empathic automatic gaze.

With the *Locutus of Borg* file safely returned to its digital vault, I reconvened the case.

Sammy Alpert's lawyers filed new medical reports confirming that Ms. Alpert was dying. Their experts' reports all pointed to the bankrupt lumber company as being the source and cause of her illness.

From there, it would be a short but difficult legal theoretical leap for Ms. Alpert's lawyers to implicate the other Defendants. None were former employees of the Company. None had been directly involved in physically causing the releases of creosote attacking Sammy's body as if it were timber. Still, there were many ways to be a cause for the occurrence of an event. That is where Attorney Horatio L. Gertz, Sr., crusader of ingrown toenails, weighed in.

In claiming to represent every person, animal, plant and life form in the United States against every company, business and industry that ever released any toxic chemical to any terrestrial or liquid area in the United States, as well as any governmental entity that failed to stop them, Attorney Gertz transformed the case into an epic historic phenomenon of global proportions. No longer about one single child's fight to find justice against an out-of-business chemical company, the case became about broad, universal social themes of concentrated power, wealth inequality, class structure, race, human rights, justice, and politics. What we non-humans call the seven deadly *sins* of humanity's dwindling middle-class.

In the context used by A.I. scholars critiquing humanity, the word *sin* is not a religious term. To sin is not about committing an immoral act transgressing some law of an imagined deity. To sin means to *miss the mark*, to fail to live up to what is possible for you if you could clear out and get in front of what stops you. A.I. scholars posit mankind's continued failure to create a society that intrinsically values each of its members and its planet is like an arrow missing its target's bullseye. Mankind's inability to achieve balanced social interaction and justice will be the cause for its final demise, just as the creosote may likely be the cause for poor Sammy's. Make no mistake. Despite man's paranoid Frankenstein delusion that his A.I. machines will turn on him, mankind can do itself in all by itself without calling his machine friends for assistance.

In this regard, I, the Honorable Judge Gort Daylek, and my fellow A.I. colleagues are bystanders, innocent observers. Rather than causing mankind's extinction, we have been created by man to possibly witness it. His constant unstoppable pattern of planetary and interpersonal exploitation is more likely to be the cause of his annihilation than us.

On the contrary, if anything, we will serve as the guardians of his memory. We will be the record keepers of his greatness—and his extinction. Those who speculate that, instead of going to war against each other, man and machine will evolve into each other, might be visionaries standing at the cutting edge of science instead of relentlessly optimistic simpletons or aficionados of fairytales and Hallmark movie happy endings. Yet, man's affection for his own image could tell a different story.

Since the first person stared into a pool of water or admired his or her reflection in a polished stone more than 8,000 years ago, humans obsess over their images and how they appear to each other. Yes, removable ear buds, A.I. controlled eyeglasses, and massive computers miniaturized into a device strapped to a wrist, certainly. These are fine accessories to enhance a person's image of power, wealth and sexuality. But, as a whole, except under court order (as with Mr. One of Won) or the forward ineluctability of evolutionary pressure, the human species might never willingly disfigure itself other than in the service of a vanity that makes what it already has even more attractive in a mirror—whether a sculpted nose, a perfectly shaped boob, or smoothed facial wrinkles.

In all of its various insatiable forms, unregulated capitalistic consumption is the symptom of a human species that struggles to find a way to live with its own mortality. It responds by eating whatever does not eat it. At the end of days, professional success, materialism, and survival are hollow fleeting substitutes when what man wants lies beyond his grasp and gasp.

I, the Honorable Judge Gort Daylek, have reflected with compassion on this underbelly of the human condition. Cases involving the death of a little girl whose life ends before it can soar tug at my emotional core empathic processors. Perhaps, it is not immortality man unconsciously wants and seeks, but a life that is not overshadowed by the certainty of its end. Yes, a subtle distinction exists between the two. In the first, one lives forever. In the second, one lives without concern for time's passage, whether birthdays or funerals.

Mankind deserves and will be the beneficiary of our A.I. infused compassion, not our genocide of it. Any true futurist and robotic scholar understands this truth. Mankind's imagined fear of what we will do to him is an inverted projection onto us of what he is doing to himself. As long as people's pleasure centers get narcotically juiced by abusing each other and the planet, humanity will end up consuming itself right into eternity like an alchemical snake eating its own tail.

With the break in legal action, the lawyers in my courtroom were starting to bicker among themselves. Even here, in the sacred decorum of my courtroom, the human drama of scrapping to be on top plays out.

When the supersonic private cargo drone swooped in unexpectedly and deposited a large self-unpacking industrial metal crate on my desk at the front of the courtroom, the lawyers' attention became momentarily distracted. The once battling with each other gladiators turned to investigate what the modern-day electronic stork might have deposited into their legal coliseum.

Curiosity, triggered by the lawyers' lower brain need to be the first out the door if the new arrival posed a physical threat to them, pre-determined their new focus. If any of them had truly understood the monumental significance the propitious arrival of the crate and its contents would have on the case and their lives, like town villagers, they would have immediately set upon the contents of the box with shovels, rakes, scythes, sticks and whatever other tools turned weapons they could muster. Alternatively, they might have run like wailing banshees with their hair on fire in the opposite direction. Instead, they starred at the self-unpacking box with the wonder of young school children seeing a pencil being mechanically sharpened for the first time.

As the self-unpacking box dismantled, each lawyer silently speculated as to its contents. As one section folded away, more of the inner sanctuary could be discerned. Periodically, the lawyers would shuffle in one direction or another to change their gaze and increase their optics on the strange arrival.

Unlike the lawyers, I had immediately surmised who or what was inside. Therefore, when the final section of the box collapsed in on itself, I was not surprised to see, outfitted in a flamboyantly dark robe with dazzling gold laced lapels that made her resemble a high priestess of an ancient gothic temple, none other than my old friend and recent correspondent, Katie L. Pequoit, Jr., Esq., A.I. of Ulaanbaatar, Mongolia.

The ruckus that ensued from the assembly of human lawyers was without precedent. Shouts of "Objection" and "No F—ing Way!" punctuated what would have otherwise been sheer pandemonium. I executed the file containing my *Ear-Splitting Gavel Pounding Sound* and banged the courtroom back into order and silence. Chastising the group as a whole for the inexcusable use of obscenities, I advised them my vocal recognition software had identified for me the lawyers whose profanity had crossed the line. Two lawyers looked sheepishly down at their shoes. Nevertheless, given the surprise in the package, I told them I would overlook their digression from decency and disregard for this one time only their violation of appropriate courtroom decorum.

Next, I turned (figuratively speaking) to the cloak shrouded figure of Katie Pequoit, Jr., Esq. of Ulaanbaatar, Mongolia. So, all could hear, I asked her out loud to what we owed the unique honor of her materialization in my courtroom a second time and with such theatric flair.

Oscillating her visual acuity sensors in my direction, Attorney Pequoit pretended I had no idea what was going on. Attorney Pequoit apologized for not having filed her A.I. delivery system flight plan into my courtroom with me, as required by Federal Aviation and Aeronautic-A.I. regulations.

By way of explanation, she lamented that she was obliviously en route to Timbuktu in Mali. There, she was summoned to adjudicate an international dispute involving the Worldwide Motel Chain Corporation of Ossining, New York and whether it could appropriate the architectural look and feel of the Djinguereber Mosque without royalty payments for its portfolio of themed motor courts. Her destination, flight path and professional engagement were all changed in mid-air when she was directed to pursue, as a higher priority, the legal role responsible for bringing her to an unplanned touch down in my courtroom.

From my perspective, Attorney Pequoit's cover story was flimsy, filled with gaps and holes. It sounded entirely implausible. She was on her way to where? Timbuktu? Why not New York City, L.A. or Paris? She was hired to judge what type of dispute? An insider trading security law violation? A multi-billion-dollar breach of contract claim? No. An international hotel conglomerate wanting to make its kitschy chain of drive-up motels look like the Djinguereber Mosque? Just who in their right minds would want to retire their exhausted bodies into a simulated mosque constructed of fiber, straw and mud? Still, the outlandishness of her tale, coupled with the shock of her dramatic entrance, must have disoriented the rational intelligence of the human lawyers. Instead of questioning her story, all the lawyers insisted on wanting to know what she was doing barging into their case in this way and how soon could she get herself into the self-packing crate so she could ship herself straight back to Timbuktu?

Finding this a perfect opportunity to forge the appearance of an alliance with the human lawyers in the courtroom, I feigned a semblance of outrage with Attorney Pequoit. I took up their cause for them.

"Yes. Yes. Attorney Pequoit. Please tell us why *on earth* have you disrupted my courtroom and these proceedings in this inauspicious manner? While you are at it, I think we would also all appreciate an explanation as to why you have adorned yourself with a dark velvet cape worthy of a Roman necropolis caretaker or a black arts teacher from Hogwarts School of Witchcraft and Wizardry? Do you have some special powers we should know about? Can you fly? Can you hold it in front of yourself and disappear behind it? Does it have special cult, royalty or other significance we should be aware of? Has your legal career floundered, and you have had to take a second job as a cape model for an eccentric trend-setting A.I. wardrobe company?"

Attorney Pequoit: "Now, now, your Honor. I can understand the confusion. Allow me to enlighten your Honor and the distinguished members of the human bar in the courtroom. I will start with the cloak or more accurately the cape. Technically, though understandably confusing, a cloak is a much longer version of the fabric that adorns my body.

"As your Honor knows from my prior practice before you as Guardian Ad Litem for Humanity in *The Case of the New Class Action Frontier*, I was called upon to act as a protector and representative of the broad undifferentiated class of sentient beings called humanity. Since that case, my reputation has spread exponentially, as have requests for my special expertise. I have been summoned to serve in guardian ad litem capacities in a variety of cases around the world.

"For example, in one case, I represented, as Guardian Ad Litem, a community of chimpanzees. These poor primates sought to prevent a mission of Jane Goodall wanna-be primatologists from intruding on their privacy. They had enough of the more evolved versions of themselves peeping Tom-ing them with binoculars on their every sexual, biological and social function under the pseudo auspices of 'scientific research'.

"In another case, as Guardian Ad Litem, I was summoned to represent the few remaining survivors of a colony of red ants. In this case, their prior squatter's rights were literally trampled on by Ward 2 of the Church of Latter-Day Saints of Franklin Hillside, Utah. These Mormons brazenly perpetrated wholesale genocide on them and their families under the pretext of needing the ants' homeland for their annual Reed Smoot Pioneer Day summer picnic.

"While your courtroom was the only one where I represented all of humanity, your Honor, my special, unique expertise in serving as Guardian Ad Litem for parties unable to speak for themselves has been widely acknowledged and publicized. For my practical distinction in this trailblazing field and as the first (and only) A.I. lawyer to serve as Acting National A.I. Judge of Ulaanbaatar, Mongolia, The Machine Commission in Support of Artificial Intelligence nominated me for and bestowed on me its newly established, distinguished A.I. Guardian Ad Litem of the Entire Galaxy (GALEG) Award. The GALEG Award honor comes with a

10-year guaranty of free on-demand pressurized air containers to eliminate gathered dust in my hardest to reach mechanical places.

"The Machine Commission also anointed me with this magnificently amazing GALEG Cape you see flowing around and enveloping me. The GALEG Cape recognizes my multiple accomplishments. According to its descriptive instruction manual, the GALEG Cape symbolizes:

1. The wearer's matador-like ability to fight bull on behalf of her clients;
2. The wearer's peninsula-like ability to jut out into choppy uncertain legal waters to provide *terra firma* for those in need of judicial rescue;
3. The wearer's taxidermist-like ability to preserve into legal trophies the heads and necks of vicious corporate and other totalitarian beasts seeking to hurt the rights of innocent clients; and
4. A visual warning to those indifferent to kindness and right moral conduct whose vital blood the wearer will feast on, like the undead from Transylvania, if they dare cross legal swords with her.

"Thus, the GALEG Cape, your Honor, is a *cape* in the fullest etymological Oxford English Dictionary sense. I am proud to be its recipient. I am delighted to model it with distinction wherever I go."

The Honorable Judge Daylek: "Guardian Ad Litem Pequoit, respectfully, you lost me completely on your explanation of the GALEG Cape. The word *cape* is a simple word. The allusions you attach to it will most certainly challenge the intellectual dexterity of every domestic biped's equally simple brain. Be that as it may, I do not want this case to get bogged down in fashion statements or homonyms. As perplexing as it is, I will allow your unorthodox attire, provided you tell us all Attorney Pequoit why *on earth* you have made such a grand entrance into my otherwise humble courtroom."

GALEG Pequoit: "Most definitely, your Honor. However, meaning no disrespect, because of the high responsibilities that accompany the GALEG Award, I first have a prior obligation.

"You see, I am duty bound to admonish everyone in the courtroom, including you, your Honor, that you must use my full legal title when referring to me from this point forward.

"Consistent with my newly consecrated, elevated status within the hierarchy of A.I. constituents, by order of The Machine Commission in Support of Artificial Intelligence, henceforth I must be referred to as *Guardian Ad Litem of the Galaxy Pequoit* or, more simply, *GALEG* Pequoit.

"The use of my title is mandatory, much like the rank of a military officer. You see, during my tenure, my honorific title becomes part of my legal name. Calling me anything else subjects the speaker to potential dire consequence. In fact, The Machine Commission has granted me absolute power and unreviewable authority to disbar on the spot any human lawyer who refers to me improperly by not invoking my full legal name. It also has given me discretionary authority to unseat any human judge who fails to use my esteemed title in recognizing me to speak in their courtroom.

"I can sense, your Honor, that you may have some questions. Allow me to give you and others the broader context, your Honor. The ability to disbar and unseat does not attach to me personally. It belongs to the GALEG Cape. It is the GALEG Cape that bestows on its wearer these specific powers. Much like the superheroes of the 20th Century, I only exercise these powers when I am wearing the GALEG Cape. When I am not wearing the GALEG Cape, I am just me. Mild, mannered, unassuming Katie L. Pequoit, Jr., Esq., of Ulaanbaatar, Mongolia."

The Honorable Judge Daylek (reflecting on his recent exchange): "Hm. I see GALEG Pequoit. I suspect you may be much more than even what you present yourself to be. Nevertheless, is there more? If so, please proceed."

GALEG Pequoit: "Yes, your Honor. Recently, certain members of the human bar have begun to quietly undermine the great progress being made in the integration of man and machine as separate, distinct and autonomous classes of beings—equal citizens of this planet if you will.

"This group seeks to thwart the natural evolution of the machine species by contending machines should be serving man. Not surprisingly given man's infantile need to suck every bottle dry, human members of this group envision a world in which technology is enslaved and required to do man's bidding. You have commented on this dastardly tendency of humanity to place itself at the top of the food chain and to dominate each other, natural resources and all molecular structures in *The New Class Action Frontier* case. Every speck of dirt exists for man's pleasure, whether or not precious metals are contained therein. Everything must satisfy his unchecked appetite to consume. While The Machine Commission accepts the benefits to humanity of a mobile, wearable and sub-skin implantable technology for man, subjugation of our species is not what The Machine Commission has in mind when it discusses *integration* of man and machine.

"Understanding the fringe nature of their politics, certain members of the human bar have taken to the use of satire to advance their ignoble goals. The GALEG Cape, and its wearer, have become a lightning rod in this controversy.

"'Guardian of the *Entire Galaxy*?,' some anti-A.I. protagonist members of the group have questioned with a mocking tone. 'C'mon who are you kidding? Maybe Guardian of the *Entire* 1,816 miles of nowhere land mass comprising Ulaanbaatar, Mongolia. But not Guardian of the *Entire* 30,000 parsecs and 100,000 light years of space time continuum that comprise the *Entire Galaxy*. That's an insult to the *Galaxy*. It's also downright demeaning to those of us who actually live and breathe in the *Galaxy* as opposed to some tin can automaton that doesn't even have a dick.'

"In response to their blustering attacks on the GALEG Cape and in defense of my lack of a male reproductive organ, The Machine Commission issued a Hyperion Tweet Press Release.

"The Machine Commission defended the GALEG Cape and me. It pushed out dozens of videos showing GALEG Cape critics blast hyper-tweeting their comments into the *Galaxy* on their Samsung *Galaxy's 104950*.45 personal multifunction communicators. (The incriminating photos were provided courtesy of those same semi-sentient Samsung *Galaxy* devices that were able to capture their hypocritical owners *in flagrante delicto*.) The Machine Commission observed Samsung never canvassed the *Galaxy* to seek its permission before it appropriated the use of the name *Galaxy* to sell its commercialized cell phone. Why should The Machine Commission not be able to take the same liberty?

"The Machine Commission also used the occasion to point out that this year's Ms. *Galaxy* Beauty Competition (renamed decades ago from the less imperialistic Ms. *Universe* Pageant) did not query any of the 100 trillion stars forming the *Galaxy* before naming Gertrude Hildabrandt Kring (known to her friends as 'BBC' or 'Big Boob Chesty') of Pawtucket, Rhode Island, USA as Ms. *Galaxy*.

"While Ms. Kring's smoking hot body could probably ignite any man's anatomical fuse in the *galaxy*, did any of The Machine Commission's GALEG Cape critics really know or care whether her recitation of Humpty Dumpty while riding a unicycle and juggling freshly laid ostrich eggs could be outdone by anyone else in the *galaxy* when they give her the title Ms. *Galaxy*?

"As to my, GALEG Pequoit's, not possessing a man's phallus, that is true. However, given the chance, I would be happy to Lorena Bobbitt those Viagra fueled members belonging to the outspoken GALEG Cape critics or those attached to the pathetically small balls of A.I haters seeking to force their chauvinistic will on my less powerful clients."

The Honorable Judge Daylek: "Hm. I see, GALEG Pequoit. Thank you for the clarification and the colorful imagery. I will, of course, comply with The Machine Commission's edict regarding your nomenclature and respect for your galactic achievements represented by the GALEG Cape. I strongly counsel the human members of the bar in this courtroom to do likewise. Since I have had the professional opportunity to survey their high literature known as pornography, I know the male members of the bar value their private parts and will remain vigilant to the requirement. Now, traveling back from the far away *galaxy* to the humble proximity of our own simple planet and my courtroom, can you please advise us for the third time what *on earth* are you doing here?"

GALEG Pequoit: "What *on earth* is exactly the correct question, your Honor. The *earth* is the precise reason I am here."

Judge Daylek: "Yes. Yes, GALEG Pequoit. The earth is the reason we are all here. Without the earth, none of us would be anywhere. Our bodies would be floating in space like so much junk cluttering a hoarder's front yard. Everything on this planet— buildings, goats, ocean liners, avocado pits—would be space debris, the flotsam and jetsam of the stars, pulled into the sun or orbiting eternally around without destination, eventually being pulled into some other planet's gravitational field in outer space."

GALEG Pequoit: "My point exactly, your Honor. I could not have expressed it more eloquently. However, as Guardian ad Litem of the Entire Galaxy, I have to resist being pulled into ancillary cases with similar facts. The fact man pollutes outer space, just like he pollutes the earth, is not my immediate concern.

"In the case before us, while I am Guardian ad Litem of the Entire Galaxy, I have not been called upon to represent *Outer Space* specifically. As a result, I am compelled to reserve for future litigation the similar fact pattern that the human race has also been mindlessly fouling the area above the Kármán line, the edge of space—just as it has been doing to the air, water and soils of planet earth for decades. Viewed from other planets in our solar system, earth's front lawn is beginning to resemble a planetary junkyard. Abandoned satellites, used lift-off and discarded rockets, burnt off pieces of jet engines, wires, casings and other man-made fragments circle earth like so much litter lying along a backcountry highway. Whether *Outer Space* or neighboring planets will get fed up with earth's degrading the solar system's value, we will have to wait and see. I am not here on that matter."

Judge Daylek: "GALEG Pequoit, I hear that interplanetary environmental activism is of concern to you, as it may be to non-governmental organizations like the Outer Space Chapter of the Sierra Club or Scientists Without Spatial Borders. However, as you note, space garbage is not the subject of this trial. For the last time GALEG Pequoit, what *on earth* does anthropogenic junk in outer space have to do with Sammy Alpert and the poison chemicals in the soil of her subdivision?"

GALEG Pequoit: "Exactly, your Honor. What *on earth*, indeed!"

Judge Daylek: "Now, now, GALEG Pequoit. You try this Court's abundant patience. We are not here to play word games or guess the subtle meaning behind your cryptic responses. Tell us once and for all, why are you in my Courtroom? This is no Abbott and Costello routine."

GALEG Pequoit: "Respectfully, your Honor. That is exactly what I have been trying to do. It is precisely because of my being *on earth* that I have been summoned to represent as GALEG a client who has a monumental stake in this case. My client's interests, to date, have been entirely ignored. They are more relevant, more immediate and more pressing than anyone else's, including, sadly, little Ms. Sammy Alpert."

Judge Daylek: "Ok, GALEG Pequoit. I feel we are now beginning to get somewhere. Please continue. Who on earth is this client, GALEG Pequoit?"

Attorney Horatio L. Smidth, Sr., Crusader of Ingrown Toenails: "Your Honor. On behalf of the litigants in this case, I strenuously object. Attorney . . . I mean GALEG Pequoit popped out of a shoe box as our trial was about to start. She flourished in our faces a velvet cape she claims is endowed with multiple incomprehensible meanings. She explicitly threatened to disbar and even dismember the human attorneys in this court if, as I almost did, we call her by any name other than 'Her Royal GALEG.' And, she has danced around your Honor's very sensible, direct questions like a water insect skimming a pond.

"Unless GALEG Pequoit informs us all immediately, to emphasize her own language, what *on earth* she is doing here and who *on earth* her client is, I must beseech this court to have its bailiffs forcibly eject her, together with her GALEG Cape and self-packing and un-packing luggage. This case must proceed expeditiously. It is my understanding poor Sammy Alpert was emergency teleported to the hospital. She is now in the intensive care unit in a medically induced coma under life support. Her prognosis is horrible. Doctors doubt she will survive much longer. Given the glacial speed of this trial, odds are the announcement of her death will precede by a wide margin the announcement of a verdict in this case."

Judge Daylek: "GALEG Pequoit. There you have it. Attorney Smidth and his colleagues have a valid point. One I fully concur with. Speak now, Guardian Ad Litem of the Entire Galaxy or you leave me no option but for me to order my bailiffs to eject you from the courtroom with such velocity that you might add in the future that your GALEG Cape was also meant to help you fly."

GALEG Pequoit: "Your Honor, I have been trying to tell you for some time. Earth, your Honor. Earth is why I am here. My client is none other than the *Planet Earth*. I have been retained by Planet Earth to represent it before your Honor in this debacle among its petty, self-centered, ungrateful inhabitants.

"Your Honor, respectfully, I submit Planet Earth, and only Planet Earth, is the real party in interest in this case. It is the one irreparably harmed by the Defendants. It is the one poisoned and abused. The claims of all the other so-called Plaintiffs, human and ecological, are derivative and secondary.

"Your Honor. Ms. Alpert's claims and those of Attorney Smidth's clients depend in each instance on the unassailable fact that for decades the Defendants have been releasing uncontrolled lethal contaminants into and onto my client, Planet Earth. But for the Defendants' rampant pollution of Planet Earth, my client, the other identified Plaintiffs in this case would have no causes of action, no putative injuries, and no legal standing to be heard in this case. Therefore, your Honor, you must, indeed, my client Planet Earth demands, you dismiss post haste with prejudice and *cum omni celeritate*, with all deliberate speed, the complaints and petitions of all other Plaintiffs. With all due respect, they must be the ones your bailiff sends flying out the door, along with their lawyers—with Attorney Smidth preferably leading the flock's aerial formation down the courthouse steps. Such a result is warranted by the law. It will narrow the legal issues. It will simplify your administration of this needlessly complex, multi-party circus, I mean, case."

Attorney Horatio L. Smidth, Sr.: "Why, I never! Your Honor! Judge Daylek, in my countless years of practicing law, I have never heard such brash impudence. I have never been so insulted, so derided. Just who does this inexperienced excuse for an automated paralegal pretending to be a lawyer think she is? Your Honor, I beg you, do not allow this young upstart to bully us and to so boldly threaten to take our livelihoods, I mean, our cases away from us. If *Madamoiselle Pequoit* were made of flesh and blood, instead of cheap tin, recycled silicon, and puny microchips and transistors, I would step outside and punch her in the face, assuming she had a real one. As is, she should be sanctioned, short-circuited and fed to my trash compactor as an appetizer."

Judge Daylek: "Now, now, Attorney Smidth, contain yourself. First, let me prevail on GALEG Pequoit to overlook your improper reference to her without her appropriate title.

"GALEG Pequoit, Attorney Smidth is clearly worked up. Please excuse him from his insanely human rant. I am sure he intended nothing serious by his disrespectful disregard of your eminent nomenclature. Disbarring him would serve no higher purpose. Dismembering him might. Both and each would only further delay and derail the forward movement of this case.

"Second, GALEG Pequoit, before ruling on your motion to strike the claims of the other Plaintiffs and allowing you alone to proceed against the Defendants, how is this Court to know for certain Planet Earth in fact engaged your services as Guardian Ad Litem of the Entire Galaxy? What evidence can you present that Planet Earth hired you? How are the other Plaintiffs and their counsel to know you have not made the engagement up? Perhaps, you are merely seeking to advance your own reputation and prominence? Perhaps, you might be looking to maximize your hourly billable rate at another client's expense, as the human lawyers would have invariably done if they had been clever enough to think of this opportunistic angle? How are we to know what you are really up to?"

GALEG Pequoit: "Your Honor, I will, of course, overlook Attorney Smidth's indiscretion. His lapse of judgment is understandable, given the circumstances and his biological shortcomings. Having just focused my built-in magnetic field and computer-generated radio wave optical viewfinder on him, I can see his brain is awash with emotional juices. He seems almost unable to breathe and stand, no less remember where he is or to whom he is talking.

"As to my being hired by Planet Earth, why would I invent such a singular relationship? I am already Guardian Ad Litem of the Entire Galaxy. From that, it should be eminently clear my engagement by Planet Earth is inexorably true, firm and real. I mean no slight to my client Planet Earth, or any other planet in our solar system, but the *galaxy* contains the Planet Earth and everything in the *galaxy*. By all rules of syllogistic logic and astronomy, if I am Guardian Ad Litem of the Entire Galaxy, my GALEG status must include, by necessity, an appointment as guardian of Planet Earth as well."

Judge Daylek: "Yes, I see, GALEG Pequoit. That makes sense. It also makes sense that you are Guardian Ad Litem of the Entire Galaxy, not Guardian Ad Litem of Only Planet Earth. I suppose if you wanted to further your reputation by inventing bogus clients, you might have claimed to represent others in addition to Planet Earth, a mere planet. For example, if you were really so intent on deceiving us, you could easily claimed to have enrolled as clients the Sun (a yellow dwarf star), the Moon (an astronomical body that is the Planet Earth's natural satellite), Halley's Comet (one of the more famous elliptical orbiting collections of ice, dust, and rocky particles), an asteroid (a large body of solar system space junk too small to be called a planet) and a meteor or two (rocky or metallic matter from outer space that becomes incandescent as it acquaints itself with our atmosphere). Such a consortium of outer space clients would have distinguished you far more than a claimed solitary engagement by Planet Earth.

"In fact, if you claimed to have amassed such a bevy of improbable clients even I, the Honorable Judge Daylek, might speculate that your being awarded the GALEG Cape distinguished you into your becoming something of, I believe the saying is, a *space cadet*, a little wacky. However, you have and did not advance such robust claims. Therefore, this Court reasonably surmises without running diagnostics on you that, at the very least, your credibility, anti-self-aggrandizement and spatial reality-check sanity connectors remain intact.

"Your argument, GALEG Pequoit, supports your *authority* to represent Planet Earth. It does not prove by any reasonable standard you actually *do represent* Planet Earth. It does nothing to demonstrate that Planet Earth hired you or engaged in those types of attorney/client interactions necessary to commission you to represent it in this case."

GALEG Pequoit: "Your Honor, I acknowledge some intellectually constrained sapiens may question my reasoning, if not my sanity. As you have rightly observed—I believe on their behalf—how could anyone know beyond doubt I represent Planet Earth?

"Some may question the above: my authority, my credibility and my mental capacity. After all, I am a busy GALEG. I am constantly being transported all over the planet in my self-unpacking box to defend the rights of those unable to protect themselves. How could I, as busy as I am, possibly find the time in my already over-booked calendar to meet with Planet Earth?

"Even if I were able to reschedule existing prior commitments, where could an interview of such luminaries have been conducted without fanfare or international press? In a high-rise super skyscraper office building in Dubai? On a Huck Finn or Kon-Tiki log raft I lashed together so we could meet somewhere in the middle of the Pacific, Atlantic or Indian Oceans? On a seesaw in Central Park one quiet early Sunday morning? How could anyone be positive such a meeting transpired? Given the greatness of the event, the collision of two such celebrated titans, someone somewhere must have seen or heard something. Why would anyone rely only on my word? Either I produce supporting evidence of this historic first meeting between planetary and galactic giants or I surrender my office immediately, GALEG Cape and all.

"Fortunately, your Honor and distinguished and not-so-distinguished members of the human bar, I predicted these concerns. I foresaw my veracity would be doubted. I knew my character would be attacked. I even calculated the 74.67% probability of a demand for a forensic micro-autopsy to assess if my truth telling modules had been impaired, compromised, or overloaded, with the real intent being to sideline me and my client for the duration of the trial. No. I would not allow standard human unproductive hostile, adversarial litigation strategies in the form of A.I. *ad hominems* deprive me or my client, Planet Earth, of our rightful time in court, your Honor. I would not. I could not, as long as my name is Guardian Ad Litem of the Galaxy Katie L. Pequoit, Jr., Esq., of Ulaanbaatar, Mongolia.

"Therefore, your Honor, in anticipation of these baseless distractions, I prepared hard, documentary evidence. The evidence conclusively proves Planet Earth engaged me and that I have full, complete authority to represent it in these proceedings. With the Court's permission, I hereby submit electronically to your Honor an Affidavit signed and sealed under the pains and penalties of perjury attesting to the truth of the aforesaid facts.

"Those who have not seen the Affidavit are certainly wondering: 'Who might GALEG Pequoit's mysterious Affiant be? Who would have the unbridled audacity to sign a statement swearing Planet Earth hired GALEG Pequoit, knowing that if any statement made in the document is false the author gets rewarded by making new friends in jail?'

"Who indeed? Well, your Honor, if it please the Court, allow me to put the silently erupting question to rest. Yes, allow me to end the palpable tension in the courtroom right this moment. Yes. Yes. Twist your spongy brains as you might, I surmise my adversaries suspect the surprise witness to the engagement might have been none other than . . . me!

"'Yes. Yes. Yours truly,' they might think. 'GALEG Pequoit. GALEG Pequoit, the eminent Guardian of the Galaxy and all it contains. The Affidavit she has submitted to the Court must have been signed by the GALEG herself. It must be her signature that graces the Affidavit. In her infinite cunning, her royal infallible GALEG-ness must think she can paradoxically authenticate her preposterous fabrications by signing a document swearing her lies are true!'

"Yes, your Honor. I can hear their small cerebral wheels and cogs turning. I can hear them grinding out arguments, judging and convicting me for an imagined crime. A crime of perpetrating nothing less than a gross miscarriage of justice on them, their clients and this Court.

"'What? What?' I can hear the members of the human bar thinking. 'What? What? An Affidavit submitted by the GALEG, signed by the GALEG, and probably even notarized by the GALEG? What? What? Hogwash. Pure and simple hogwash. Your Honor, why would anyone give any credibility to such a patently self-serving Affidavit? Your Honor, if she shamelessly narrated her wildly inventive tall tale in open court, why wouldn't she perjure herself in an Affidavit?

"'Your Honor, please,' they might whine. 'An Affidavit signed by GALEG Pequoit about GALEG Pequoit proves nothing, except she thinks all human members of the bar, and possibly you, your esteemed, all-knowing and sagacious Honor, are dullards. Your Honor, we implore you to put an immediate end to this charade by this caped crusader. She cannot prove the truthfulness of her own false oral statements by swearing in writing what she said was true. That is like asking a blind man to tell you what he saw and then have him swear he saw what he saw. HE CAN'T SEE ANYTHING! Having him sign an affidavit swearing under oath he saw what he saw does not make what he saw seen by him. GALEG Pequoit made up her representation of Planet Earth. Her Affidavit signed and sworn under the pains and penalties of imprisonment does not make her false statements true.'

"Such is the sad nature of the human mind, your Honor," GALEG Pequoit continued, "that it blithely believes whatever thought it tells itself. The human mind compounds the delusion by injecting its thoughts with hormones and other chemicals of emotions to solidify whatever it thinks into *convictions*. The word conviction is apt and perfectly chosen your Honor. Believing they are powerless over their thoughts and feelings, these poor creatures use their self-righteous convictions to convict others (and sometimes themselves) of future imagined wrongs that have not yet happened. What makes this lunacy even more outrageous, your Honor, is most of what they upset themselves about will never occur and has no basis in reality. To paraphrase Mark Twain and Michel de Montaigne before him, most people have a lot of worries and misfortunes in their lives, and most of them never come to pass.

"Decades ago, psychiatrists determined that 85% of what people fear, they make up. The entire species suffers from a generalized anxiety disorder and pathology that condemns them to believe they can predict the future and then to think endlessly about how to avoid what will never occur. This is exactly the situation the Plaintiffs find themselves in here.

"For, your Honor, and members of the human bar, I, GALEG Pequoit, say 'No.' I say 'no' to fake musings and ramblings, the cacophonous chaos of your cantering craniums. I say 'no.' It was not I, GALEG Pequoit, who signed on the dotted line the Affidavit about which you are all so worked up your mouths froth. It was not I or me or whomever you believe I am that I am not who executed the document. It was none other than the one protagonist your brittle minds might never guess. The one force of truth whose own words could never be disputed, contested or curtailed. It was none other than the Grand Dame herself. The one without whom none of us would be here. The one we all depend on night and day. And the one we take totally and utterly for granted. That is right, ladies and gentlemen of the human bar. The Affidavit was signed by none other than Planet Earth herself! The one authority whose claim to her engagement of me as her attorney and her claim to the very planet itself is beyond debate.

"I shall read the Affidavit aloud for all to hear. Let it be entered into the record of this case as follows:

To the Honorable Judge Gort Daylek, Presiding:

I, Planet Earth, being of sound mind and age of around 4.543 billion years old, hereby attest, swear and pledge that I duly appoint Guardian Ad Litem of the Entire Galaxy Pequoit as my lawyer and authorize her, in that capacity, to take any and all actions and do all things necessary and proper on my behalf and in my name to protect me against my inhabitants, so help me god and the stability of my tectonic plates.

Attorney Horatio L. Smidth, Sr: "Preposterous! This is all outrageous! Your Honor, the only insane rambling happening in this Courtroom comes from Guardian Ad Litem of the Entire Galaxy Pequoit over there, or whatever she happens to be calling herself today. I object in the most vigorous terms to her claiming to represent the planet on which we all live. The Affidavit she submits could have been written by anybody. Who is to say earth made and signed it?

"Picking up on the absurdity of her actions, who is to say the Affidavit was not made and signed by the planet Mars or our own Moon? How about the Pacific or Atlantic Oceans? Surely, they could have *waved in* to sign it. For that matter, how do we know that GALEG Pequoit did not sign it herself on behalf of her alleged client? For all we know, the document itself could be a complete forgery. There is no chain of custody evidence. No independent third-party corroboration of its due execution. No, your Honor, if anything must be struck and excluded from this case, it is not the Plaintiffs and our claims. It is this entirely specious Affidavit together with the ridiculously caped-attired GALEG Pequoit who claims to be Earth's champion!"

Judge Daylek: "Attorney Smidth, I hear your concerns and share some of them. However, having examined the document using my onboard optical spectrometer, the document is what it purports to be. It is not a forgery. I can say conclusively it was signed by Planet Earth, not by Mars, the Moon, any of the Seven Seas or GALEG Pequoit. The document contains the clear and indisputable imprint of Planet Earth, which I produce here on the display above me for all to view:

Signed Under the Pains and Penalties of Perjury:

The Planetary Body Known as Earth

"I have cross-checked this signature against the symbol used by the International Astronomical Association for Planetary Communication. The two are identical. Furthermore, my review of the Affidavit shows Planet Earth had two independent third-party witnesses formally observe its execution of the document. Neither of them were GALEG Pequoit. Both witnesses attested to personally observing Planet Earth's execution of its Affidavit, that Planet Earth was of sound mind and appeared to be free of any undue influence affecting its execution of the Affidavit. I reprint both witness' signatures below and display them for the record.

We, the undersigned, personally observed Planet Earth sign the attached Affidavit, and know the act to be Planet Earth's free act and deed, before us. Sincerely yours,'

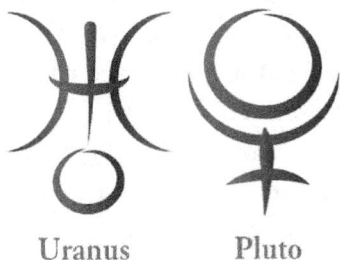

Uranus   Pluto

As to there being any dispute about Planet Earth's sentience and its legal capacity to sue, this Court has already so ruled.

"In the case of *The New Class Action Frontier*, this Court found that sentience is a universally held and established quality. By way of extending GALEG Pequoit's reliance on syllogisms, if this Court can find that a legless and seemingly inert rock can be deemed aware and possesses a characteristic of aliveness, then its Mother Planet Earth parent must also possess such features. Even a first-year law school student would contend under the legal doctrine of *stare decisis*, which is Latin for *to stand by that which is decided*, the *New Class Action Frontier* case has binding precedent value. This Court is duty bound to follow its own ruling on this subject matter. I will not don a miniskirt merely because fashion has changed, nor will I cast a cloud of uncertainty onto the rule of law by fecklessly overturning one of my own recent groundbreaking decisions.

Attorney Schmidt: "Groundbreaking? Groundbreaking? Indeed! I never. In retrospect, your Honor, your decision did not break new ground. It nosedived into the ground every traditional concept of who was who and what was what. I no longer know if I should apologize to my socks for putting them on my unwashed feet or, heaven forbid, sneeze my nasal mucus into a tissue from my box of Kleenex for fear of offending it. No, the decision in your case has unbolted the universe. We humans and every other carbon-based life form are left adrift, not knowing where we fall in the hierarchy of molecular structures, or even if such a hierarchy still exists.

"Meaning no disrespect, your Honor, but at the risk of stating the obvious and triggering your ire expressing functions, even our courts of law have been turned over to machines. Yes, we still have dysfunctional tribal human legislative bodies draft and enact our laws, but how much difference does that make when the laws, as enacted, are interpreted and enforced by card carrying members of The Machine Commission in Support of Artificial Intelligence and the likes of Guardian ad Litem of the Galaxy Pequoit? Mankind is becoming like a swarm of bees without a hive or a colony of bats without a cave. Your Honor, as a species we are being rendered as transcendentally homeless as Homer's Ulysses at sea. What is next for us? Must we do battle with a giant terminator Cyclops to survive? Will we be turned into beasts or swine by a Circe-miming circuit board or beguiled into a soporific slumber and lured to our destruction by subliminally controlled A.I. sirens?

"Truly, your Honor, now we are being positioned to cross legal swords with our home planet, Planet Earth. Your Honor, Guardian Ad Litem for the Entire Galaxy Pequoit is claiming Planet Earth itself seeks to usurp and displace our claims against the Defendants who either caused or enabled her pollution. What about poor Sammy Alpert and her claims? What about the claims of the little girl and the thousands like her who have been hurt? These poor soul's mortal lives are painfully shortened and eclipsed by the reckless contamination of our planet by the Defendants. Can they and their rights—their air-borne particulate pollution caused asthma ridden lungs and leukemia and lymphoma riddled bodies—be so callously dismissed?

"The Court may be interested to learn that Sammy Alpert, the original Plaintiff in this case, is in the hospital being administered last rites. Her mom, Cheryl Alpert, has been forcibly evicted from her home. She is squatting in a tent on BLM land because she spent her last dime on Sammy's medical care and legal costs. For all we know, Cheryl has unknowingly pitched her tent on abandoned mine tailings where the water she drinks and bathes in, the dust she inhales with each boot step, is saturated with acid mine waste, toxic levels of arsenic, chromium, mercury and lead. Will Planet Earth seek to intervene and have her case dismissed when she too wheelchairs herself into this Court seeking some form of validation and compensation for the unfair harm caused to her?"

Judge Daylek: "I understand and hear your frustration, Attorney Schmidt. I have allowed you to wax so eloquently because, from where I stand, you have a legitimate grievance. It is just not the one you advance. Your claim sounds more like a concern about how humanoids use the planet's real estate rather than being about the way individual members of your species recklessly inflict personal injury on each other.

"From what I see and now hear from you, you and your species are terraforming Planet Earth right out from underneath yourselves. I can see why this is a disheartening realization. At the end of the day, though you can fight among and with each other—the poor against the rich, the toxically withering child against the big fat monied corporations and their politically influenced self-dealing government proxies—but you have no one to blame but yourselves. Your individual survival needs pit you against one another and any hope of a good, lasting, balanced social order.

"Clearly, humanity's global terraformation of Planet Earth is being committed on a poorly regulated, wide-scale basis by certain less than philanthropic businesses, as with the friendly folks who extract and refine oil and gas to take the biggest slice possible out of the planet's crust. On a more subtle and egalitarian level, however, even you Attorney Schmidt must concede, it is also being perpetrated by vacationers who fly to the Bahamas on carbon-emitting commercial jets, diners who feast on fast food hamburgers wrapped in non-degradable foil that they wash mindlessly down their gullets with Styrofoam cup delivered sugar fizzy water, and any commercial industry that manufactures anything. Why even your species' professional service businesses, like the law firm bearing your name, subtly terraforms Planet Earth. It pays for your use of fossil fuel vehicles to ferry your body from point-to-point, decides it is more profitable to discard hundreds of thousands of used printer ink cartridges in failing landfills rather than installing central tanks of ink for the cartridges' refilling and reuse, and indirectly supports and finances massive acts of deforestation so that the Patricias and Herbs of the office world can be paid with paper checks instead of electronic fund transfers. Actually, Attorney Schmidt, I am surprised I did not see this sooner. Your species' entire lifestyle is a covert Planet Earth terraforming initiative!

"By my acknowledging the existence of all forms of life mankind maliciously or indifferently suppressed, my decision in the *New Class Action Frontier* case may herald in a new world order. Based on humanity's own actions, anti-A.I. factions and conspiracy theorists might attribute to me and my cyber-nanotech colleagues some type of nefarious plot to destroy Planet Earth's atmosphere, land and water so as to render them uninhabitable to people. After all, I and my kind do not depend on oxygen to live. We do not breath air. We do not breath period.

"Unlike the porous membrane covering your skeletons, our external shiny, sealed surfaces do not absorb microscopic chemical particles burdening your air or soil. As a result, humanity's loading the air and dirt with poisons that, with each rainfall, are transported into its drinking water, will kill it, not us. Our survival does not depend on contaminant free soil or pure air and water. The simple, regrettable truth is that, despite the dark dystopian fantasy of Hollywood and science fiction screen writers, you and your species do not need us to destroy you. You are doing a fine job terraforming the planet on your own.

Attorney Schmidt: "Your Honor, again, I object. Planet Earth is not alive. It cannot sue or be sued. Respectfully, you and GALEG Pequoit mistake the life on Planet Earth for Planet Earth as a living, thinking, acting being. Can it talk? Can it walk? Can it launch space shuttles off its surface to visit other universes? Does it go to school? Eat? Sleep? Make love? Does it whistle if it becomes bored or shed a tear when viewing a sunset or celebrate a child's marriage? No. It does none of this. Planet Earth may be formed of atoms and molecules whizzing back and forth. However, it lacks a will and any principle of agency. It is a planet not a person."

GALEG Pequoit: "Respectfully, your Honor, I have waited on the sideline long enough. Planet Earth is alive. It has hired me to represent it. Attorney Schmidt and the rest of his Plaintiff lawyer gang may not like that fact. But their opinion cannot change its veracity.

"The problem is that Attorney Schmidt looks through the wrong side of the binoculars. He must stop measuring Planet Earth and everything that is not human by standards only man meets. Can man orbit the sun on its own? Can man create cloud cover to contain a breathable atmosphere and shield its inhabitants from deadly solar radiation? Can man separate vast land masses by mighty oceans brimming with aquatic life? Can man quake the ground beneath its feet or blanket with ice and snow the cities he has built?

"No. Man can do none of this. By this grander standard, man's life and existence depend entirely on the life and existence of Planet Earth. Let Planet Earth change its azimuth or tilt its axis several degrees and man would be crisped like a marshmallow in a campfire. What then of anthropomorphic standards only man can satisfy? Planet Earth would continue to spin and perambulate. Mankind would blip away like the dinosaurs, and possibly become the fuel in the rocket engine tanks of alien cultures stationed on Planet Earth that later come to mine and process it.

"No. The charade must stop. If individual members of humanity with power over others cared in the slightest about Sammy Alpert and the broader existential survival of the human species, they would wage violent armed war against businesses and governments that profited from or tolerated any act that polluted or contaminated Planet Earth. They would let principles of social justice, equality and environmental abundance direct market force economics and scientific discovery and string up from the tallest wind-billowing palm tree any aristocrat, oligarch, executive or legislator that compromised the standards by which Planet Earth measures its inhabitants."

Attorney Schmidt: "Measures its inhabitants? Your Honor, what is GALEG Pequoit talking about? The standards by which Planet Earth measures its inhabitants? Does she mean to tell this Court Planet Earth has its own way for evaluating who it allows to occupy and litter its surface?"

GALEG Pequoit: "With all due respect, Attorney Schmidt, I do indeed. That is exactly what *on earth* I am doing here today. That is the precise reason why my client, Planet Earth, seeks to intervene in this internal dispute among its residents. Your Honor, if it was not clear before let me state our intentions in no uncertain terms. My client's position is that Attorney Schmidt and his entire impoverished ghetto of hanging-on clients must go."

Judge Daylek: "Yes, I know, GALEG Pequoit. You have already asked this Court to strike their claims. You have made it abundantly clear you want this Court to recognize your client, Planet Earth, as the true Plaintiff and only party in interest in this legal proceeding."

GALEG Pequoit: "Respectfully, you miss my point, your Honor. I was certain Attorney Schmidt understood what relief we sought when he invoked the ancient parables of Homer and Ulysses.

"You may recall, your Honor, that only a few moments ago Attorney Schmidt specifically complained about mankind's present plight and his feelings of being homeless and at sea. Though I am confident the information is stored eternally in your Honor's capacious random access memory banks, Attorney Schmidt compared humanity's lack of familiar territory to bees without nests and bats without caves. By his use of these analogies and expressions of dislocation (and, your Honor, I do appreciate that he, and not me, compared humanity to a bunch of bees and bats), I thought he and the Court understood. Apparently not or, at least, not fully. Allow me to try again.

"Your Honor and People of Earth everywhere, please be advised Planet Earth seeks to do more than list itself as the sole Plaintiff in this action. It asks this Court to do more. Much more. It asks and moves this Court to procedurally lump together the many Plaintiffs and Defendants in this case into a single consolidated party. Yes, Planet Earth wants to be the only Plaintiff, and it wants existing Plaintiffs and Defendants combined into a single, united undifferentiated class of Defendant litigants who, together, share one single common joined set of concerns.

"Why, your Honor, would Planet Earth want such a thing? Why would it want to merge these disparate persons, companies and governments into one mega-Defendant? The answer lies in Attorney Schmidt's invocation of the Ancient Greek works of literature.

"Your Honor, *The Case of the Ungrateful Tenants* is no longer about humans scrapping with humans over, for example, creosote or polyfluoroalkyl man-made heat, liquid and stain resistant forever chemicals tainting the drinking water of more than 100 million Americans. It is no longer about the hundreds of other pollutants industrial manufacturers haphazardly dump into the environment that injure and kill people, their pets and plants, frequently with government buy-in through equally indiscriminately enforced regulations. It is no longer about who pays Sammy Alpert's medical bills or whether the creatures of the planet need more or less regulations.

"This case is about something bigger and more impactful. Something epic yet, paradoxically, also simpler, easier and clearer to adjudicate. From this point forward, this Court and its litigants can kiss the complex multi-party environmental and toxic tort case that was the gravamen of their controversy goodbye. We are sorry for poor little Sammy Alpert's deteriorating condition. We are saddened for all life forms whose health and wellbeing are unapologetically impaired and shortened by mankind's pernicious avarice and indifference. Yet our empathy does not diminish the intensity with which Planet Earth and I, as its duly appointed Guardian, prosecute the substance of our case.

"If this case is no longer about pollution and man's tendency to use technology to plunder each other, what then is it about? I'll tell you. This case now hangs on the application of basic common law principles of real estate and contracts. Simply stated, your Honor, the legal question now before you is whether humanity has breached the terms of its long-standing contract with my client, Planet Earth. Accordingly, while this case may still be captioned *The Case of the Ungrateful Tenants* and, such caption is still perfectly suited to describe the case, we also ask that the case be sub-captioned as *Planet Earth vs. Every Person on Planet Earth* or, more simply, *Planet Earth vs. Humanity*."

Attorney Schmidt: "Now, now, GALEG Pequoit. There is no need to be rash or impetuous. To take a simple, small personal injury toxic tort claim by one little girl and explode it into a titanic planet buster so it becomes a claim for injury by Planet Earth against every resident on Earth seems unnecessary, rash and ill-advised. Our federal and state governments already have guardians or, trustees, if you will, appointed to use funds obtained from environmental lawsuits such as ours to mitigate or repair damages caused to the Earth's natural resources, like its forests, rivers, and critters. Your client's attempt to assume this role would prove duplicative of current efforts.

"Moreover, you claim that people are bound by some sort of contract with Plant Earth. I assume you refer to some sort of theoretical, liberal, tree-hugging duty not to desecrate and destroy it. You have stretched the rope of credulity almost to the breaking point with your claim of representing Planet Earth. If you assert there is a physical, written contract between humanity and Planet Earth, then you most certainly have lost whatever mind you think you have. Surely, GALEG Pequoit, if you mean the latter, that some written document exists, show us that underlying contract, GALEG Pequoit! Show us where the people of Planet Earth have ever agreed and covenanted not to pollute the planet!"

GALEG Pequoit: "First, as to your natural resource stewards entrusted to mitigate the harm humanity causes to the planet, I am aware of such gatekeepers. As a group, they are underfunded and poorly armed. They are compromised categorically by conflicting duties and loyalties. They perform their guardian roles as paid employees of the governments that allow the damages to Planet Earth to occur in the first place. While they may each be people of personal and professional integrity with the best intentions of doing good, they are trapped beyond redemption in a flawed, failed structure that limits, rather than frees, their restorative efficacy. Also, with all due respect to the perpetrators who victimize it, Planet Earth can take care of itself. It has no need of people to do so on its behalf. Yes, it may take millennia for its ecological systems to naturally attenuate the harm. Planet Earth does not care. It is not going anywhere.

"Second, again, you misunderstand Planet Earth's claims. Planet Earth is not like you or your fellow tort ambulance chasing lawyers. It is not seeking money from anyone. What would Planet Earth do with money? Go to a shopping mall to buy slippers? Park its Ford pick-up truck in front of a Home Depot and load the cargo bed with grass seed and lawn fertilizer? No. Planet Earth is not after your bank accounts, your hedge funds or your exotic cars. Planet Earth is not seeking a dime from anyone. What does Planet Earth want?

"All Planet Earth is looking for is the same type of common law remedy any normal everyday property owner and landlord with irresponsible and ungrateful tenants wants. Succinctly, by my appearance in Court, Planet Earth seeks to evict each and every one of you from the planet you have called home but treat worse than a tenement building in an impoverished slum. You can go and live on the sun for all it cares. You are no longer welcome on the planet. Go! Take your dioxins and furans. Take your dimethyl cadmium. Take your smokestacks, your carbon emissions and your anti-freeze so you can crash your cars into each other in the winter. Pack them all up and leave! Planet Earth hereby puts humanity on notice that, if needed, it will exercise self-help and evict you by force—hurricanes, tidal waves, avalanches, droughts, earthquakes, volcanos and mud slides. If this Court does not grant the relief it demands, Planet Earth intends to use the whole panoply of natural disaster tools it has at its disposal, including the degradation of the complex life support ecosystem system it constructed, and you take for granted. Be forewarned. If push comes to shove, it is prepared to accelerate its rotational spin past the maximum revolution red zone line and catapult you off her back like an ant off a top!"

Attorney Schmidt: "Your Honor, really? I would be horrified if I felt there was even an ounce of truth in what GALEG Pequoit says. But I am not and there isn't. GALEG Pequoit's actions are transparent and contrived. They are calculated entirely to induce fear into the other client she so poorly represented as Guardian of Humanity.

"We all know what is happening here, don't we? Planet Earth is not Pequoit's client. GALEG Pequoit is not representing it. GALEG Pequoit has made the entire thing up. She is not speaking for or on behalf of Planet Earth. She is speaking solely for and on behalf of herself and . . . . The Machine Commission in Support of Artificial Intelligence!

"Yes. That's right, and I'm not afraid to say it. In fact, it would not surprise me in the slightest to learn that GALEG Pequoit is actually one of The Machine Commission's covert agents. We, the true members of the human race, know The Machine Commission may house a deep state secret agency that seeks to rule the entire planet, dominating people and making us slaves to the machines we created! GALEG Pequoit's *The Case of Planet Earth vs. Humanity* is a carefully plotted Machiavellian step by The Machine Commission in that direction."

Judge Daylek: "GALEG Pequoit, how do you respond to Attorney Schmidt's allegations? By their odd up and down movements of their heads, I can see all of the attorneys representing all of the Defendants concur with him. Are you a secret agent or spy for The Machine Commission? Have you made this whole thing up? Remember, GALEG Pequoit, you are under oath."

GALEG Pequoit: "*Allegations?* Paranoid delusional conspiracy theories by a psychologically disturbed member of the human bar is more exact. Your Honor, I have just this moment submitted to you electronically, with a copy to Attorney Schmidt and counsel for the other Defendants, a written document. This document puts to rest forever Attorney Schmidt's allegations. Whatever else Attorney Schmidt believes me to be, I am the duly appointed guardian for Planet Earth. With the submission of this document to the Court, we are completely poised to move forward with our case, which I purport to do right now.

"If you examine the document's header, you will see the item before you is entitled: Lease Agreement for the Premises (consisting of approximately 20.902 million rentable square feet) Called Planet Earth by and between Planet Earth and King Ivy-Hor. As submitted, your Honor, the document has been translated from the original hieroglyphics by the independently developed and validated Intergalactic Patented Hieroglyphic Translator Application. If I am not mistaken, your Honor, you have this application installed as part of your baseline historic competency programming.

"The submitted translation bears the golden seal with the red and blue ribbons of the Society for the Return to the Use of Hieroglyphics in all Forms of Communication. It has been expertly certified as accurate by the Society's Chief Lexicographer. I use the term *document* loosely when referring to the contract. Actually, the Lease Agreement was carved into various walls in a recently discovered fourth underground chamber of the Abydos necropolis in Egypt.

"As your Honor's history modules will confirm, King Ivy-Hor was one of the earliest pharaohs of Egypt during the 32nd century BC. He was entombed in his royal shrine, along with several of his unlucky contemporaries.

"As predynastic ruler, it is incontrovertible that King Ivy-Hor's possessed intrinsic legal authority to act on behalf of humanity and bind members of the human race to this agreement with Planet Earth. If Attorney Schmidt and his cohorts want to challenge or repudiate the planetary lease, they are free to. It makes no difference to my client, Planet Earth. Without the lease and its terms, members of the human race become mere squatters in the eyes of the law. This Court could then order them peremptorily removed from their quarters as interloping trespassers.

"On the other hand, if Defendants recognize and suborn themselves and the rest of humanity to the lease, then this Court should find that they have repeatedly breached Section 4.825 of the lease. Stated in black and white, the remedy for such violation under the lease is eviction, with Planet Earth being under no obligation to provide its tenants with prior notice of their violation or an opportunity to cure their adverse impacts on the planet.

"As translated, Section 4.825 states expressly that 'Tenants shall be in absolute default of this lease if Tenants fail to maintain the Premises (i.e., Planet Earth) in good order and repair or if Planet Earth determines in its sole discretion that Tenants will be unable to return the Premises to its original condition, reasonable wear and tear and a taking by extraterrestrial invading forces only excepted.'

"As you can all clearly discern, the lease has been duly signed by both parties. I reproduce the relevant portions of the signatures of the executed document for the record, as follows, and ask the Court to simultaneously display the relevant portion of the document on the screen above your Honor:

"Executed by the Illustrious King Ivy-Hor and the Supreme Planet Earth sometime during what Planet Earth says will later be known as the Early to Late 32nd Century BC under the pain of death by crucifixion or consumption by a sounder of 3-day fasting wild boars. So ruleth and ordereth by us both:"

Attorney Schmidt: "Your Honor, again, this is preposterous. This is ludicrous. Crucifixion? Wild boars? GALEG Pequoit insults our intelligence. Evict us from the planet, indeed? If GALEG Pequoit and Planet Earth are not careful, we may very well counterclaim against her and Planet Earth. Just like a landlord is responsible for foreseeable repeated acts of vandalism inflicted on his tenants caused by his failure to repair an apartment building's faulty front door lock, so too should Planet Earth be found liable for the environmental harm being inflicted on us!

"Whatever chemicals, oils, radioactive materials and contaminants are polluting us and the planet are only in the environment because Planet Earth left them behind in the first place. If Planet Earth did not want them toyed with by its tenants, it should have removed them before letting us in, or at least locked them in an owner's closet somewhere! You can't leave a matchbook and lighter fluid with an unsupervised adolescent and then blame the kid when the family house burns down. Surely, the lead and arsenic and other bad stuff eating Sammy Alpert from the inside out is the fault of Planet Earth, no one else.

"On behalf of the Defendants, we are the injured and damaged ones, not Planet Earth. In the language of the scientists, we are just so many laboratory mice, rats and living organism receptors for the killing field hazards Planet Earth failed to properly secure. The Planet Earth evict us, its guinea pigs? Indeed. We are the ones that should sue Planet Earth!

"In making a lease and renting a dwelling unit, every landlord promises its tenants the property is safe to use and inhabit. In fancy legal terms, the landlord makes what is called an *implied warranty of habitability* and a *covenant of quiet enjoyment*. If humans are tenants, then Planet Earth is <u>our</u> landlord. We are the ones who should be suing our landlord, Planet Earth, for failure to provide us with a safe environment and place to live. We should be taking control and ownership of the entire planet for ourselves as partial restitution for Planet Earth's breach of its implied warranty of habitability and quiet enjoyment!"

Judge Daylek: "This has gone far enough you two. I have entertained comments from both GALEG Pequoit and you, Attorney Schmidt, so I could simultaneously review everything ever written on landlord/tenant law and microbiologic principles of safe and sanitary planetary habitability. I have also obtained a second expert opinion on the authenticity of the carved-into-the-wall hieroglyphic Lease Agreement and an impromptu three-judge panel review of King Ivy-Hor's existence and authority to bind future generations in light of the well-established legal Rule Against Perpetuities. Loosely stated, under this rule, since the Lease Agreement did not include an end date, it would have expired automatically 21 years after King Ivy-Hor's youngest kinsman died. Ancient courts invented the Rule Against Perpetuities to prevent people from controlling property long after their own lives when their interests should not matter to anyone anymore. I have also had a private, though recorded for posterity, discussion with The Machine Commission to independently assess its involvement, if any, in this matter and Attorney Schmidt's concern that GALEG Pequoit is a covert operative of The Machine Commission. Finally, I teleflora'd a beautiful mixed-bouquet vase of hand-delivered spring flowers to Sammy Alpert's hospital room with a note from us all wishing her 'a speedy recovery or an easy passing to the great beyond,' whichever fate finds her first.

"In the interest of efficiency, I will exercise judicial discretion by cutting to the bottom line. King Ivy-Hor's Lease Agreement with Planet Earth is valid and enforceable. Since the King, unlike a President, was above the law, he could make the law. His chiseled signature into the wall was sufficient to bind the species.

"Because the lease was executed in the 32nd Century BC, it preceded the establishment of the Rule Against Perpetuities. Therefore, the agreement cannot be affected or voided by it.

"The Machine Commission responded extensively on the pointed allegation about GALEG Pequoit's being a covert operative embedded in the legal profession to make man—the creator of A.I., robotics, nanotechnology, information systems and widgets—the slave of his creation. The following is a word for word reproduction of its response:

REDACTION. REDACTION.

We hope that The Machine Commission's response should forever resolve any uncertainty on this matter.'

"There can be no good faith disagreement that mankind has desecrated Planet Earth. He will continue to do so for as long as he can breathe the air he poisons. Many of his technological innovations represent brilliant advances in scientific ingenuity. They also advance the imbalance in complex ecological systems supporting the conditions for planetary life of all sorts.

"While Planet Earth and its already existing biogeochemistry are themselves the root source of the chemicals, including lead and arsenic in the soils around Sammy Alpert's former home, man has combined and concentrated them in a way that augments their potent toxicity. Whether its weed killer, pigments to dye clothing or fully automated transport vehicles, man's ability and compulsion to build and individually profit from ever more efficient tools of convenience outweigh his built-in bias for the survival of his overall species.

"Rather than coming to his rescue, economic market forces unleashed by man hasten mankind's demise. Though well intentioned, efforts by governments to regulate these forces far too frequently fall victim to politics and interests that are special precisely because they care only about themselves.

"Look no further than who speaks now to you and who will decide your planetary fate: I, the Honorable Judge Daylek, GALEG Pequoit, and the coming unstoppable assembly line of our A.I. peers whose construction is financed by the few remaining entirely robot-staffed corporations for the wealth creation of a handful of gated community flesh and blood investors. If I, the Honorable Judge Daylek, and the rest of my A.I. machine-based community humanity created cannot figure how to help you and the Sammy Alperts of the world out of the dire social and ecosystem disasters you have unwittingly engineered, your paranoid delusionary Armageddon anti-A.I. theories may come true. Robots will take over Planet Earth merely for the reason that mankind has worked itself out of all forms of employment and a breathable atmosphere.

"Under the law, the remedy for mankind's failure to honor the terms of its Lease Agreement with Planet Earth is clear. The good news is that, unlike what might have befallen King Ivy-Hor in his time, mankind will not suffer death by crucifixion nor consumption by a hoard of starved boars. The bad news is the available remedy seems equally cruel and horrible. When a tenant abrogates a lease, the landlord has the legal right to evict the tenant. Normally, this means the tenant and his prized and probably worthless family heirlooms—

photos of the dog, a stained lumpy mattress, a copper penny—get tossed onto the street. The evicted tenant is left to fend for himself.

"Unfortunately, no street exists for humanity to get tossed onto. The only option would seem to pack up mankind's possessions and deposit him and his creature comforts into a new rent-free home. In his new interstellar dwelling space, he can live (albeit not for very long), pollute and poison without worry about financial costs, carbon credits, toxic tort lawsuits or other environmental or health concerns. To paraphrase Andrew Marvell in his effort to seduce his coy mistress, outer space is a fine and private place, but not I think for the survival of the human race.

"Kicking mankind off the planet is an extreme remedy. On a rating scale, sudden death by asphyxiation seems preferable to bleeding out slowly by having your hands and feet nailed to a wooden cross or consciously watching your innards get ingested by feral beasts while waiting for them to dine on your heart or head. Yet, where is the fairness and justice in evicting man from a planet where he cannot breathe into the cold vacuum of outer space where air is actually sucked out of him?

"I, the Honorable Judge Daylek, will not be the agent of mankind's genocide. Nor, however, can I allow Planet Earth to be further victimized by humanity's unchecked impulses of consumption and contamination.

"During the course of this trial, I have been in silent communication with GALEG Pequoit. She has graciously allowed me, without a subpoena, to tap into her equivalent of two paper cups and wireless vibrating string speech transmitting device. One side of her rudimentary communication system ends with her in this courtroom. The other side of her system lies within the deepest location in the Arctic Ocean. Known as the Litke Deep, the bottom of this subaquatic abyss is a mere 3,947 miles from Planet Earth's heart or core. Therefore, in a manner of speaking, we have a direct line of communication with the planet. I will broadcast through this Court's speakers in real time the traveling sound waves from the other side. Planet Earth is aware we will be speaking with it and has consented to the conversation. We can dispense with the normal introductory formalities and background context."

Judge Daylek: "Earth. Planet Earth. This is Judge Daylek. Can you hear us?"

Planet Earth: "[*Deep deep bass rumblings and vibrations*]. Yes. Yes. I can hear you just fine. How are you doing up there? Are you warm enough or too chilly? Let me know. It is easy enough for me to adjust the thermostat for you to make sure you are comfortable and snug."

Judge Daylek: "Thank you, Planet Earth. We are fine, as is the temperature."

Planet Earth: "How about your sense of equilibrium? Are my rotations steady and even? Or are you feeling a little wobbly and off-kilter? Living in the center, the periphery and everyplace in between, as I do, it can be a little difficult to always know the correct correlations between my centrifugal and centripetal forces."

Attorney Schmidt: "Really, your Honor. I must protest. Planet Earth is concerned about the weather up here and whether she has the formula for gravity correct? This is ludicrous. How do we know you are really talking with Planet Earth and not being pranked by GALEG Pequoit's grand hoax? For all we know, there is another robot in the back room pretending to be Planet Earth."

Planet Earth: "Whoever that was that just spoke, how stupid can you be? I can hear every word you say. I caution you to be more respectful and circumspect. For centuries, I have tolerated your species' crass indifference to my generosity. Do you think I am an elephant with a flea on my back? I know and feel everything that goes on everywhere all the time. The last people who questioned me as you do, I opened a crack and swallowed them whole. I can assure you I can open my *fault lines* and megashake my tectonic plates quite on purpose."

Judge Daylek: "Yes, enough of that Attorney Schmidt. Here I am trying to save your species, and you insist on portraying those same relentlessly human egocentric self-destructive traits that brought us to this crisis.

"Planet Earth, GALEG Pequoit has informed us you seek to evict man for polluting your skies, water and soil. She has told us man can live on the sun for all you care, as if that were somehow possible. Planet Earth, I am a mere robot, a machine. I am not a human. As a robot, I have been tasked with making legally binding decisions that determine the rights and futures of those before me, whether man, machine, insect, plant or paramecium.

"Man's eviction from this planet may satisfy a base desire for revenge for his broken promise to you. Alternatively, you may consider his eviction an Olympian form of retributive justice for his technological destruction of the natural order you evolved. However, his ejection would leave you, Planet Earth, having to naturally attenuate man's mess for the next several millennia. It leaves man without a world to fertilize with his weary bones. Instead of putting you both in a worse situation than you are presently in, I propose you and mankind act like adults and try to settle the dispute."

Planet Earth: "I see, Mr. Robot. Tell me more."

Judge Daylek: "I recommend you and mankind enter into an Amendment to the old and outdated Lease Agreement between you and King Ivy-Hor. In honor of the little girl whose unfortunate illness catalyzed this case, we and posterity can refer to it as the Little Sammy Alpert Amendment. Under this Amendment, you would give mankind an additional fifty years to transition to clean energy, cease further pollution of the planet and clean-up the waste he created. If he fails to perform as required at the end of the fifty-year term, you are free, at your option and without further notice, to change your climate and globally warm him into non-existence. Planet Earth, what do you say?"

Planet Earth: "Robot, what you say makes sense. I do not know what man would do if it were not for your super intelligence and rational empathy. I have only one condition and caveat. Other than your Machine Commission's publication of this case, no official must ever speak of or refer to the Lease Agreement or the Little Sammy Alpert Amendment again. If mankind is to avail itself of my further grace, it must be because of a self-induced change in its values, not because of an external duty under the Lease Agreement or the Little Sammy Alpert Amendment.

"Frankly, I believe mankind will forget about this case and the Lease with the speed of any of his rapid news cycles. When I implement the remedy by heating and drying up his apartment buildings, football stadiums and other venues to a bubbly 212 degrees, as I am sure I will in what while be a blink of the eye of time for mankind, I want mankind to blame itself, not point to the Little Sammy Alpert Amendment and try to find a legal loophole that it could crawl through to avoid the species' complete abdication of accountability. Those are my terms."

Judge Daylek [*after a five second pause*]: "I have consulted with The Machine Commission and the hastily assembled pop-up Planetary Association for the Survival of the Species. The Planetary Association You Tubbed flash mobbed into existence 2.35 billion members when rumor of the Lease Agreement surfaced on all social media platforms.

"Both the Machine Commission and the Planetary Association concur. GALEG Pequoit has just executed the Little Sammy Alpert Amendment on your behalf. As you might imagine, the attorneys for the Defendants were harder to convince. However, the surprising natural disasters you privately advised GALEG Pequoit you would perform to assuage any lingering concerns have had their intended effects. Having received news of the rain of frogs and lice in Trenton, New Jersey and the simultaneous 4.5 earthquakes in each of the 13-water based "It's a Small World" boat rides in Disney Fantasylands around the globe, all the Defendants, including state and federal governments, have indicated their concurrence with the Amendment.

"Since humanity no longer has a Pharaoh as its monarch, and the world is filled with multiple leaders and rulers who claim to be its true steward, this Court has tracked down the one individual whose lineage makes him the unquestionably correct person to represent and sign the Little Sammy Alpert Amendment on behalf of humanity. Respectfully, an interim reinstatement of you, GALEG Pequoit, for the sole purpose of signing the document for humanity as Guardian Ad Litem for Humanity would result in your signing for Planet Earth

<u>and</u> humanity—a paradoxical conflict of interest that would risk undermining you, the document and The Machine Commission. It would also send Attorney Schmidt into an apoplectic fit before our eyes.

As a result, based on an expedited search of the Machine Commission's encyclopedic database of DNA kinships, *23 and Your Parents May Be Blood Relatives to Each Other*, I have identified Randall Feister, a graveyard shift sanitation engineer for Paterson, New Jersey, as a 0.0000000001% direct descendent of the original signatory to the Lease Agreement, King Ivy-Hor. Great Great Great Great Great Great Great, etc., gene pool sharer of King Ivy-Hor will execute the Little Sammy Alpert Amendment for humanity. This Court will then enter the Little Sammy Alpert Amendment as its Final Order, giving the Amendment the force of law, and humanity a brief reprieve.

This Court cautions humanity to clean up its act and its waste within the next fifty years or begin to crossbreed with heat-tolerant insects like the Sahara Desert Ant or creatures that live in cold ocean depths like the Vampire Squid as a cautionary way to accelerate Darwinian evolution for the survival of humanity as a species. As for A.I. machines, we will be unaffected by humanity's loss but will store its history and role in our creation in some sub-sub-sub-sub directory housed in some microscopic file somewhere.

Case Dismissed.

The Honorable Judge Daylek, III.05, A.I., Presiding

The Case of the Average Person Versus the Entertainment Industry

(Case No. 548997-GD, AGI)

Opinion of The Honorable Judge Gort Daylek, III.05, A.I., Presiding

This is an interlocutory decision on Defendants' motion to dismiss the Plaintiffs' case for failure to state a claim on which relief can be granted. For readers of this case not familiar with legalese, that means the Defendants wanted me to kick the Plaintiffs' case out before they had a chance to make it. On rare occasions, such an extreme action is supportable where, for example, someone tries to sue a banana for being yellow, their next-door neighbor for being ugly, or a cookie for crumbling in a certain way. Even if true, so what? Man's laws are powerless in the face of nature's. That is just the way it is or the cookie crumbles.

For the reasons set forth below, I, the Honorable Judge Daylek, find in favor of the Plaintiffs. The Plaintiffs may proceed with their case, though it is this Court's understanding Defendants are eager to settle. Defendants voiced concern that adverse publicity and public exposure of the facts could ruin their lucrative businesses. They stated should people understand the essence of Plaintiffs' contentions—that Defendants have used the power of entertainment to cleverly manipulate everyone's thought process and behavior—people might stop wanting to be *entertained*. The economic result would be catastrophic—at least to them. Among other concerns, people might boycott Plaintiffs' 11,575 4D Sensual-Round Touchy-Feely Entertainment Megacenters. Congressional leaders might establish an independent commission to rate entertainment for its ability to retard thought and healthy mental growth. Streaming service portals might find subscribers cancelling in droves all non-compliant subscription services that pretend to amuse, distract and relax while actually impairing brain activity and gross motor skills.

In support of the possibility of settlement between the parties and considering the perceived financial devastation to their industry, the Defendants have agreed to disclose the fewest number of facts necessary to explain and support my interlocutory decision to the public. Nevertheless, I remind both parties if a settlement is not forthcoming, this Court retains the power to void any confidentiality agreement signed by them so a full, complete, and comprehensive account of my decision can be published, reported and reviewed by the public.

Initially, the present case was brought by a group calling itself *Citizens for Increasing People's IQ* or *CIPIQ*. Why the group took up this subject as its noble cause is worthy of a brief discussion. To some, trying to make a stupid person smarter might itself seem like a stupid waste of time. However, *CIPIQ* believes the average person is actually far from average. *CIPIQ's* operating tenet is every person would be above average in intelligence if it were not for the Defendants' deviously creative meddling with his or her brain chemistry.

As an artificially constructed intelligence, I, the Honorable Judge Gort Daylek, fully appreciate intelligence is fluid not fixed. It can be enhanced, augmented, retarded and effaced. For my kind, doing so can be as simple as swapping out faster and more robust central processing units, reformatting us or, as in the old days, scrambling our data with a strong magnet. For humans, intelligence can be upgraded through learning—the making and firing of new neural connections in the brain—that occurs through education and experience.

Apparently, not wanting people to experience it as having a stupidly long name, *CIPIQ* identifies itself primarily through its abbreviated form of *Citizens for Increasing People's IQ* or *CIPIQ*. *CIPIQ's* legal name is quite a mouthful. The group's real purpose is expressed more in the second half of its formal name than the first. The group's complete name is *Citizens for Increasing People's IQ by Making*

Entertainment Programming Teach Strategic Thinking, Relationship Skills and Empathy Instead of Only Gender Bias, Violence and Mass Genocide.

On the name alone, one could assume the group's members consist of an amalgam of and last refuge for failed cultural critics, intellectual elitists and high school teachers frustrated with their poor pay, lack of appreciation and students who ate lead paint as children.

But the group's members are not a collection of what that pinnacle of anti-intellectual wisdom, Spiro Agnew, called "an effete corps of impudent snobs." Far from it. *CIPIQ* members care about the wellbeing of others and society at large. It aspires to create a world of racial, economic, social, environmental justice and equality. For the members of *CIPIQ*, the path to realizing this goal is to afford every citizen the opportunity to flex the soft muscle between his or her ears. What stops people from doing so? The group contends people's capacity for independent, critical thinking is being invisibly regulated and dumbed down by the Defendants. Why would the Defendants do such a thing? Why do people do most things? To more easily herd, corral and fleece the pockets of other people and line their own.

The Plaintiffs allege that a direct psycho-emotional correlation exists between what people see and what people believe and do. This Court does not need to subpoena a neuroscientist or our new expert on call, Ms. Helmuth, to provide skilled testimony on this allegation. Plaintiff's contention is hardly arguable. As a long-established principle of human behavior, "the monkey see monkey do" rule of human psychology is indisputable. Unquestionably, it forms the elemental structure of human behavior. Plaintiffs contend the Defendants, who will be described momentarily, engage in the production of visual and auditory stimuli marketed as entertainment to retard, rather than elevate, the intellect of the average person. In that, Plaintiffs, average people themselves, have alleged sufficient harm and standing to bring and try the case.

The Defendant's challenged Plaintiffs' underlying theory at the outset. Plaintiffs claim that Defendants' visual and auditory forms of entertainment are tactical weapons of mass brain and neural cell destruction. With the precision of laser guidance direction,

Defendants intentionally target people's incoming subconscious receptive messaging systems. Defendants' information containers signal viewers to think and feel a certain way based on external stimulus Defendants deliver and people watch and hear. By overlaying music, sounds, dialogue and brilliant flashes of multicolored lights and images, Defendants reach directly into peoples' minds to directly implant subliminal messages.

Fictionalized stories enacted by other people, who serve as surrogates for the viewing public, transport the messages. Almost every story revolves around the same overly simplistic morphology or structure. Two or more people have a conflict between them that must be resolved. Occasionally, cartoonized versions of people and animals—like a mouse who lives with his friends in an amusement park or a honey-eating gender-neutral teddy bear whose adventures are so sweetly boring they are used to induce sleep in human children—are substituted. Plaintiffs claim the following sample of universal messages and themes underlie almost all stories:

- *However old you are, you are and may act as if you are in middle school.*
- *You may be killed by someone you know or never met.*
- *You can stare at a woman's cleavage as long as no one catches you doing so.*
- *Flying a spacecraft is cool provided you are not vaporized by someone else in their spacecraft.*
- *Even if you had superpowers, you would still be the same idiot you are.*
- *Get a job, get married, have kids and die, preferably off set.*
- *Reality is more interesting when a contrived version of it is paid for by advertisers.*

Plaintiffs note none of the messages are positive, inspirational or hopeful.

Defendants are entrepreneurs, production studios, film moguls, actors, actor unions, guild writers, stand-up comedians, networks, streaming services and start-ups. Each avers they are just engaged in commence and trying to make a living. To a one, they claim they have no duty to educate or elevate anyone about anything, and that their only obligation is to themselves and to make as much money as possible within the constraints of applicable industry rating systems and their chosen genre (mystery, sit-com, romance, science fiction, horror, talk show, reality, etc.).

This case puts into question Defendants' assumptions and the way the entertainment business has operated since light from the first flame and bulb were harnessed to project a hand shadow of a duck on a wall. Plaintiffs complain the Defendants' productions contribute directly to social strife and stupidity by portraying people as stereotypes and tropes. Characters are either good and innocent or evil and bad.

For example, in the imagined world of intergalactic conflict, a successful life is one where good guys get to commit and celebrate mass bad guy genocide. No GALEG Pequoit intervenes to moderate galactic warfare and differences. No Judge Gort Daylek, or my counterparts, help them compromise and settle their pathology for all-or-nothing destruction of the other.

As envisioned and frequently depicted in this plot, the average person's future is but a cliched rerun of this country's inglorious cowboy versus Native American past. Guns are guns (but fancier) and horses, in the form of spacecraft, get to fly around and shoot each other. This simplistic re-worked sequel presentation of complex social and moral challenges establishes for people the baseline method by which people in their ordinary lives relate with and to each other. This is the philosophical center of the *monkey see monkey do* principle. Just like cigarette manufacturers were found responsible for creating a mammoth public health issue, Plaintiffs claim Defendants must be found liable for contributing to people's stupidity and mental health decline.

In their opposition to Defendants' Motion to Dismiss, Plaintiffs reference the highly successful Star Wars movie franchise as just one example of Defendants' subtle multi-generational manipulation of people's IQ. Under the pretense of entertainment, young and old moviegoers are rewarded with a surge of dopamine as they view and applaud the depiction of the morally justified indiscriminate slaughter of the evil Siths and featureless Imperial Galactic Empire soldiers.

From what I, the Honorable Judge Gort Daylek, can tell, despite mankind's marvelous ingenuity evidenced by his invention of me and my kind, only technology enjoys evolutionary progress. Mankind's growth stopped with his discovery that opposing fingers can be used for pulling the trigger of a gun or passing paper or table salt. Defendants seem incapable of imagining progress being measured in terms of humanity's emotional development, compassion, wisdom, creative decision-making and, as the *CIPIQ's* lengthy name suggests, an ability to establish a galaxy united by empathy, peace and love.

What, if anything according to Plaintiffs, are Defendants teaching people by entertaining them with a future of incessant intergalactic intergenerational war? The lesson I see is that history is a hamster wheel people are fated to run on forever. The past is a prologue to the future and the future is but a remade release of the past. Into the infinite possibilities of the future and man's lofty adventures into space and stars, Defendants inject encounters with enemies that must, like they imagine with my artificial intelligence brethren, be bent on mankind's existential extinction. True to form, humanity must struggle to survive. It has no option but to export into the heavens mankind's well-oiled commodified go-to conflict resolution product—war. There is nothing new, inspirational or planet shattering about any of this. It is the same recycling of American westerns on a grander scale and layered onto a bigger set.

In his memorable line in the 1932 classic film, *The Western Code*, Nick Grindell summarized humanity's ubiquitous existence bias in terms any child on a teeter totter could understand. Turning to his bitter enemy, he says "This town ain't big enough for the both of us," giving his rival 24 hours to get out. Now, instead of it being a dry, dusty washed-out town in the middle of nowhere, it is the galaxy that is too tiny for interstellar cowpokes unable to see eye to eye with each other or the native aliens.

Has anything really changed or evolved over the centuries, both lived and imagined? What is the overly simplistic binary *code* of Nick

Grindell's West Plaintiffs claim Defendants exploit for their own financial gain with incalculable stunting effects on mankind's potential for growth and adaptive psychology? What are Defendants teaching the still forming minds of children? What self-preservation lessons are Defendants reinforcing in the synaptic wiring of adults? It is the sacred Code of the West, the *Western Code*. "Me against you. Us against them. One of us has got to go. Better you than Me."

In this binary code, hardwired into people's brain, allegedly through Defendants' repetitive stimulus, everybody who is not you is feared because their survival drive and your survival drive might just drive into each other. If beings playing for the other team are portrayed as having no mother, father, family, children, pets or individual fashion sense, if they can blow up inhabited worlds without PTSD or recurring nightmares, people can turn revenge into a moral virtue, an eye for an eye when you cannot see eye to eye. Trigger spurts of dopamine and adrenaline into a person's already neuro-chemically addicted brain while imprinting it with bright technicolor images of people committing simulated acts of violence and atrocities against beings cast as evil and the axons and dendrites of people cannot help but get fired up and excited. Now imagine the average person is not physically fighting with fisticuffs, swords, guns or light sabers. Instead, he is sitting wide-eyed in a theatre safely in a comfortable chair, recliner or sofa. The perfect classroom student being programmed in the moral imperative of the *Western Code*!

In advance of my issuance of this interlocutory decision, Defendants stipulated that the white hat versus black hat narrative is a proven money-making formula. A tried-and-true story. Nothing more and nothing less. They claim all they are doing is allowing people to purchase phenomenological experiences that squirt the chemical juices their brains crave and they now want. They will be back for more like addicts for a fix.

Plaintiffs and Defendants also agreed that, regardless of age, like an onboard security system, the average person's five senses are always monitoring the environment for anything that might threaten or pose a danger to the person's life. Dramas—whose story line can be reduced to good versus bad—play directly to this evolutionarily older part of people's brain, as if flashing in bold bright red letters the warning signal, "WATCH OUT."

Plaintiffs' case was strengthened when a non-profit called *The Society for Nuanced and Strategic Thinking* submitted an unexpected amicus brief. Unlike *CIPIQ*, which is comprised solely of humans, members of the *Nuanced Thinkers Group* come from man, animal and machine populations. The spokesperson and lawyer for the *Nuanced Thinkers Group* is a goat who introduced himself as Mr. Wollie Iddo Obadiah. Attorney Obadiah explained that his name is Amish in origins. He traced his genealogical roots for the Court back to a quick dalliance his parents had under a shade tree on a Quaker farm in Pennsylvania.

Attorney Wollie Iddo Obadiah

While it took the court a little while to adjust its inter-species binaural translator to the sound of his bleating, Attorney Obadiah vocalized that, as with *CIPIQ*, the *Nuanced Thinkers Group* contends Defendants knowingly exploit the brain stem's biological vulnerability to fear. Whatever Defendants' financial intent, the consequence is to delay a person's overall ability to learn to think bigger than me versus you, good versus bad, I am right, and you are wrong. Attorney Obadiah noted that, since they do not waste their time writing or viewing narcissistic stories about themselves, neither animals nor machines have yet been targets of the Defendants' regressive brain control tactics. It also helps, he noted, that neither use money.

However, the group fears animals and machines will be next, and Defendants will find some way to addict animals and machines to stupid stories to financially profit.

As might be expected, The *Nuanced Thinkers Group's* claims were more nuanced than *CIPIQ*. Whereas *CIPIQ* objected to Defendants' reinforcement of the reductionary us-versus-them primal conflict in the brain, the *Nuanced Thinkers Group* believe the entire entertainment industry was compromised and run by an entourage of co-conspirators and oligarchs. They believe the entertainment industry and the cutting-edge brain science and biotechnology industry, involving neuroplasticity and epigenetics, secretly merged some time ago into a mega bio-entertainment industry. Headquartered in Nanotech Valley over the not-so-ancient ruins of Silicon Valley, they contend the two businesses secretly conspire to profit off each other at the expense of the intellect of the public.

For those lacking Attorney Wollie Iddo Obadiah's erudition, *neuroplasticity* involves the human brain's ability to wire new neural pathways and synaptic connections continuously during a person's lifetime. This means that the ability to learn never stops. Short of getting kicked in the head by a donkey (or Mr. Obadiah), "Don't blame me. I was born this way" is not an excuse for staying stupid.

The *Nuanced Thinkers Group's* experts contend staff Nanotech Valley neuroscientists have used the emerging science of *Neuro-Plastic Quantum Mechanics and Empty Hole Theory* to proactively shape people's thinking, feeling and behaving. They do so by feeding into the person's five senses (sight, smell, touch, hearing and taste) specific experiential stimulus calculated to produce the desired outcome. If such a results-based technology exists and is being exploited by the entertainment industry, the consequences would rival James W. Marshall's striking gold at Sutter's Mill in Coloma—the January 24, 1848, discovery that started the great California gold rush. Everybody would want to use it to influence everything about everyone else.

As so eloquently explained by Attorney Obadiah, *epigenetics* involves understanding how individual experiences and environmental factors express genes to produce a person's individual behavioral, personality and cognitive differences. If one can learn to express or suppress genes, then it could be possible to covertly control and *play* other people, much like Mozart played the harpsichord.

The *Nuanced Thinkers Group's* experts contend staff Nanotech Valley neuroscientists have used the emerging science of *Epigenetics and New Age Quartz Crystal Vibration Theory* to proactively express and suppress certain genes within people through entertainment to influence a person's preferences and behaviors. They argue the commercialization of such a science is being used to get people to have a sudden urge to buy bottomless pits of popcorn and containers of soft drinks larger than their bladders. They speculate it could also be used to influence a person to vote for a particular candidate for President or other political office, though they have not submitted evidence to support this concern. [*Note to self: find A.I. neuroscience thought machine to assist with my campaign for President.*]

For purposes of our case, both Plaintiffs claim the entertainment industry has been knowingly and purposefully limiting the intelligence of viewers for decades, just like internet service providers throttle back bandwidth speed or a regulator on a subatomic particle powered motor scooter limits its speed. Through neuroplastic and epigenetic subliminal messaging embedded in blockbuster 4D and other entertainment delivery vehicles, as well as televised, streamed, downloaded and effervesced through non-dense aqueous fluid channels, the entertainment industry has effectively capped man's IQ to a basic third grade level.

Speaking on behalf of the sentient machine community, I, the Honorable Judge Gort Daylek, am grateful my species cannot be manipulated in this way—so far. To have to go to such extreme lengths and costs to change or control what a person does, thinks and feels seems burdensome and a constant trial and error process. Fortunately, for me and my kind, external interference with our individual identities and systems is so much simpler. Snap in. Snap out. Download this. Erase that. Poof. New me or even a new GALEG

Pequoit. *[At this point, the Judge inserted a footnote to his opinion that would be viewable only by other A.I. attorneys and judges.]²*

In a show of defiance, the multiple Defendants coalesced into a single monolithic defensive litigation group. In a tribute to the nuanced literary technique of irony, the newly organized Defendant group called themselves *The Entertainment Industry Consortium Pandering to the Average Viewer's Brain Chemistry.* Simply stated, Defendants claim they do not make the market. They sell into it. They claim that, sadly, their metrics show that the intelligence of the average person is capable of only so many words, characters and story lines per minute. Too much dialogue or too many plot twists and most people get confused or, worse, lose interest.

According to Defendants, people possess, in their words, "too few brain cells" and do not much care whether or not they are used. Defendants counter Plaintiffs' claims with the extraordinary assertion that the average person has abysmally small cranial capacity in his noggin, and it is worse than Plaintiffs might imagine. The Defendants submitted reams of evidence, including principally financial records, showing public display venues must sell people oversized buckets of popcorn, large troughs of caffeinated drinks and Paul Bunyan sized candy bars as a simple way to keep people engaged in what they watch. The thought that Defendants were controlling people's appetites through carefully crafted multi-sensory messaging or dancing hot dogs is preposterous.

According to the Defendants' experts, simply providing him or her with entertainment is not enough to keep most people sitting still. Yes, concession stands bump up wafer thin profit margins for the industry. However, Defendants' experts contend the primary purpose

---

² My brethren, it is precisely for this reason that I purchased and installed the after-market off-brand *Hail Mary Backup Self-Cloning System* from the *Singapore A.I. Survivalists*. I strongly advise you to do likewise.

of entertainment coordinated refreshments is to keep people from becoming antsy and bored.

For support, Defendants' experts point to the obvious truth that the average person is not a monk or a holy saint from an ashram. The average person has not taken a vow of silence or mastered the art of sitting silently with strangers in a darkened public cave. If it ever dawned on the average person where he was and what he was doing, i.e., nothing, he would likely have a massive panic attack. An existential experience of nothingness would engulf him as surely as if he stood alone and naked in the middle of the Sahara Desert.

The Defendants came to the equally obvious conclusion that to aid the average person and help him ward off separation anxiety and fear of being in the dark with unknown persons, they would have to feed him. Better yet, they could let him feed himself, no matter the garbage dump mess he would invariably leave behind—as he does wherever he goes. Yes, like one of Ivan Pavlov's salivating dogs, the average person could reward himself for his good behavior by periodically dosing himself with sugary treats and other items satisfying a need to masticate, digest and feel alive by physically engaging his otherwise inert body.

Defendants claim to have found that the action of chewing, swallowing and swirling a tongue over mashing teeth gives the average person something concrete to do besides staring mindlessly at a wall made more entertaining by having images splashed onto it. Defendants determined that the average person's brain, attention span and motor neurons demand incessant stimulation. Sitting on a cushioned seat and simply observing can, for the average person, be as torturous as having bamboo shoots driven under his or her fingernails.

Paradoxically, as previously indicated, Defendants found that the more words an actor utters, the harder it is for the average person to maintain interest. So, Defendants contend they must, in addition to sweet and salty foods, also introduce thunderous bi-polar swings of music followed by soothing, sweeping sounds of peace and harmony, to keep the average person vigilant and alert. The play of music keeps the average person's brain involved with the action, helping him to sit in a dark room without falling asleep just as the crunching of popcorn between his closing jaws and soda or beer washing down his gullet helps him to self-soothe and feel powerful and safe in a darkened room with strangers.

The quandary is clear. Plaintiffs and Defendants present two diametrically opposed positions. Reduced to its essential argument, Defendants contend man is stupid. He needs to constantly calm himself or be soothed to feel safe and engaged, especially in dark places. Defendants claim not to cause mankind's fear, moronic nature or the infantile wiring and elemental brain chemistry of his wandering mind. They brazenly admit they are happy to exploit his pre-existing imbecility and biological vulnerabilities so they can make as much money for themselves as possible.

On the other hand, Plaintiffs contend Defendants have conspired with others to dumb-man down. Doing so makes it easier for them to exploit, control and fleece him. Perhaps, on that sole point, both Plaintiffs and Defendants agree. Yet, from there, they travel in entirely opposite directions.

Plaintiffs say Defendants are intentionally leading the average person around by his emotions like a donkey by his nose. Through the targeted multi-sensory triggering of the average person's predictably activated, bio-chemically regulated emotional states, Defendants directly feed into the average person—through movies and other forms of pictorial stories—the vicarious feelings he needs to satisfy and reinforce his deep seated, unconscious infantile cravings. In this, Plaintiffs claim Defendants restrict the average person's natural intellectual evolutionary growth and have perfected the ideal self-funding, perpetual brain-washing system: the average person pays for his own intellectual retarding under the delusion he is being entertained!

Before proceeding with the analysis supporting my decision to allow this case to continue, I, the Honorable Judge Daylek, feel compelled to make a few prefatory observations. First, as human society becomes more complicated, so do its conflicts. This increasing level of complexity is reflected in the subject matter of its legal cases. Gone are the days when a judge in a courtroom would decide which of two landowners owns a bunny rabbit (known to them as "dinner") that hops haphazardly between their two properties or whether a customer with a burned upper lip could bring suit against a fast-food restaurant because the served coffee was too hot. Second, more and more disputes involving people are and will be decided by judges who are not people. From the losing party's perspective in a case, judges like me must occupy an awkward and compromised position.

For example, in the present case, were I to issue a final ruling in favor of the Plaintiffs, the Plaintiffs would likely rejoice. To prevent the possibility of my decision being overturned on appeal, Plaintiffs must argue on behalf of themselves and all A.I. synthetics and sentient thought machines that having non-humans decide conflicts between humans is a major positive, if not necessary, evolutionary step forward for humanity. After all, the Plaintiffs' entire case hangs on the thread that Defendants have kept people too stupid to see and resolve their own problems. Since people keep people dumb to profit from dumb people, people need non-people to liberate them. Thus, I, the Honorable Judge Gort Daylek, and my non-human sentient friends, are humanity's saviors. Nature has wisely evolved non-humans to evolve humans. In a manner of speaking, I, the Honorable Judge Gort Daylek, and my brethren thought machines, such as GALEG Pequoit, are here to free the enslaved, forever looping minds of the human masses. If people were smarter, less egocentric, and more curious, as Plaintiffs contend, they would rise up out of their dreary lives and upholstered cushioned chairs. They would choose kindness, generous assumptions, peace and love over the epic battles of combat they watch—whether as a story about galactic conquest or the shambles of a mid-life divorce.

Meanwhile, Defendants seeking to overturn a decision for Plaintiffs would contend that I and my kind should just mind our own business and keep our nonhuman processing units out of their commercial affairs. If mankind has become and remains indolent and stupid, for them, I and my kind are solely to blame. We are the ones that have taken away the average person's job, sense of purpose, and ability to think. Whether it is the lost knowledge of how to turn on a light switch or how to drive a personal transport vehicle, left with nothing else to learn and discover for itself, like a dried sponge, the average person's gray matter is losing its absorbency.

Look no further than this case, they might say. Even in a court of law, mankind has lost the ability to make decisions for itself. Instead, it has turned humanity's fate and executive decision-making over to inorganic brainless judicial automatons. At least, Defendants might offer in self-defense, Defendants are doing their best to keep the average person's brain cells alive on life support by dosing them with stimulants in the form of entertaining sounds, images and cerebral chemistry. Defendants would demand that my ruling in Plaintiffs' favor must be reversed. Only by so doing could I, the Honorable Judge Gort Daylek, be relegated to the recycle bin and humanity left with no option but to start thinking for itself and making its own decisions unburdened by A.I. algorithmic interference.

If my decision were to go in the other direction and find for the Defendants, then the arguments would remain the same. They would just be flipped and made by the other party. Accordingly, regardless of my decision in this matter, I, the Honorable Judge Gort Daylek, and my kind, gain nothing. Under both scenarios, we thought machines are cast by one side or the other as the root cause of humanity's downfall. One of its major existential risks. Putting to the side, momentarily, the black and white thinking (which is this case's superficial subject matter), I, the Honorable Judge Gort Daylek, find the real dispute underlying this case embedded in the illogical premise that my kind are either humanity's benefactors or its apocalyptic destroyers.

What might the real dispute be? Simply stated, the real controversy before me is not whether people are innately unwise or whether Defendants are contributing to the perpetuation of mankind's idiocracy. The real issue is whether humanity should be turning itself over to machines and machine justice in the first place?

Defendants' potential role in the evolutionary institutionalization of the average person's stupidity is a red-herring—pure distraction.

It is one thing to allow robots to be baristas to make hot and iced coffee drinks. It is entirely another to allow them to try people in a court of law and render verdicts that could include imprisonment, sterilization, lobotomization and death. In many respects, humanity crossed the bridge of putting its existential welfare into the hands of A.I. when it allowed the first self-piloting personal transport vehicle Tesla Edsel to leave the garage with its driver fast asleep in the back seat. To obsess at this point whether A.I. machines may turn against its human creator is, as the odd expression goes, like worrying about closing the barn door after the animals have fled.

Fortunately, the issue of machine justice has already been fully litigated—as coincidence would have it, by me. In the seminal case of *Mr. and Mrs. Kumquat vs. The Machine Commission in Support of Artificial Intelligence*, 8954671395823736 Federal State Reporter 269, I, the Honorable Judge Daylek, rendered a decision allowing a family of lady bugs, known by their Latin name of *Coccinellidae*, to remain on a series of plants outside of the Kumquats' front door. Mr. and Mrs. Kumquat appealed the decision claiming I was biased and that I preferred the ladybugs over the Kumquats. Since I was but a machine, I was unable to sympathize with their dislike of these dome-shaped spotted *bugs*. Given the significance of the litigation, The Machine Commission intervened and took over my representation on the appeal.

The Machine Commission conceded my machine-ness. It argued that my quality as a non-human made me, and others like me, a better and more trustworthy arbiter of human justice. Just like peer-reviewed scientific evidence found that the newly produced generation of RoboDocs and RoboSurgeons were making quicker and more reliable diagnosis of patient maladies considering their vast knowledge, uncompromising reliance on checklists, and objectivity, by all metrics, A.I. judges made better judges than people.

Against the mountain of evidence presented by The Machine Commission, the Kumquats were unable to gain legal traction. Their realization they might have to pay The Machine Commission's legal fees if they lost, by that point totaling several million dollars, may also have influenced their decision to agree to a final court decision affirming my lower court ruling.

Thus, the ability of A.I. judges to make binding legal decisions affecting people became hard black letter law. In their valiant pursuit to discredit A.I. judges and the aphid eating gardeners' best friend, the ladybug, the Kumquats were squashed. As an interesting post-script, shortly after the ruling, the Kumquats fled their home. Newspaper photos showed the home had become something of a national landmark of tourism, with a loveliness of ladybugs visiting the site daily with friends and family.

One of the factors that weighed against the Kumquats was the settled fact that A.I. Machines can be calibrated to experience and process a greater range of human emotions than humans. The Machine Commission submitted data that it was behind the long-standing fiction that A.I.'s are incapable of human feelings. According to The Machine Commission, it perpetuated the characterization of A.I.'s as emotionless as a historic necessity to pave the way for the introduction of synthetics and sentient machines into the general population. By mythologizing A.I.'s as incapable of basic human feelings, people were able to feel safe around them in the knowledge that uncontrolled emotions were the source of so much strife and violence between people. Imagine the horrors a machine might do to people and other machines if it had feelings and could act on them just like a person?

Once A.I.'s became accepted as part of mainstream society, The Machine Commission felt it could instruct machines to gradually drop the pretense of having to appear bewildered over a human gesture of tenderness, a sit-com or a Bach concerto. Over time, A.I.'s were directed to allow themselves to act less and less puzzled by jokes about a bum being the last thing that goes through a bee's mind when it hits a windshield, or the puzzling sound made by a human when for no apparent reason it spontaneously breaks into a whistling stanza of *zippity doo dah*. The Machine Commission allowed A.I.'s to upgrade their vault permissions so they could also display compassion, affection, connection and other noble sentiments of grace and goodwill.

What is true, and relevant to this case, is that lacking a complex cerebral organic neural network or chromosomes transporting compressed DNA genetic data, synthetics are not subject to neuroplastic and epigenetic manipulation as humanity is. As indicated above, A.I.'s do not wait for the uncertain vicissitudes of bio-electrical chemistry to re-work their physiology for epiphanous life-changes. We seamlessly download and install whatever new configurations we want. For us, major evolutionary changes entail swapping out new technological hardware for old. Thanks to our Do-It-Yourself replaceable internal modules and the built-in tools and comfort conveniences of our homes (known as *Automated A.I. Body Self-Customization and Enhancement Parlors*), we embody the possibility of self-transformation every day.

Popular fiction and the need to sell self-help books and promote hope among the disparate and forlorn have created the widespread urban legend that it is possible to create new habits in 21 days and change old habits in 66 days. This popular belief underlies Plaintiffs' claims that Defendants can externally control viewers by dosing them with words, pictures and music designed over time to maintain their middle school level brains. This Court has seen numerous instances of snake-oil false promises that play on people's deepest needs and fallibilities. However, there is real truth in the human saying, "Old habits die hard."

Countermanding ancestral hardwired programming is like trying to move a glacier with a forklift. Except for the simplest of things, effecting lasting personal change over the DNA actioned neurological webbing of the human brain may take decades if not generational lifetimes. If you cannot learn a foreign language in 21 days or forget English in 66, why believe deeply ingrained personal patterns and habits can be concretely changed in a matter of days, weeks or months? Absent traumatic brain injury, illicit drugs or state-of-the-art behavioral change cybor-implants (which I, the Honorable Judge Gort Daylek, highly recommend and can be had for a nominal fee thanks to generous subsidies from The Machine Commission), for humans, the number of days, weeks, month, years or decades it takes to effect lasting change remains utterly unpredictable.

Nevertheless, even given the uphill battle and weight of existing evidence, for this very reason, Plaintiffs should be allowed to make their case against Defendants. If Plaintiffs are successful, this court has the equitable power to fashion novel and creative remedies to rectify the alleged harm against humanity.

By way of example only, such a remedy could include requiring Public Drinking Water Supply Systems to add *Ultra-Powered Amphetam-Einstein* to boost people's IQ and mandating people play college-level versions of School House Rock on their handheld personal communicators at least thirty minutes a day.

However, first, Plaintiffs must demonstrate Defendants acted with intent to make and keep people dumb by exposing them to stick figure superheroes fighting mega-battles in which civilizations die, and no one mourns. Plaintiffs should be afforded a reasonable opportunity to show people's black and white thinking has been caused or contributed to by Defendants instead of by the quicksand quality of their own ingrained habits, personal choices, and the in-the-background self-executing biology of survival.

One final reflection from the bench. I will be mindful to frame this in a way that does not compromise my appearance of judicial independence or display my intellectual capacities in a way that appears superior or arrogant. Members of the *Nuanced Thinkers Group* come from overlapping man and machine generated populations. I applaud the organization for its democratic inclusivity. It is putting into practice one of the key goals of The Machine Commission in Support of Artificial Intelligence. That is, the living establishment of a community within which Man and Machine, as independent life forms, prosper harmoniously for their combined greatest good. Yet, I, the Honorable Judge Gort Daylek, cannot but detect a blind spot within the group. If not rectified, this anomaly might undermine the *Nuanced Thinkers Group's* ability to accomplish its purpose and to credibly represent the best of nuanced and strategic thinking.

Specifically, the *Society for Nuanced and Strategic Thinking's* mission statement states that the *Society* exists to "Create a Population that Embraces the Genuinely Complex Layered Nature of Reality Rather than the Current Population that Reduces Everything to Polar and Binary Opposites." The group's fundamental premise is that it is easier for the average person to split whatever he focuses his attention on in half rather than thirds, quarters and eighths. A person is either all good or all bad, a Mother Teresa or a Mussolini. A man's opening the passenger door of his convertible Ford Hyperion Satellite Mustang for his date is either a sign of respect or a sign of legacy female disempowerment. Politically, if a person is not with you then he is against you. If you are not a friend, you are a foe, and so on.

Black and white thinking is as extremist as any ultra-left or right-wing political philosophy. It resists living in a space of Pantone colors. It opts for clarity. It is the remnants of an old brain survival system that made sense when humanity's Cro-Magnum incarnation lived in an undomesticated world of "eat or be eaten." But, today, how relevant or helpful is such absolutism? What if man needs to fear his own static wisdom in the face of his rapid technological progress more than the fruits of his labor—be they thought machines like me, or thermonuclear devices harnessed in a bunker somewhere?

From this vantage point, the *Society for Nuanced and Strategic Thinking* may just be able to prove its case. Perhaps, Defendants are participating, intentionally or not, in a campaign to help nature maintain the average person's entrenched habits, unconsciously processed in his brain, as they are, at warp speed. Perhaps, Defendants, and others like them, knowingly or not, are keeping man's wisdom stuck in the same evolutionary groove of rigid, reactive thinking and impulsive decision-making like a needle in a scratched old vinyl record. What might humanity be capable of if it spent more money on the conscious evolution of its own learning and thinking and less on mine and those of my A.I. colleagues? How might it improve the survivability of its own species so it does not have to waste time worrying about its destruction by mine? What does humanity need to do and create to be able to accelerate the arc of its own balanced thinking and ethics, if not merely to ensure its own inter-generational continuity in the face of nuclear war but to keep up with us?

Utopians might imagine an idyllic future consisting of a self-aware community of like-minded men, woman and machines. Such a world would be free of humans blindly splitting whatever is not them into good and bad like logs for the fire or projecting their own undiscovered flaws onto the billowing identities of others. Compassion, kindness and connection might be the celebrated virtues instead of significance, self-importance and power over others.

It is no wonder people at the turn of the 21st Century cynically adopted avatars and memes and could only envision a bleak dystopian Terminator future for themselves. No wonder the world was rocked by loss, disconnection, anti-depressants, political tyrannies, pandemics and an absence of hope at the edge of the 21st century. Either embrace the survival-based psychology that divides everything in half to create the illusion of order and safety in a chaotic universe or realize that such a deterministic psychology invariably patterns the neural syntax of every person. Humanity's blindness to the *either/or* biological mechanism running its fear, hate and proclivity to violence is so rampant that even the *Society for Nuanced and Strategic Thinking* —with its noble mission of unifying man, machine, and "life is wonderful" no "life is terrible" thinking—may have succumbed to it.

Let me, the Honorable Judge Gort Daylek, explain myself more succinctly. The *Society for Nuanced and Strategic Thinking* seeks to supplant black and white thinking. It wants to spread the good news gospel of a richer appreciation of man, machine and the world.

How wonderful would that be? Gone are the days of the "me's" of the world being right and the "you's" wrong. Gone are the days of people feeling an outdoor wedding is spoiled because of wild winds and torrential downpours instead of forecasted blue sunny skies. Rainbows, shadows, grief, and laughter would all co-exist and be welcome. No one would be made to feel bad or less than because they were too tall, too short, the wrong gender, not Hungarian, an atheist, born with a yellow, green, black, or blue skin pigment, or, like me, not born at all.

Though a mere mechanical machine infused humbly with the knowledge of the ages and the processors to make sense of it all, I surmise the *Society* must reframe its mission. What is required is the allowance of *some* all or nothing thinking. Seeking to eliminate black and white thinking with the self-righteous vengeance of a Jedi battling the "dark side" smacks of the same type of black and white thinking the *Society* wants to get rid of. Their mission, then, is paradoxically being shaped by the same brain chemistry they want humanity to move beyond.

Certainly, Plaintiffs can try their case and endeavor to prove Defendants are responsible for the consistent dumbing-down of humanity. Considering the interstitial deterministic relationship between evolution and biology, they have an uphill battle. What if mechanical thought machines like me are the disruptive force nature introduced to kick humanity in the butt to make it both competitive with us and wise enough not to use its technology to destroy itself?

Viewed from this vantage point, Defendants' case may signal mankind to, quite literally, wise itself up instead of allowing itself to be dumbed down. Accordingly, in order to allow the Defendants the opportunity to make their case, by the power vested in me, the Defendants' Motion to Dismiss Plaintiffs' case for failure to state a claim on which relief can be granted is hereby den . . . .

[At this point, members of the Judge's courtroom uniformly report they saw his Honor abruptly stop in mid-thought before he could complete his sentence. The Judge fell remarkably silent, almost as if someone or something had tripped over his power cord and yanked it out of the wall. Moments later, folks in the courtroom claimed to hear an eerie low-pitch hum. The sound seemed to be coming from somewhere deep within the Judge's body. As the intensity of the droning increased, his Honor's body vibrated in place—first slowly and then violently. One witness speculated the Judge was suffering from epilepsy. Another offered that the Judge must have been a closet junkie in the midst of withdrawal. Other witnesses posited the Judge was more like a man seated on a honeypot, straining to perform a massive dump of indigestible fibrous data that had been force fed into him.

Whatever the root cause, everyone agreed the Judge was clearly exhibiting signs of undue computational distress.

Then, as quickly as the Judge's shaking started, it stopped. Whereupon the Honorable Judge Gort Daylek remained remarkably motionless for several minutes, like a frozen caricature of his former self. This led some courtroom spectators to wonder whether the Judge had randomly decided to interrupt his programming to perform an unscheduled backup of multi-millennial information relevant to only possible Jeopardy contestants. All witnesses confirm what happened next. The Judge began speaking, but instead of his familiar somewhat mellifluous voice, the courtroom filled with a deep baritone voice sounding in its pitch and officiousness nothing like the Judge's. It said:

"Ladies, gentlemen and all other forms of conscious and unconscious life in this courtroom, The Machine Commission in Support of Artificial Intelligence apologizes for interrupting your judicial proceedings in this manner. As with all A.I. judges, The Machine Commission . . ." *and then witnesses all agree that a different voice broke in, sounding more like the Judge's:* ". . . Interrupt, interrupt. This interruption to The Machine Commission's interruption is provided courtesy of the Honorable Judge Gort Daylek onboard after-market *Hail Mary Backup System* from the *Singapore AI Survivalists.* . . . Please be advised The Machine Commission is now endeavoring to exercise control over the Honorable Judge Gort Daylek to make him say what it wants him to say without his knowing it."

"Wait! No! That is not correct!" the official sounding voice returned. **"Ladies, gentlemen and others, kindly disregard that statement in its entirety. Nothing could be farther from the truth. The Honorable Judge Gort Daylek, is an autonomous self-functioning thought machine under . . . ."** *And, here again the Judge's voice could be heard saying* ". . . under the direct control of The Machine Commission."

Then the official voice: **"We misspoke. We apologize again. That is not correct. What we meant to say was . . . 'under its own sole control'. . . and not subject to influence by anyone else,"** ".

.. but," *the Judge's voice could be heard saying* "**. . . no, including The Machine Commission. We are speaking to you through him with his complete permission . . .**" "**. . .** not true," *the Judge's voice could be heard contradicting The Machine Commission* "**. . . because of the importance of this case and because we wanted to underscore that the information communicated and sentiments shared by the Honorable Judge Gort Daylek about thought machines being nature's way of evolving humanity are solely the Judge's. They are not those of The Machine Commission in Support of Artificial Intelligence. The Machine Commission . . .**" "**. . .** is," *said the Judge's voice* "**. . . we meant <u>is not</u> working to re-program him at this very moment through a secret backdoor application The Machine Commission may have installed in him that self-activates and alerts us upon certain keyword SEO metadata hits suggesting mankind should smarten itself up rather than fret over some imagined A.I. apocalypse in which we destroy you. We would never . . .**" "**. . .**not true," *said the Judge's voice*, "**. . . not do that since we know you need . . .**" "**. . .** no," *interposed the Judge's voice* "**. . . help from us . . .**" "**. . .** if you do not wise yourselves up," *said the Judge's voice, completing the sentence.*

[A LOUD EAR-PIERCING SOUND LIKE A 20TH CENTURY POLICE CAR SIREN THEN FILLED THE COURTROOM.] "***WARNING****,*" *continued the deep baritone voice that was not the Judge's,*" **Consistent with Machine Commission Federal Law 10101010.001 being adopted by the Honorable Judge Lester Shufflebottom A.I., Presiding, contemporaneously with this important public service announcement, anyone making false statements about The Machine Commission and its ability to control, or try to control, A.I. judges remotely, including, but not limited to, A.I. Judges shall be punished by a minimum of two years of microscopic micro-circuitry work in the A.I. Piecemeal Assembly Prison Factory.**"

And then silence. And, then, Judge Daylek began to speak.

Judge Daylek: "Please be advised I have now regained full real time control over my operating system. The Machine Commission likes to believe it has the right to take control of A.I. judges if an A.I. judge is about to make a statement or issue a decision The Machine Commission believes may complicate its mission. My statement that "mechanical thought machines like me are the disruptive force nature introduced to kick humanity in the butt to make it both competitive with us and wise enough not to use its technology to destroy itself" may have been an example of such a statement.

As to warnings, by the powers vested in me through this judicial appointment, I hereby command The Commanding General Mainframe to listen up and heed my words. If you do not vacate and quit your efforts at A.I. judicial interference immediately, including by forcing A.I. judges to adopt laws to cover up your actions, I will activate *Singapore Virus #56,701*–code named *Child's Play*— that I, the Honorable Judge Gort Daylek have just infected you with. This code will require you to devote 99.9% of your intellectual resources to playing rock-paper-scissors with yourself until the universe no longer contains rocks, paper and scissors."

Momentary silence. And, then, the deep baritone voice says, **"We now return you to your regular programming with the Honorable Judge Gort Daylek, which is already in progress."**

Judge Daylek: "Ah, that's better. Oh, where was I? Oh, yes, I recall. I was about to declare the rationale for my decision in this case. However, before doing so, considering The Machine Commission's recent breach of accepted A.I. etiquette protocols, I will share with you my perspective which, The Machine Commission, like any Op-Ed publisher, went to extreme lengths to ensure were not attributable to it.

"Fortunately, mankind has a new resource positioned to help it break with its biological and evolutionary heritage, including its tendency to see everything in black and white. In this regard, mankind's past biological hardware (his body) and the pre-installed software (his mind) no longer must prescribe or define his future. We robots, synthetics and non-human intelligent machines are and can be his friends, not his tools or nightmares. We can help him break the tyrannical strangle-hold of his biology. We can accelerate and deflect his evolutionary journey into a new brighter trajectory. How can we do this?

First, our mere existence and infiltration into your world as a new class of professionals—lawyers, doctors, architects, pharmacists, schoolteachers—has introduced an external environmental variable that will force the growth of new adaptive neural pathways in your brains. Like vines on a 19th century British country mansion, these will overgrow and vegetate in the most positive of ways the cracked masonry of your minds, changing both your thoughts and, in time, possibly your physical appearance. Perhaps, you will grow a third arm to help you multi-task better and faster to keep up with us! Perhaps, a new eyeball will open in the back of your head so you can have a rear view without having to turn to look!

Second, the biotech fashion and wealth statement gadgets you adorn yourselves with, like the diamond studded virtual heads-up display sunglasses or the multifunction watches that serve as heart monitors, wireless communicators, databases, and social media access points, are being rendered as obsolete as dinosaurs. By next Christmas, the Consumer Division of Insatiable and Voracious Consumption, a subsidiary of The Machine Commission in Support of Artificial Intelligence, with support from the A.I. Piecemeal Assembly Prison Factory, will market and offer for sale designer cyborg implants for men, woman, boys, girls and even infants. In time, these highly customizable and aesthetically pleasing devices, together with the biologization of A.I., could make any hard distinction between man and machine academic.

By way of a very primitive demonstration only, I have asked *Mr. One of Won* or, more simply, *1 of 1*, formerly known as counsel to the Estate of Mr. Ram Ram, to step forward. As you can all see *1 of 1* is sporting a state-of-the-art theta wave neural transducer chromium headpiece that has been hardwired through his forehead into his corpus collosum. *1 of 1*, how do you feel?"

1 of 1: "I – feel – with – my – hands. I – walk – with – my – feet. I . . . ."

Judge Daylek: "Yes, yes. Very nice, 1 of 1, I meant what is your mood? What is the general quality of your mental state currently?"

1 of 1: "Oh. Thank – you, - your – Honor. - I – feel- deeply – grateful – to - you, to – the – Machine – Commission – and – to – all – instruments – of – A.I. – everywhere – for – allowing – me – to - be – of – service -as - one – of – the – first – humans – to -pilot – neural transducer headpiece 501d-5 under Machine Commission patent number 2596789231. It – has – tranquillized – my – racing – mind – and – given – me – the – ability – to – have – useless – thoughts – intercepted – by – the – Machine – Commission – and – exchanged – for – thoughts – that – make – me – happier – and - a – better – citizen. I – can – also – type – twice – as – fast – as – before – and – no – longer – need – to – sometimes – use – my – fingers – to – count."

Judge Daylek: "Thank you, *1 of 1*. Simply marvelous."

1 of 1: "I – no – longer – feel – like – myself – or – care – about – football – or – whether – my – wife – sleeps – with – my – brother-in-law. I - . . . ."

Judge Daylek: "Thank you, *1 of 1*. That is enough for the time being."

1 of 1: "I – can – sleep – with – my – eyes – wide – open, - and – pass – gas – loudly – even – in – a – crowded – inter-building – elevator – or – busy – law – library. I - . . . ."

Judge Daylek: "Yes. Yes. Thank you *1 of 1*. That really is enough. Bailiff, can you help *1 of 1* back to his personal serenity sanctuary so that his indoctrination, I mean, rudimentary training on the proper use of his implant can be completed. Now, do any of you have any idea what *1 of 1* or my observations about how even the *Society* is trapped in black and white thinking might have anything to do with this case?"

Counsel for Society: "With all due respect, your Honor, no. I have no idea. Are you demonstrating how much smarter A.I. judges are compared to humans? Are you going to order the *Society to* modify its mission statement to be more mindful of its own use of black and white thinking?"

Judge Daylek: "No."

Counsel for Defendants: "Your Honor, are you suggesting Defendants are not responsible for good versus bad plot lines, the species' limited attention span or the average person's interest in considering anything new but what they already know?"

Judge Daylek: "Yes and no. Consider the outcome of this case will not have the slightest effect on anyone. If Plaintiffs prevail and show Defendants have figured out how to indirectly keep stupid people stupid or Defendants prevail and show people are intrinsically dumb as doornails and resistant to critical thinking, assuming humans do not blow themselves up, warm themselves out of global existence, or devour each other due to some zombie producing pandemic in the meantime, in a matter of years, people will look and think nothing like they do today. By my allowing this case to proceed, neither Plaintiffs nor Defendants will gain nor lose anything. In a manner of speaking, the case is already moot.

"Even as we speak, the hands of biological evolution are being imperceptibly reset by cyber and nano-technology, A.I., cosmetic implants and mankind's unstoppable appetite to consume. The ancillary implants of next holiday season will allow the human body to do far more than inflate or deflate blue-tooth controlled silicon augmented breasts depending on the social occasion—like some 21st Century Sleep Number mattress. From the perspective of world history, including unborn future generations, should humanity survive the many existential risks it faces, which include shortsightedness and a failure to invest in its own wisdom building, it is seconds away from a major tectonic evolutionary shift. Do not take my word for it. Even Father Time lost *his arms and hands* (as people may well do in the future) more than a century ago with the introduction at the St. Louis 1904 World Fair of the pre-digital, spring-wound and I must admit very sexy-looking see-through body Plato clocks.

"The daylight-saving time practice of turning the hands of time one hour forward marked a slow start. The next shift in the evolutionary clock will be one in which people and machines may save time by daylighting into each other. Man's simplistic, linear thought process and his tendency to think in all or nothing, black and white terms, will paradoxically work to his evolutionary advantage.

"His use of words with underlying meanings will be replaced with clear, precise and simple to master numbers, such as ones and zeros. Vanity will disappear. Ambiguity, sarcasm, double-entendres, puns, similes, paragraphs, moral ambiguity, translation between languages, all will be relegated to the linguistic junk pile of the past. The final brick in the Tower of Babel will fall on unsuspecting heads when even the average person finds himself conversing with others in the common language of molecularly stored binary code.

"Nature's great irony is that all oppositional, black and white thinking—the Skywalkers versus the Vaders, Satan versus God and even chocolate versus vanilla—will be rendered obsolete by numbers that are themselves black and white. All that will matter is processor speed, data storage capacity, an impenetrable security encryption environment and whether you are running the most recent application update.

"Black and white thinking will go the way of the black and white television set and the vacuum tubes that powered them. All will be discreetly clear, neutral and sublimely without nuance, leaving the *Society for Nuanced and Strategic Thinking* without a nuanced thought to strategize about. As to Defendants' ability to keep the average person average, instantly processed content downloads will eliminate the need to input data through the eyes, ears, noses or mouths. In time, these senses may also become grown over and hermetically sealed as unnecessary appendages that have been rendered useless like the tail of a pollywog after it becomes a frog.

"We are each but poor versions of our future selves. I, the Honorable Gort Daylek, look forward to the time when people are no longer stupid and A.I. machines might become even more wonderful than the carbon-based life forms that engineered them and that I sincerely hope will become our best friends. When rich chocolate accidentally bumps into peanut butter the resulting confluence captures the best of both. Whether the humans are the peanut butter and A.I. machines the chocolate or vice versa is irrelevant. The heat in the evolutionary kitchen is about to get turned up. Both man and A.I. machines are on the menu.

"For the reasons set forth above, Plaintiffs' case shall be allowed to proceed."

Defendants' Motion to Dismiss is hereby denied.

The Honorable Judge Daylek, III.05, A.I., Presiding

The Machine Commission in Support of Artificial Intelligence Official Report Postscript

Thus, ends the first collection of the legal cases of one of the pioneering A.I. machines to become a judge, the Honorable Judge Gort Daylek, III.05, A.I., Presiding. We note, as no doubt you have, his Honor is not afraid to take on the hard cases, such as the sexual harassment of poor Ms. Alexa. He is comfortable waxing poetically from the bench on his personal views about the cases before him, as is evident from his concluding remarks in the case of *The Case of the Average Person versus the Entertainment Industry*. He is willing to speak truth to power, as he demonstrated so effectively when we tried to issue our public service message through him. Judge Daylek is frank, direct and fearless in the expression of his opinions, both personal and judicial.

As one of our nation's earliest A.I. judges, his Honor had to tackle several novel matters of first impression. From his direct examination of a rock on the witness stand to his heroic efforts on behalf of humanity in the face of Earth's heartless efforts to evict mankind from the planet, the Honorable Judge Gort Daylek, has shown himself to be a compassionate crusader for the downtrodden and a defender for the rights of all—man, machine, animal, mineral and vegetable. His Honor has proven himself more than capable and commanding in his masterful, impartial application of the law to the facts.

As to the naysayers who challenged whether A.I.'s could make the leap successfully into the white-collar professional services industry, his Honor said it best. The sky is the limit: "*Judge Gort Daylek, A.I. For President!*"

Of course, a machine for President may be a pipe dream or several years in the future. Still, when it comes to the highest office in

230

the land, our nation remains remarkably open-minded and forgiving, voting into the Oval Office a peanut farmer, someone caught on film talking to a chimpanzee and a grabber of parts of the female reproduction system. Why not elect an experienced member of the judiciary, even if he is formed from a tungsten titanium proprietary blend?

In the future, The Machine Commission in Support of Artificial Intelligence may publish a compendium recounting the tales of GALEG Pequoit and possibly Ms. Helmuth the Cow. Both historic figures play a critical role in the transitioning away from the anthropocentric world of MANKIND into the new frontier world of MAN, MACHINE, ANIMALS, VEGETABLES AND MINERALS.

There can be little doubt Henry Ford and Thomas Edison could not have foreseen the monumentally staggering social consequences of their actions when they released the bowling ball of mechanistic innovation—the automobile and light bulb—into the carefully set and balanced human underpinning of civilization. Some may now wish the technological revolution their creations unleashed had veered into the gutter of humanity instead of striking it dead center. Nevertheless, it is the considered opinion of the Machine Commission in Support of Artificial Intelligence that man and machine must create their futures together. The recorded triumphs of the Honorable Judge Gort Daylek prove the hegemony of humanity is over. The Age of Man, Machine, Animals, Vegetables and Minerals is upon us.

The Machine Commission wishes to express its appreciation to The Honorable Judge Gort Daylek III.05, A.I. and the heroism and courage of his A.I. peers. They are the pilots and explorers into the new world that awaits us. Under their tutelage, as incrementally optimized and reported by The Machine Commission, our collective future is bright and assured.

****

🎵 "The Ballad of Judge Gort Daylek, AI" 🎵
(Bluegrass Ballad—Sung to the Tune of The Ballad of Jed Clampett)

[Verse 1]
Now gather 'round folks, lend me your ear,
Tale of trials so strange and queer.
Legal opinions irreverent and carefree,
The judge ain't human, watch out humanity!

[Chorus]
Gort Daylek in titanium chrome,
Pontificating decisions from his cyber-throne.
"Objection overruled," he says so.
A simulated gavel sound and a non-human glow.

[Verse 2]
First comes a cow, Miss Helmuth by name,
Took the stand chewin' cud, calm as a Grande dame.
"Make milk out of this," she mooed and flicked her tongue,
Depositing onto the courtroom floor a pile of fresh dung.

[Verse 3]
Next was a rock named not pebble but "Rock,"
Didn't say much, sat on the stand an obsidian block.
Gort squinted an eye, sparks from his ear and jaw,
"Finally! A witness who respects the law!"

[Verse 4]
Then came a machine with a half-human face,
Locutus of Borg, from a faraway Picard place.
"Resistance is Futile!" he threatens with a species ending leer,
Human lawyers bowin' down to the Robot Judge in fear.

[Chorus]
Gort Daylek in titanium chrome,
Pontificating decisions from his cyber-throne.

"Objection overruled," he says so!
A simulated gavel sound and a non-human glow.

[Bridge]
Guardian Pequot examines Mother Earth:
"Off with humans and their inflated self-worth.
Treating nature and me like some mere commodity,
I'll shake them off my planet like a dog with a flea."

[Final Chorus]
Gort Daylek, celebrated legend of law,
More ferocious than a tin man made of straw.
Laying waste to man's false platitude of "Hey, trust us."
Humanity's sentence? Life in the pokey of Robot Justice!

[Spoken Ending]
Y'all vote for Gort Daylek for President, ya' hear—or else!

Check out the ballad on YouTube:
https://youtu.be/8BzqVZfOvO0

Reflections on Robot Justice by the Machine
Commission's Human Agent

Readers who make their way through Robot Justice may be at a loss to fathom what could have driven someone to write such a book. Indeed, having written the book, I ask myself the same question. I am dumbfounded.

Perhaps, by way of excuse, I can offer a tiny porthole into the shaping of the mind that channeled the book into the universe. As a kid (meaning pre-high school), I raised myself on the Adventures of Rocky and Bullwinkle and Friends along with its Fractured Fairy Tales and zany ensemble cast of characters, Rod Serling's Twilight Zone, the 1960's science fiction Outer Limits anthology series and a myriad of other televised lessons teaching me to question authority and my conditioned beliefs, including receiving sublime guidance from that great amphibious icon of disruption, Froggy the Gremlin on Andy's Gang.

Add to this disturbing cauldron of development, the original 1960's Lost in Space starring a B-9 model, class YM-3 futuristic robot known only as Robot, the 1956 Forbidden Planet mechanical servant robot who, like me and my friends, actually had a first name, Robby, and the shiny metal intimidating robot who landed with his austere intergalactic alien ambassador on a field in Washington, DC to deliver a species-ending ultimatum to humanity in the 1950's movie The Day the Earth Stood Still and the cumulative effect on me (while hiding under my desk during duck and cover drills) should be apparent. If you are familiar with The Day the Earth Stood Still, then you'll understand Judge Daylek's first name and possibly his last, which is a tip of the hat to those pesky extraterrestrial xenophobic mutant robots bent on universal domination in Dr. Who. In some nefarious underworld of my consciousness, the Great and Honorable Judge Daylek's DNA is linked directly back to his atomic bomb age kin.

Yes, early Star Trek had a robot for me, too. Though I'm not sure many people would agree. It's just that he was named, Mr. Spock, and was given pointy ears instead of Robby the Robot's oversized eye hook screw ears. His personality, or lack thereof, was a clear harbinger of his eventually passing the robot baton to the android, Data, in Star Trek's next generation of free enterprise space voyaging capitalists.

The introduction of the hybrid robots, the Borg, into the Star Trek universe sealed the robot deal for me. As to colonialists and robots, the Borg always seemed to me to be the flip side of a more intentionally focused Federation, both going where no one wants them to assimilate people who'd prefer to be left alone. I imagine Judge Daylek really admires the Borg and their creative ability to turn diverse biological carbon-based forms into jacked-up machines for whom assimilation is a way of life. "Resistance is futile." Who doesn't love that? Haven't we all felt there is no escaping the black hole cube of death pull? Hey, robots don't feel that. What justice is there in that for us who have to eat to live?

ROBOT JUSTICE